ASHBURN

by

Julia Erickson

Chinquapin Press

United States of America

ISBN-13: 978-1-942006-11-4

©2014 Julia Erickson

All rights reserved. No part of this book may be reproduced, stored in a retrieval system, or transmitted in any form without the prior written permission of the author, except by a reviewer who may quote brief passages in a review to be printed in a newspaper, magazine, or journal.

This novel is a work of fiction. Though actual locations may be mentioned, they are used in a fictitious manner and the events were invented in the mind and imagination of the author. Similarities of characters to any person – past, present, or future – is coincidental.

Cover design by Julia Erickson

First Printing

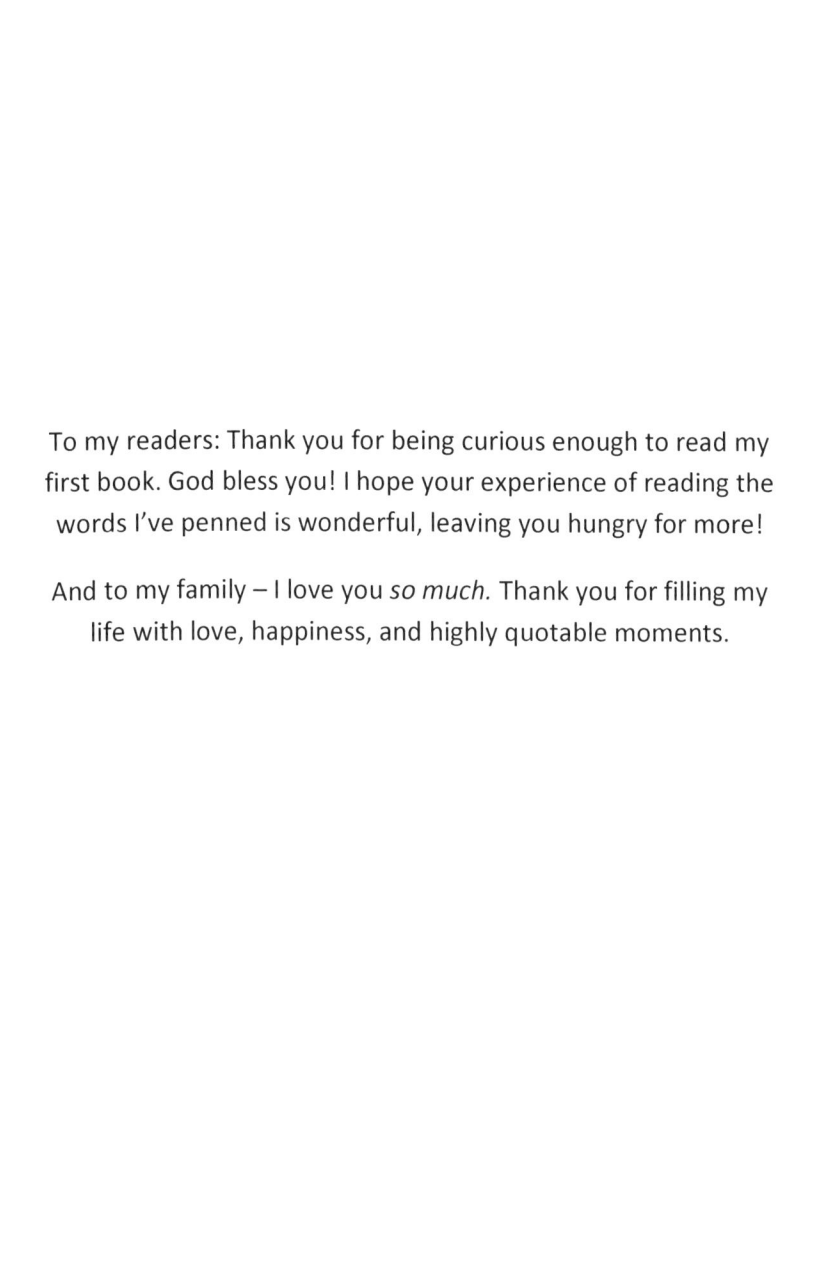

To my readers: Thank you for being curious enough to read my first book. God bless you! I hope your experience of reading the words I've penned is wonderful, leaving you hungry for more!

And to my family – I love you *so much.* Thank you for filling my life with love, happiness, and highly quotable moments.

Chapter One

So, We Meet Again

5:00 AM on Monday morning, and already he was running for his life. Gunfire pierced the foggy air from the direction of the battered van with murky-tinted windows. It chased him through the clamoring throng of activity on the pier, screams echoing in their wake. Shanghai was awash with traffic. On foot, he had the advantage of agility, able to squeeze through pinholes of clear space, but that meant constant weaving. At this rate, it would take too long to reach the rendezvous point.

He only had 90 precious seconds.

A left turn landed him squarely in the center of a market square, smelling strongly of fish and ripe fruit. There was no way to avoid crashing straight through a stand specializing in ginger root and pomegranates. 4 seconds wasted in rolling to his feet and regaining his momentum.

He vaulted onto the nearest car and used it as a springboard to flip up on top of the market stalls. Bouncing wildly from one to the next, he flew from canopy to canopy above the crush of people and carts. His pursuers fell farther behind, and the gunfire ceased, for the moment.

Breathe. Remember to breathe. One last leap and he'd reached the correct street that led to the right dock... and there it was. The *Stingray*. A ticket to freedom in the shape of an outsized speedboat.

But they had company. With the squeal of burning tires against rough concrete, the van's occupants resumed their target practice. A bullet whooshed past his ear as he sprinted for the end of the wooden dock.

"Not today, guys!" He launched himself from the last board and hurtled through the air, barely managing to catch hold of the steel railing on the side of the boat.

A firm hand grasped a fistful of his jacket and hauled him the rest of the way onto the craft. "Cutting it kind of close, aren't you? We had orders to split in ten seconds if you didn't show!"

Gravity shifted, the boat wheeling away from the pier and zooming out into the dark waters. He turned to look into the face of his friend and fellow counterintelligence operative, finding concern written there.

"I know, I know." Chest still heaving, he filled his lungs with the fresh salty air, trying to slow his speeding heartbeat. Before he could explain himself, his pocket buzzed. Extracting his phone, he answered the call.

"Ashburn."

"You made it?" The gravelly voice of his boss held an undertone of worry. "Ryan Black's men are out for your blood."

Do they all think I've lost my touch?!

"Of *course* I made it. By the skin of my pearly whites."

A rich chuckle. "Business as usual, then."

ASHBURN

"Yep. I collected the information. I'm giving it to Agent Markdown to analyze." He slipped the microdisk to his friend, who nodded and headed into the small cabin. He followed.

"Well done. I know you're due some vacation days, but something has come up that requires your attention."

Collapsing into the soft leather of a bank of seats embedded in the hull, he sighed. "Not to be rude, but it'd better be important." This last mission nearly ran him into the ground. Literally.

"It is." His boss lowered his already deep voice. "It involves someone from your past."

"Who?"

"Someone named Cara."

~*~

6:00 AM. Cara awoke to the sound of her alarm playing a classical piano serenade. Light from the street lamps filtered through the sheer curtains at the window. She sighed as she slipped from the comfort of her soft bed and dressed for the day. For a few seconds, she eyed the woman in the mirror, who appeared confident, put-together, and chic with her hair swirled up in a braided bun. She allowed herself a nod of approval.

Right before heading out the door, Cara stopped to glance at the photo frame that rested on the small IKEA table by the front entryway. Her mother and grandmother's faces smiled up at her in monochrome. She paused to smile back for an instant before locking the door behind her.

She descended two flights of steps before reaching her car. Living right on the outskirts of Atlanta was no picnic, but she had been lucky to get her apartment. She made it her own with little personal touches of décor, and it was a welcoming environment to come home to... although there was no Mom or Nana. They were still back in the slow, sedate hometown of Alvaton. Sometimes Cara missed them so much she ached inside. But she had a great job and was putting money in the bank every month. Surely that counted for something.

Cara drove through the morning traffic with a practiced grace. She changed lanes around the choking sludge of commuters and intuitively found the open spaces she needed for a quicker commute.

Skyscrapers towered on both sides, glimmering in the faint light of the rainbow-hued dawn. The shiniest building was the Silver Strand Technologies tower. It looked like a giant silver pencil, poking through the sky and writing its mark in the heavens.

Cara locked her car in the parking garage and made her way through the maze of the building until reaching the familiar arts department. Striding into her office, she set her briefcase on her desk and dropped into the comfortable desk chair. The atmosphere was clean, sterile, a blank canvas from which to create the art she was born to design.

Her official job description was "Director of Graphic Arts", but in reality, she did many things at Silver Strand Technologies. Everyone who worked there wore several 'hats', but sometimes Cara felt that she wore everyone's in turn, except for perhaps the janitor and of course... the boss. Everyone came to Cara when in need of someone to help them out of whatever hole they had dug themselves into.

"Hey Karen, check out the new guy on campus." One of the secretaries, way down at the bottom of the food chain, stuck her head through the door to Cara's office and gave her a too-friendly wink. She reminded Cara of the 'mud-sucker' fish she used to keep in her aquarium, the ones that swam near the bottom, vacuuming up all the dirt.

"It's Car-*a*." Cara emphasized the last A.

"Yeah… there's a cute new guy who's just been hired on in the arts department." The woman leaned one bony elbow against the edge of Cara's door and lowered her voice.

"He's quite a looker… and word is he'll be working pretty closely with you."

Cara flicked her gaze up from the paperwork in her hands to the pointed, over-eager face in front of her.

"Is that so?" She purposely infused into her tone all the indifference she could.

"Here he comes now!" the secretary scuttled away, now rather like a cockroach fleeing the light. She was, of course, supposed to be hard at work instead of trotting about spreading idle gossip in between flirt-fests at the water cooler.

Cara rose from her desk and went to the doorway. She glanced through the arts department and saw her boss, Mitchell Gungerson, Sr., escorting a man through the arched glass-and-steel entryway, approaching at a swift trot. Cara darted back to her desk and seated herself just as they reached her door. She looked up as they came in and manufactured a tranquil smile.

"Ah, Cara. You're looking lovely as usual."

Cara's shoulders tensed. When the boss tossed around compliments, it was well to keep one's eyes peeled for bitter pills hidden in the strawberry jam. Mr. Gungerson folded his thick hands across his substantial midsection and turned his gaze to the man beside him. Cara took her first good look at him as well.

Gulp. Shock pulsed through her. Was it answering surprise she saw in his face? She already knew the tall man standing beside the owner of Silver Strand Technologies, Inc. ... but she hadn't seen him in a long time.

He's here. Right in front of me. After ten years.

"Bryce!" She greeted him with just a hint of warmth in her voice, standing and reaching out a hand.

He took it in his own warm, strong one. "Cara. It's good to see you again." Bryce's smile looked a little tight... cautious, maybe.

As he released her, Mr. Gungerson darted his eyes from one to the other.

"So, you two are acquainted?"

She stopped studying this grown-into-a-man Bryce and gave her full attention to Mr. Gungerson.

"We shared a hometown." Slow, poky little Alvaton, Georgia, where the most excitement happened around the fruit stand where one could buy fresh peaches grown in local orchards.

"Ah. I see. Well – Cara, meet our new head of design research."

ASHBURN Julia Erickson

Cara risked a glance at Bryce. His new title meant he was the new head of the group that studied rising patterns in the design world and how customers responded to the less technical aspects of technology. Ensuring the designs flowed along with the data. As one of her coworkers on the tech development side said, "You design the part that makes the part we design look good." It covered a broad range, from web design to concept art for phone and handheld device design... including most of the graphic design *she* was already working with.

"Now, if you don't mind, I'll leave Mr. Reynolds with you to finish his tour. I'm a busy man, you know."

When Cara inclined her head in a nod, the boss smiled in satisfaction. "Good, then. I'll see you both later." He moved away, with a smooth stride despite his imposing bulk.

"So..." Cara broke the silence Mr. Gungerson left behind. "Where have you been for the past ten years?"

Bryce laughed, and smiled for real this time, exposing the familiar dimple in his left cheek. An ache went through her at the sight.

"Has it really been that long?"

He's being evasive. That's annoying. And it doesn't feel long to him? It feels like forever to me.

"The last time I saw you, I was twelve, and now I'm twenty-two. So... it's been ten years."

Bryce's eyebrows rose. "Wow. Well, we moved to Colorado, and I spent the remaining part of my growing-up years there until I went off to college. I've only recently moved back here."

Suddenly it was difficult to look at him. Her gaze wandered the office furnishings, searching for what, she didn't know... yes she did. The courage to ask. Why shouldn't she? A bubble of frustration rose to the surface and burst without warning.

"*Why* didn't you contact me, somehow? Facebook! Heard of it?" *Ten years.*

Her gaze met his eyes, and something flickered behind his hazel orbs.

"No, wait, forget about that – for a second..." there was something more important to ask. "Why didn't you say goodbye?"

She'd walked inside one day to find her mom and Nana talking quietly at the kitchen counter, whirling in surprise when she dropped her sketch pad on the table. Noticing their startled, guilty silence, she'd asked what was the matter... and had been told that the Reynolds family had "up and moved across the country." Rumor speculated about a divorce.

He'd been her best friend. Well – except for Penny, of course. But they had been close, her and Bryce. Close enough to deserve a goodbye.

He opened his mouth to speak, then froze, staring into her eyes.

She waited.

"I... Cara..." He exhaled, lowering his gaze. "I'm sorry."

Almost as if she'd been dashed with cold water, Cara realized in an instant that she didn't want to be interrogating Bryce. What she really wanted to do was give him a huge hug, but doing that now would be too much of a radical shift in behavior. *He'd think me schizophrenic.*

"Well... welcome home." Cara offered in a quiet voice, silently extending a truce. *For now.*

Bryce looked as if he didn't know whether to be relieved or confused. "Thanks. It actually does feel like a homecoming, in a way."

Cara liked that thought. But then she realized that she, the girl who prided herself on not wasting time at the water cooler, was standing there doing – *what am I doing, anyway?* – when there was work to be done.

"How much of the company have you seen already?" Cara asked. After all, her boss had told her to finish Mr. Reynolds's tour.

"Not much. I came straight here from the parking area."

His 'tour' hadn't even begun. She drew a deep breath. "Well then. I suppose we had better get started." She walked around her desk.

"Right this way." She gestured out the door.

They walked together through the building. Cara straightened her shoulders, trying to coax herself to relax. She took a few brief seconds as they walked to study the guy beside her.

Bryce had grown into a very tall, impressive man, something there had only been hints of in the 14-year old she'd known. There was an air of capable strength about him... and a firm jaw. His hazel eyes still shone in his face with an intelligent light, and his sandy brown hair was cut in a short, clean-looking style. He was dressed in impeccable business attire – understated, yet sophisticated.

He's still cute, Cara mused. But then she deleted that thought from her mental inbox. Ignored the attraction she felt. The last thing she needed was another distraction at work. *But who knew Bryce, of all people, would show up?* Delete! Again. Her calm inner strength took over once more.

Letting another person into the small circle of people she loved would only create another option for heartbreak.

People get hurt. People die. She knew that all too well... after what happened to her father.

The less people I let myself get attached to, the better.

They breezed through Accounting, Tech Support, and Development & Research, and took a swift look at some of the massive conference rooms.

Bryce seemed fascinated. "You know, I can hardly believe I'm really working for Silver Strand." He told her on the way back to her office.

She gave him a brief smile. "It's an amazing company, on the upward climb." She agreed.

"I'm still not sure why they even hired me." Bryce donned a self-deprecating grin.

He would never last with that kind of attitude. How had he even gotten *hired* without the typical cutthroat maneuverings?

Cara looked at him. "Hey. You have to believe in yourself a little more than that if you want to stick around."

He nodded, seeming to catch the gentle warning in her tone and glance.

"You're right. But don't worry... I think I can handle it." He winked.

Why did he have to be so charming? When did he learn not to be shy?

Cara looked up just then to see Mr. Gungerson actually *waiting* in her office. An uneasy feeling in the pit of her stomach signaled her alarm. Her boss never waited for anything. He barked orders all day long and people jumped to do his bidding. This was very strange.

"And how did you enjoy your tour, Mr. Reynolds?" Mr. Gungerson asked as they approached.

"Very much," Bryce replied politely, "You have a most impressive company here, Sir."

Mr. Gungerson looked flattered, a gratified look on his round face.

"Here at Silver Strand, we take pride in everything we do." He stated grandly. The man was ridiculous in his pomposity.

"And now, as for your office space. It's right next door." He led Bryce out of the room to a door a few feet from Cara's.

Mr. Gungerson could have given him a temp office down the hall until it was certain that Bryce was staying... that's what the boss usually did with brand-spankin' new employees.

Not this time.

Laney, her favorite coworker, had left work to become stay-at-home mom to a newborn son. Cara secretly envied her. Bryce was taking Laney's old position, but she hadn't realized he would also be in her office.

"We'll see you later, Cara." Mr. Gungerson nodded over his shoulder. "Come, Bryce, I'll show you some of the projects we have for you to start with."

They disappeared into Bryce's office, and Cara knew Mr. Gungerson would pull up the project specs on the ultra-sleek computer waiting inside.

Cara turned back to her own ultra-sleek computer and tried to go back to work. Those exciting projects that she'd focused on all week seemed dull. No inspiration would come. Her mind stubbornly kept wandering back to what was going on next door.

She almost felt like going to Bryce's rescue. He seemed too innocent to be left alone in a den with a lion like Mr. Gungerson. He might say something or do something to jeopardize his job and then he would be out of here like yesterday's canned ravioli. The old Bryce had needed her.

Just as Cara was actually considering intervening and taking Bryce away by some clever ruse, a tap came at her door and Mr. Gungerson poked his head in.

"Cara, my dear, will you come assist us?"

She popped up like a jack-in-the-box.

"Of course." She kept her voice cool, hoping to offset the spectacle she'd made of herself by leaping to her feet.

Mr. Gungerson escorted her into Bryce's office, where Bryce sat in one of the desk chairs. Bryce stood up as they entered.

He's a gentleman now?

"Cara, please update Bryce on some of the current work you and the previous Head of Design Research were accomplishing together. I'd also like you to show him our processes and formatting." And then her boss was gone.

"So…" Bryce tilted his head towards the computer.

Cara's jaw dropped, stunned. She had just been assigned enough work to keep them busy for the rest of the day.

"Well." She seated herself in one of the desk chairs. "We've got a lot to do, so here we go." Bryce joined her at the computer, sitting in the other one.

She started at once on the projects she and the late Lead Designer Laney had been working on together. There were nine at present, ranging from a design for the new logo of an online video messaging program to the home screen for a brand-new mini tablet scheduled for release in November.

Even with Cara's concise way of relating information, it was hours later when they took a break. They had missed lunch, and she was ravenous. And then Bryce's stomach growled.

"Care to join me for lunch someplace?" Bryce asked with a charming tilt to his head.

Cara thought about it, and then smiled. "Sure."

She buzzed Mr. Gungerson's personal secretary, Matilda, to tell her that they were stepping out for a bite to eat and would be back within an hour if Mr. Gungerson asked about their whereabouts. She grabbed her purse from her office and they left the building together.

~*~

Bryce drew in a deep breath of the air as they entered the parking garage. The noxious odor of gasoline and rubber tires permeated the area, but at least the air was richer in oxygen out here.

"Shall we take my car?" Cara suggested.

She seemed to have shelved the issue of his – what could he label it? – avoidance, for now.

In truth, he didn't want to think about why he hadn't said goodbye. The pain was too much.

He agreed with a nod and followed Cara to the silver Jetta, waiting against the side of the garage. The bright light glittered on the silver paint job and showed off the car's sleek lines.

He released an appreciative whistle. "Cute. It looks new."

Cara smiled, slipping into the driver's seat. "I've had it since I was sixteen."

Sweet Sixteen and never… has she been kissed? He had missed so much of her life. He'd never know the 16-year-old Cara.

He got into the passenger side, noting that the dash simply sparkled and the carpet and seats looked spotless. There was even a hint of 'new-car' smell inside. Was Cara a neat freak now? Or lying?

They pulled out into the ceaseless stream of cars that was Atlanta's streets. Cara tapped the steering wheel in a motion that could almost have been classified as a caress.

"I know it looks new. I like taking care of it." She fished a spray bottle from somewhere next to her and held it up for inspection. "Behold, my secret weapon."

ASHBURN — Julia Erickson

The label read "New-Car Air Mist".

He laughed, and she laughed along. *How long has it been since we've laughed together?* They were always laughing, way back when...

He'd woken up on that blackest of days to find his family ripped apart like so much wreckage from a ship's sinking. His father was gone, with only the most cryptic of notes in his wake, and his mother floated about like an ashen-faced ghost, drifting without purpose. His younger brother Blake locked himself in his bedroom, weeping, and little Bethany's moaning wails pierced the air like a seagull's mournful cry. The mantle of family leadership settled around his thin 14-year old shoulders as a great weight to be borne, and he nearly broke under the burden of it.

The move to Colorado had been their only choice. Moving in with Gramps and Gram, his mother's parents, had brought faint rays of sunshine into their lives... rays that warmed and grew stronger as the jagged edges of pain from his father's abandonment smoothed, over time, like nuggets of sea-glass.

Bryce studied her for a moment, taking advantage of the fact that her gaze was captured by the road. Cara was a woman now, tall and statuesque. He had to look hard for hints of the girl who had lived down the road. Gone were the faint freckles and crooked teeth, replaced by creamy skin and a perfectly straight white smile.

His heart nearly stopped when he realized he'd forgotten to do a ring-check.

A clear view of Cara's bare left hand perched on the wheel restarted his ticker. *But that doesn't mean there isn't a guy in her life.*

"So." She threw him a look before zipping around a slow-going van with practiced timing. "Where do you want to eat?"

Obviously his 3-minute introspective silence hadn't sat well. She looked bemused. Or maybe she was just irritated by the awful traffic. How Cara had maintained a dent-free car driving in this mess was beyond him.

"How about somewhere with pizza?"

She looked at him, something coming alive in her eyes. "You still love pizza?"

She remembers.

She took him to a place that looked promising, and upon entering, they breathed in the heavenly aroma of yeasty crust and the tang of fresh spices.

In a remarkably short time, they were eating the most delicious pizza he had ever had the pleasure of tasting. The flavors burst in his mouth like colorful fireworks.

"So… how do you like Antico Pizza Napoletana?" Cara's eyes glinted as if already guessing his answer. She sipped her lemon water through the straw, and then delicately patted her lips with the napkin.

Wonder where she learned the dainty manners. He smiled at her. "I'd say this is lunch and dinner rolled into one, right here."

Cara's laughter spilled out of her like a brook tumbling down a mountainside.

Wow. She's so gorgeous. But that could be bad… distractions are dangerous. He gulped. In his line of work, losing sight of the goal… making a mistake, slipping up, could mean death. It had nearly happened to him quite recently. "Delicious, really. What's their secret?"

"The ingredients, the preparation, the atmosphere..." Cara waved a hand at the basil-scented surroundings. "They love what they do... every batch of dough is hand-kneaded. They fly in fresh ingredients from Italy every week, and their special ovens were brought from Italy by sea and weigh over 10,000 pounds each." She stopped, as if realizing how long she'd rattled on. A smile tipped up the corners of her mouth.

They ate in contented silence for the next few minutes. He finished off a last slice and sat back in his chair, stuffed to the gills. "You have to love how most of the menu is written in Italian." He glanced at his.

"I love coming here. It's almost as good as going to Italy." She looked around, her gray eyes shining. "But we've probably used up our lunch hour by now."

Was it just him, or did her voice hold a hint of regret? They'd kept the conversation light, but her unanswered question – *'why didn't you say goodbye?'* – still hung in the air.

"A very good point." he agreed, rising in tandem with Cara from their table. She was right, the time had melted away. But he wished they could have lingered over their empty plates.

It had been *more* than a coworker-to-coworker lunch out.

Back at the office, Cara briskly wrapped things up and Bryce found himself clued in on everything about his new job.

"I already feel good about working here." *Working my way to the inside should be easy, now that I've got an ally.* The Cara he knew would never let him down.

The big question was... *was* she the Cara he knew? Or had she changed?

"Great." Cara said, reaching for his hand and giving it a hearty shake. "Welcome to Silver Strand."

Bryce's grin stretched from ear to ear. "Thanks." Her hand felt cool and slender in his.

She released him and stood. "Well, I'm going to see if I can get a few things done myself before clocking out." Her tone had decidedly cooled.

Just as well.

"Okay." He turned back to the computer as she headed for the door. "Hmm." He murmured quietly to himself as he opened a few programs.

What should I pretend to work on? It would be a while before he could slip out and snoop through the offices.

"Bryce?"

He turned to see Cara paused in the doorframe.

"If you need anything, I'm right next door. Don't hesitate to ask." The look in her eyes was full of meaning. He didn't have time to analyze it – couldn't let himself drown in their deep-flowing current.

His smile was forced, and felt waxen. "Oh, I'm sure I'll have questions." *And lots of 'em.*

A brief smile emerged for an instant. She knew her unspoken offer to listen had been gently refused, for the moment. Then Cara vanished.

ASHBURN   Julia Erickson

~*~

Cara's inspiration came at last, and she managed to solve a few quirks that had plagued her for days. A rounder curve here, a paler shade there, and it was done. She sighed with satisfaction as she saved her work.

The lights were dimmed when she left the building. She had stayed longer than was normal, caught up in her art. Tucking her hands into the pockets of her pink trench coat, she hurried to her car. Sunset wasn't until another hour or so, but a stiff wind blew, teasing a few wisps of golden hair out of her bun and into her face. Winter lingered as spring gently softened the edges of the elements.

Once inside the safe haven of her Jetta, she circled the garage and began the descent to the bottom. She noticed a man on the other side of the parking level. The fluorescent lighting glinted off sandy brown hair, identifying Bryce.

What's he doing here so late?

Cara slowed as she saw him walk to a coal-black Mustang GT and open the driver's door. She stifled a laugh as he started the car with a throaty roar of the engine. Then she rolled out of the parking garage before she could be spotted.

So Bryce had a hot car. She liked it – it fit his personality. Well... it seemed to. She knew next to nothing about him now.

What has he been doing for the last ten years?

Chapter Two
The Mission of a Lifetime

Raindrops pattered on the windshield by the time she reached her apartment. Cara brewed herself a cup of Orchard Spice tea, then curled up on a chaise lounge piled with pillows by the window and pulled out a mystery that she had been itching to read.

She lost herself in the pages of her book until the stars were twinkling. Then she reluctantly closed the covers, leaving the heroine in a bit of a pickle.

She washed away the day's stresses with cherry blossom shower gel. Climbing into her big, downy bed in comfy pajamas, Cara drifted off to sleep to the sound of the rain drumming on the roof.

~*~

Bryce tried to ignore his empty stomach while he waited to be patched through to his boss. The Agency had sent him into some real dives before, but this one wasn't so bad. Though the studio apartment was awfully cramped, it was clean. Sort of.

He opened the door of the miniature refrigerator and scanned the shelves. *Meh.* A jar of olives, some deli ham that should probably be tossed, and a package of string cheese. He'd have to pick up some groceries if he didn't want to be eating out every night.

"Ashburn, I'm juggling several agent reports at once, make it snappy." Mr. Montrose came on the line in a flash.

"It was a good first day. I checked out a couple of the offices, nothing suspicious so far. Squeaky clean, in fact, but that's a little suspicious on its own. I couldn't get into Gungerson's files."

"Why not?"

"He was there." Gungerson had been sitting at his desk, nearly in the dark, when Bryce entered the room, and he'd had to quickly manufacture a question about the tablet home screen wallpapers, which had Gungerson frowning and telling him to simply ask Cara about it later. *Why* he had been sitting there in his office, so late, was a mystery. The man owned the company... and a million-dollar home.

"Well find out when he leaves his office and get in there. Just don't get caught, I need you alive." Montrose's tone was only half-humorous.

"I'll be careful."

"Good. See that you are."

~*~

Cara was drafting a preliminary sketch for one of the projects she and Bryce were going to work on together – a user interface for some advanced computer software... when two loud thumps sounded on her office door.

Cara stifled a groan. She'd barely slept last night with the thoughts careening around in her mind, questions only Bryce could answer.

I do not need this right now. But what choice did she have?

"Come in."

She hid her gaze in her computer screen and did not look up when heavy footfalls announced the entrance of ...Mitch.

"Good morning." It was a husky whisper that was supposed to be attractive, but it came across as cheesy.

She looked up for an instant, long enough to see the face that would have been handsome were it not for the insolent, pampered expression, and then looked back to the computer.

"Hi." Her tone was calculatingly ice-cold.

"Cara, come up for air. You're obviously working too hard if you don't even have time to give me a proper greeting."

She could hear the petulant whine starting to creep into Mitch's voice. Cara looked up again and glared into his water-blue eyes.

"Good *morning*." She turned back to the computer and started to type, not regretting for an instant the hardness in her voice.

"Aw, come on." Mitch leaned one arm on the desk and put his other hand casually in his hip pocket. "Can't you even give me the time of day?"

"10:32 AM." She replied, "Although I notice you're wearing a watch."

Mitch's laughter, a sharp sound that grated on her ears, overtook the small office. "How about coming to lunch with me? I know a cozy little place that serves a beautiful plate of escargot."

Cara's stomach lurched at even the thought of digesting snails.

"It's a little early for lunch break." She evaded giving a direct answer.

"Sure, so I'll come back around 12:00 to pick you up." He spoke like it was a done deal, a broad grin spreading out on his equally broad face.

She looked up and stared at him in the manner of a brick wall. "No. Sorry. I already have plans."

Mitch sneered in disbelief. "Is that so? What are they?"

She kept the blank stare on her face. He had no right to know her personal concerns. Even if he was the boss's son.

"Okay, okay." He held up both hands. "You don't *have* to tell me."

"Good." She looked back to the computer.

"Good grief, Cara, I'm a human being too – you might try treating me like one once in a while!" Mitch threw the remark over his shoulder as he turned to go.

Cara breathed out a sigh of relief, but inhaled it again when Mitch almost collided with Bryce in the office doorway.

"Excuse me." Bryce gave a polite nod, even though Mitch had barreled through the opening.

Mitch ignored him and shot an accusing look at her. "And who is *this*?"

Bryce smiled and stuck out his hand. "Bryce Reynolds."

"He's the new Head of Design Research." Cara added for Mitch's benefit. Mitch shook Bryce's hand once and let go like it was a hot potato.

"Is he part of your 'plans' for lunch?" He demanded an answer with a glare at Bryce.

Before Bryce could answer, she blurted "Yes. He is. Aren't you, Bryce?"

Without batting an eye, Bryce replied. "Naturally."

Mitch's face flushed an ugly shade of puce as he glanced from one to the other.

"Aha. I see how it is. A new inter-office affair. Those never last long, you know."

With that nasty remark, he left in a huff. As the thumping sound of his footsteps faded down the hall, Bryce turned to her.

"Whew! Who was that beefcake?"

Cara looked up to the ceiling to beseech heaven for mercy. "The boss's son."

A slight groan escaped Bryce's lips as he seated himself in a chair across from her.

"I know." Cara sighed. "I've been told by some of the office scum that if I didn't play so 'hard-to-get', he would leave me alone, but somehow… I doubt it."

There was a sympathetic look in his hazel eyes. "Sorry that you have to put up with him."

Cara shrugged her shoulders. "It comes with the territory." She clasped her hands. "Did you want to see me about something?"

Bryce's expression grew businesslike. "Yes. I had a question for you concerning the specs on this website art."

When they had cleared up the problem, she asked somewhat hesitantly "I hope you didn't mind I said you and I were doing lunch, in front of Mitch. You don't have to go out to lunch with me."

A twinkle danced in Bryce's eyes. "Are you kidding? I can't wait to see what other culinary delights you have up your sleeve. The last place was terrific."

"You're on!"

~*~

Cara walked in with a spring in her step. Her favorite Mexican restaurant had earned rave reviews from Bryce. Sure, they still hadn't discussed his ten-year disappearance or why he hadn't said goodbye, but she was sure he would bring it up, soon. For now, she was at peace.

That feeling was shattered when the receptionist informed them that "Mr. Gungerson wants to meet with you in conference room C3."

They headed there at once.

Bryce held out her chair for her as she sat at the long table, and then seated himself next to her. The table's sharp edges looked like a sheet of steel, and the room was painted a bleak shade of stone-gray. Something about the tint played tricks with one's mind, casting shadows where there were none.

Cara tried desperately to hang onto a feeling of calm, but her insides quivered. And it wasn't the salsa she'd eaten for lunch. Nobody who got called into a special conference room by Mr. Gungerson ever came out thankful for the experience. Either they were about to be fired, their pay docked by half, the workload doubled with no extra pay, or sued by a rival company for designing something that infringed on someone's copyrights. None of which Cara particularly longed for.

~*~

Bryce leaned back comfortably in his chair and studied the painting of a sailing ship on the opposite wall. He was determined to keep his cool. This new development was either very good, or very bad. Either way, it might shed some light on his situation. Or... it could be nothing. He wouldn't be alarmed until he had good reason, but his senses were presently on alert. Make that a code yellow.

A lot would depend on the demeanor of the boss when he – Bryce glanced at his watch – *finally* arrived. He had learned from long experience that what a person did not say was usually twice as revealing as whatever words came out of their mouths. One simply had to read between the lines.

It was this unique ability that had earned him his code name.

~*~

"Sorry to keep you waiting."

Cara jumped, startled, and Bryce's gaze darted up to the heavy-jowled face of Mr. Gungerson. The boss's grin had a greasy sheen to it, and he wore a look of smug complacence. Cara wouldn't have been surprised if her boss had deliberately waited ten minutes just to make them nervous, although he was forever telling his employees that "time is money"!

Mr. Gungerson rolled out the chair at the head of the table and delicately sank into it, then pulled himself closer to the table and rested his elbows on the surface. "Cara, how would you like a little ...vacation?"

Cara fought the urge to scream, beg. She did not want to be fired. Leaving the company wouldn't have stung, but being fired would be a crushing blow to her ego. "What sort of vacation, Sir?" Her voice was surprisingly smooth, considering her state of mind.

"Well..." Mr. Gungerson settled into his chair as if getting comfortable for a long car trip. "I am very sorry to say that a little snag has come up in one of our recent projects." He looked into Cara's face. "Nothing you've been spearheading, my dear. Something from the development side."

Cara was thoroughly confused and was not enjoying it.

Her boss continued. "One of our field test operatives, a man named Freddie Nigel Donaldson, has... gone missing. With some very important experimental technology on his hands. We don't believe he's stolen it, but that possibility is still up in the air. We are more convinced at present, however, that he has been... spirited away."

~*~

Bryce studied the back of Cara's blond French twist as she sat up straighter. *How long is her hair, anyway? Yesterday it was a bun, today this swirly thing...*

"Someone's been kidnapped?" Cara's voice was squeaky. Her creamy skin had gone a shade paler.

Bryce reminded himself to look surprised. He thought raising his eyebrows and opening his eyes a little wider should do the trick.

It usually did.

Mr. Gungerson folded his hands across his belly. "Maybe. We think he may be held by some agents of our top rival company, Ravenmeister. But they might be paying him a steep bribe to have dropped out of sight, and in that case, he would decline to press any charges of kidnapping. We can't have the authorities getting involved."

"What technology is missing?" *I might as well hear it from your end.*

"Excellent question, Bryce. I like that. You have a good head on your shoulders." Mr. Gungerson waited a few beats before continuing.

Stalling for time, are we?

"Freddie was working on the personal ID scan implant technology Silver Strand has been developing for the past three years. He was field testing as a human experiment. We embedded our prototype chip into his arm and he went off to try out the high-tech GPS signal it sends. We were reading him loud and clear when suddenly the signal disappeared... and so did Freddie."

Mr. Gungerson sighed heavily. "It really is vexing. If we don't find him and get back the prototype, the work Silver Strand is doing on the ID implant will be obsolete. We're racing our competition on this project. Ravenmeister is trying to develop the same device. Whoever releases their technology first stands to gain control of the ID implant distribution for the whole world."

He drilled his gaze into their heads with jackhammer intensity. "Millions upon millions of dollars are at stake."

Cara drew in a long breath and slowly exhaled. "What can we do?"

Bryce was also curious about the answer to that question.

"We've noticed you, Cara. You're smart. Whenever there's a problem, people go to you. We want to use you on something bigger than handling cell phone graphics and website backgrounds. And you'll need an assistant, so Bryce here comes in handy."

Bryce held back a guffaw at the thought of being an assistant as a slight blush rose to Cara's cheeks. She pursed her lips, appearing to give her boss's last statement deep thought.

He studied Cara's classic profile. Playing an assistant should be… interesting.

~*~

"When do you need my answer, Sir?" As soon as the words left her mouth, Cara knew she'd made a mistake.

Mr. Gungerson frowned. "I thought you knew that at Silver Strand, we need *team players*. Any employee who isn't willing to be part of our efforts…" He trailed off and looked her up and down as if reevaluating her worth. "I would hate to see your bright future here grow dim."

Well, that was clear enough. If she didn't accept this mission, she could forget about a career at Silver Strand Technologies. Cara swallowed around the lump in her throat.

"Count me in."

~*~

Bryce had to hurry to keep up with her. At the rate they were going, the hallway blurred as if they were at warp speed in an old sci-fi movie.

"Cara, are you okay?"

The muscles in her face were tense and her eyes had gone surprisingly dark, changing to a more obsidian color rather than gray.

"What should we do?" She wouldn't look at him.

"For starters, how about we stop storming down the hall like Klingons are chasing us?" His attempt at a joke fell flat, earning him a glare.

"Okay, come with me." He led her out a side door and suddenly they were standing in the sunshine. Fresh air blew across their faces and Cara visibly relaxed.

"Now." Bryce took her hand in his and tapped it with his other one as he spoke. "I think we should go with the flow. Accept the mission."

"You *do*?" Cara looked taken aback, "But it sounds so... shady! What if it's illegal? I'm not happy with that part about not getting the authorities involved." She lowered her voice, glancing nervously around them at the bystanders, none of whom were in earshot.

He hastened to try and explain his reasoning. "I'm curious. I want to find out what's really going on here. If it turns out to be shady, Cara, I'll call the police just like that." He snapped his fingers, underscoring his point.

She sighed. "You will?"

"I promise." She still seemed upset, so he gazed into her eyes and spoke in his most reassuring tone. "Look. I've got some... friends ... in the Federal Bureau of Investigation."

"You *do*?" Cara exclaimed, for the second time. "When did that happen?"

His eyes crinkled at the corners with his outwardly casual grin, although his heart was racing. "I do. I'll call them in if there's trouble. And would you mind not yelling?" He glanced covertly at their surroundings. "Come on, let's find a park bench."

She eyed him as if he had taken leave of his senses. "In this neighborhood? They don't know the meaning of the word 'Park'."

"Surely there must be somewhere to sit." He drew her hand through his elbow and walked down the sidewalk with a merry spring in his step. "Or we can just stroll."

"This isn't bothering you a bit, is it?" She pulled her hand away from his arm.

"Not really." *Not at all. You're the issue.* He would be much better off if she would only cooperate.

"Why not? It's definitely troubling me."

Yeah, I can see that... He scanned his mind for a moment for a reasonable answer. "I like adventures."

"That's what you think this is? An adventure? This is not an Indiana Jones movie, Bryce!"

"I always liked Indiana Jones."

A fierce frown pulled down her blond eyebrows.

"Sorry." *Sort of.*

Cara sighed in exasperation. "What would my mother think about this?"

He looked at her. Cara's voice had held a barely concealed tremor, and her forehead was wrinkled in stress.

"Hey." He stopped, grasping both her elbows and turning her to face him. "Everything's okay."

"How do you know?" Cara nearly hissed, a tear escaping from the corner of one eye. "This is scary. I am either going to do this crazy mission or lose my job, and both options look very bad at the moment!" She shook her head in frustration. "Maybe I should just resign. It's not worth all this."

He looked up at the towering skyscraper behind them. "Well, if we can just figure out where the field agent went, and ask him politely to come back, then we can enjoy Italy for a few days and come home to find your job waiting for you intact. It shouldn't be that bad."

~*~

Cara's mouth dropped open. "Italy?" *I don't remember anything being mentioned about Italy!*

Bryce laughed, his whole face relaxing into warmth. "You really do need an assistant. Weren't you listening to Mr. Gungerson in there? He told us that Freddie signaled last from Venice, Italy before they lost contact with him. At the *Hotel Al Ponte Antico* on the Grand Canal, to be exact."

Cara shook her head. All she remembered was her head swimming, and that Mr. Gungerson had given them the rest of the day off to get ready for the trip. They would leave in the morning.

"*Italy...*" she breathed softly, "I have *always* wanted to go to Italy."

Bryce grinned, flashing white, even teeth. "See? It's not going to be so bad." He laid a comforting hand on her shoulder as they turned to walk back to the parking garage.

~*~

Mitch glared down at them as they strolled, loathing the history and camaraderie that flowed between Bryce and Cara. The Daily Office Scum reported that they had grown up together... "childhood friends" or some such rot. He pressed his nose against the cold glass of the windowpane, angling for a better view. Cara was making a very bad choice if she was trying to take up where she left off with Bryce.

"She'll regret this." His whispered threat echoed through the empty room.

~*~

Bryce escorted Cara to her car and opened the door for her.

"Thank you." Cara rewarded him with a smile before slipping into the driver's seat. She rolled down the window and he leaned his arms against the rim of the door, ducking his head in order to see her inside the car.

"Pack light, but bring a pretty dress."

Cara looked at him with wide eyes. She looked surprised, but a hint of delight lurked in the curve of her mouth.

"I just might take you out to dinner while we're in Venice." He gave her a slow wink, then straightened and stepped back from the car.

"Sounds good." Cara put the keys in the ignition and slid out of her parking space.

Bryce waved as the silver Jetta left the garage via the exit ramp.

"Smooth."

He turned to see Mitch Gungerson leaning against a chunky SUV several yards away. He snickered. The vehicle and the man had the same build.

"I'll have to study your style, and practice. She never smiles like that for me." Mitch's tone was light but the look in his eyes was anything but friendly.

"It's not a one-style-fits-all game, Mitch. I wouldn't copy me, if I was you – I've never considered myself a ladies' man." Bryce dished it back at him with a saucy grin and turned to go.

He didn't get far before a heavy hand clamped down on his left bicep.

"Listen to me, pal. If you've got any ideas about getting fresh with the little lady while you're on that dreamboat trip of yours my dad cooked up, think again. You'll live to regret it." Mitch glared and curled his lip in a sneer.

Good grief, who did the guy think he was, *Mafia*? Even they didn't use such tacky dialogue!

Bryce jerked his arm out of Mitch's grasp in one smooth motion and lifted his chin. "If you mess around with me, *pal,*" He nailed the jerk with a searing stare. *"...you* will be the one regretting it." After delivering the message in a low, deadly tone, Bryce vanished before Mitch could react.

He slid into his black Mustang and relaxed into the seat, smiling to himself at the way he'd ducked out of sight on the previous level of the parking garage. Mitch had been easily fooled by the quick one-two-double-back evasion route he'd pulled around a couple of BMW's and a Hummer.

"Just your ordinary day at the office." If you couldn't joke about it, you didn't last.

He activated his Bluetooth as he drove through the semi-clear afternoon Atlanta streets.

"International Federal Publishing, how may I direct your call?"

"Hi, Daisy."

"Bryce…" The receptionist's tone chided him for not following protocol, yet again. And for calling her by his nickname for her. The one she wasn't very fond of.

"All right. Sorry." He cleared his throat and spoke precisely. "Password of the week… Goldenrod. This is Agent Ashburn. Get me Alpha Major."

"One moment, Ashburn."

Bryce waited. He imagined Daisy patching him through to their boss. Mr. Montrose would be picking up the phone any second…

"Ashburn! What's up?"

"Hey Monty. Something big, actually."

"Don't keep me in suspense. Spill it."

"I just got drafted to be an assistant to a lovely graphic designer the boss is sending to find the guy who disappeared with valuable technology. In Venice."

A few more seconds of silence. "Interesting."

Bryce gave Monty the rundown of the meeting he and Cara had had with Gungerson Sr. in the conference room.

"This is good." His boss finally concurred. "Go to Venice, but keep your eyes peeled for bugs in the works. We still don't know if it's Silver Strand or Ravenmeister that is the front for the illegal arms dealing."

"Got it."

"And Bryce, take care of the girl. I don't want any civilians getting hurt on my watch. The minute this becomes dangerous, get her out of there."

"Will do, Sir. No worries. Cara and I go way back, I'll look out for her."

When his boss next spoke, there was a heightened level of interest in his voice.

"You two have a history together?" Monty was aware that he and Cara both hailed from tiny Alvaton, but now he sounded as if he thought there might be… *something* between him and her.

Bryce scoffed in disgust. "It's not what you think. We took homeschool co-op art class together, in like, eighth grade, lived in the same neighborhood. It's nothing."

"Ashburn, I hear you trying to be nonchalant. Watch yourself. You know better than anyone that distractions are deadly."

"Yes Sir."

"Keep me posted. And watch your back."

"Will do."

The line went dead, Montrose's signature way of ending a phone conversation.

Bryce deactivated his Bluetooth and parked in front of a department store. He'd taken everything he thought he would need from his apartment in D.C. down to Atlanta, but he hadn't realized that he would be traveling internationally. He had some shopping to do. Thankfully, his expense account was nice and fat.

~*~

Cara hummed to herself as she slipped a silky robe into her half-full suitcase. She followed it with nylons, a few pairs of shoes, and the non-wrinkling blouses and pants she'd chosen to take. She eyed the small collection of perfumes on her vanity table. She really only had room for one. But which one? She crossed to the table and picked up one, then another. Hmm. "Charmed Life" or "Paris Amour"? She spritzed a little of each on either wrist, then sniffed thoughtfully.

Which would Bryce like best?

The phone rang, startling Cara even more than the sudden question her mind had formed. Heart pounding, she answered.

"Hello?"

"Hello, darling."

"Mom! How are you?"

"I'm fine, dear. How are you?"

Cara knew they both really meant the question. It went far beyond the requisite small talk inquiry.

She sighed softly. "I'm fine."

"Mmmm-hmm?" Her mother's I-know-you tone told her she was waiting for more.

"Well, the company is sending me to Italy!" She let a little of her bottled-up excitement creep into her voice.

"Cara! That's wonderful!"

"I know! I'm packing now and I leave in the morning. I was just about to call and tell you."

"How long will you be gone? Tell me all about it."

Cara froze, staring at herself in the mirror. How much should she tell her mother? "Uh – well, I can't say exactly how long I'm going to be gone. I think perhaps a week."

"Oh, how nice!"

"The company is sending me on... a research project." True. She would be researching the location of a possibly kidnapped man.

"How exciting! Italy will be so inspiring for you. Oh, Cara, this is just wonderful. Wait until I tell your grandmother." She actually sounded bubbly.

It sickened Cara a little not to share the whole story. Ever since her father had passed away when she was five years old, she and her mother had been inseparably close.

"There's one more thing, Mom."

"What?"

"I'm going with… Bryce Reynolds."

"Oh?" Her mother sounded alarmed.

Cara felt herself blush. "No, no, I mean, not *with* him, just… *along* with him. We're both going. He was hired by Silver Strand a few days ago. Do you remember Bryce, Mom?"

"Bryce Reynolds from the homeschool group?"

"Yes." Cara sighed with relief. "You remember, don't you? He and I used to play together sometimes."

More like every *day*.

"Is he still nice?" There was an uncommon lilt in her mother's tone.

"*Mother.*"

"Well?"

"Yes, he's very nice, for a friend." Cara decided it was high time that they changed the subject. "Mom, what should I bring back for you from Venice? A little gondola?"

Her mother laughed, but was willing to let the subject of Bryce drop for now. *Thank goodness.*

"Some Venetian glass, or a postcard! Something small. But I would love a souvenir."

Cara laughed along. "I'll find something special. And I'll get a surprise for Nana, too."

"All right. Have a lovely trip, honey. You'll be in my prayers, as always."

"Thank you, Mom. I love you."

"I love you too." Her mother's voice was so sweet. Like honey and cinnamon. "Goodbye!"

The room felt hollow after she hung up the phone. Cara gave herself a little shake and turned on the radio, returning to her packing. She stared at the perfume bottles. Charmed Life or Paris Amour? Paris Amour seemed too… romantic. Should she go with something else, something plainer, like Warm Vanilla? Cara sighed.

A knock sounded on the outer door of the apartment in a 6-tap rhythm of "shave-and-a-hair-cut, two-bits."

Cara grinned. Penny was here.

"Yoo-hoo!" Penny's voice called through the door. "I know you're home, darlingest! Your cute lil' car is down there in the parking lot! Let me in!"

Cara ran to open the door, and there stood Penny in all her red-haired glory, wearing a forest-green-and-white striped top and long, flowing gaucho pants, carrying an *enormous* peach leather purse. Nobody would disagree with the fact that Penny definitely had her own style, and she made it work.

Penny stepped in and swept her into a hug. "Hey, Sugar! I've missed you."

"Penny!" Cara greeted her, returning the hug with equal warmth. "You'll never believe what I'm about to tell you."

Penny leaned back and looked at her with eyes as blue as forget-me-nots. "Try me." She grinned.

Cara took a deep breath. "I'm going to Italy." She plugged her ears just in time to muffle the piercing shriek.

"Aaaaaaaah!" Penny squealed and jumped up and down three times. "*No way!* Oh my *word!*"

"*Yes*! I am dead serious. I leave tomorrow morning."

Penny gasped, one hand flying to her chest. "Excuse me while I faint."

Cara giggled. Penny always made her giggle. "Before you faint, would you help me decide what perfume to bring?" She asked, although already knowing what Penny would say.

"What happened to that simply luscious fragrance I gave you for your birthday?" Penny's eyes danced. "You know… the *Paris Amour*?"

Cara smiled and shrugged. "I thought about it."

"Well, think no more. You're taking it, and that's that." Penny laughed, tossing her head. "Now let me see what else you're packing! Oh, I wish you would let me take you shopping."

Cara shook her head as Penny tugged her towards the bedroom. "Not with my budget and your taste."

"Oh, Pfoo, darling. You're too practical under that head of show-stopping blonde hair."

Penny looked over the clothes Cara had laid out in the suitcase with a decidedly disdainful expression. Cara's wardrobe tended towards elegant grays and pastels, lacking the bold colors Penny loved.

"Oh well. You do look amazing in these outfits. Oh! I know." Penny dug around in her mammoth purse until she emerged victorious with a gray silk peony clutched in her grasp.

"Here…" She handed the ruffly flower to Cara. "It's a pin. You can use it for a brooch, or a hair accessory, or hang it on a chain for a necklace. My contribution for your trip!"

Cara smiled. "Thank you, Penny. I'll use it."

"Oooh, you're going to have so much fun. Tell me everything. *Why* are you going to Italy?" Penny shucked off her shoes, curled up on Cara's bed, and tucked her feet underneath her, cross-legged. Cara joined her and they sat facing each other.

"The company is sending me… It's a research trip." It was getting easier to tell people about it.

Penny smiled. "All expenses paid?" She arched an eyebrow.

Cara laughed. "I wish. Just travel expenses and lodging, as far as I know. A pair of Prada shoes isn't in the budget."

"Aww, too bad." Penny pretended to sympathize, giggling.

Cara traced the floral pattern of the bedspread with the tip of her finger. "I'm going with an assistant."

Penny listened intently. "Oh?"

"His name is Bryce Reynolds."

Penny gasped and acted out a melodramatic swoon, falling slowly backwards on the bed, her auburn hair spilling out behind her. "Not *The* Bryce Reynolds?"

"I'm afraid so."

Penny sat up. "*The* Bryce Reynolds that every teen girl in the homeschool group had a crush on, *The* Bryce Reynolds who hardly even looked at any girl, ever, except you, *The* Bryce Reynolds who mysteriously disappeared and moved away to who knows where?"

"The same."

"*The* Bryce Reynolds who does *not* have Facebook, Instagram, or Twitter?" Penny shrugged mischievously. "I looked."

"You didn't!"

"Can you blame me? What's he like now?"

Cara sighed softly, trying to think of what to say.

"That good, huh?"

"Penny!"

"You lucky thing! I can't believe he just waltzed into your life like some gift from above. He's actually your assistant?" Penny shook her head.

"Man, if I had an assistant like that, I'd work without pay." Then she cocked her head in thought. "Nah, maybe not. A girl's gotta eat."

Cara found herself giggling like a little girl. Penny was so hilarious.

"You silly thing. Yes, he's my assistant. He just started working for Silver Strand, and then Mr. Gungerson ordered us both off on this… trip."

Penny put a finger on her mouth. "Hmm. Sounds like the old boy's playing matchmaker."

"Mr. Gungerson? Are you out of your *mind*?"

"Wait, what about the son? Mitch, wasn't it? Is he still hanging all over you like kudzu along the highway?"

Cara blew out an annoyed breath. "Yeah, he is… but I've told him to bug off."

"And he won't?"

"No such luck. But now he thinks Bryce and I are an item, so maybe he'll leave me alone."

"Oh he does, does he? And why is this?" Penny narrowed her eyes in mock suspicion.

"Well… he got the *impression* one day that Bryce and I were going out to lunch together…"

"*Were* you?" Penny's face lit up.

"Well, no, but then I did end up taking Bryce to *Siesta Ole*. And before that we went to Antico Pizza Napoletana."

Penny looked like she was holding in her laughter. And possibly a squeal. "Aha!"

"Anyway... typical for Mitch, he instantly turned evil and said something about inter-office affairs never lasting long."

"*Lovely.*" Penny wrinkled her button nose with the fairy-dust sprinkling of freckles over it.

"Yeah." Cara stood and stretched. "I have a little more packing to do. You really think I should take that perfume?"

Penny bounded up like a gazelle. "Yes! It's so you. Elegant... mysterious... romantic."

"Really? I'm all that?"

"And more."

Cara squeezed Penny in a hug. "You're too sweet."

"Thanks, dearie." Penny smiled her beautiful smile. "Well – the real reason I came over was to see if you wanted to paint the town red with me this evening. I just sold three of my paintings and I feel a serious need to celebrate with some cheesecake!"

Penny painted beautiful watercolors that featured adorable children and animals. She also drew whimsical illustrations for children's books.

"Penny! That's wonderful. Congratulations on the sale." Cara sighed. "Unfortunately, I do have more packing and planning to take care of... and I'm going to need a good night's rest. Can I take you up another time on that cheesecake?"

"Of course, sweet girl." Penny gave her an understanding smile. "Well, I must be off –" She scooted for the door.

"Have a beautiful trip, and come back to tell me all about it!" She shook her finger at Cara, standing in the doorway. "Now don't you go off without that Paris Amour, you hear me?"

Cara nodded. "Yes, Ma'am." She winked.

Penny grinned, her smile showcasing beautiful white teeth. "And don't you dare leave Bryce for some handsome Italian!"

"*Penny!*" But Penny was gone with a flounce of her swishy gauchos.

Cara laughed and closed the door, walking back to her bedroom with bare feet against the soft white carpet. Feeling optimistic, she smiled playfully into the mirror, and tucked "Paris Amour" into her suitcase.

Chapter Three

Investigating Venice

The doorbell rang. Cara glanced swiftly in the mirror. Her long braid passed inspection. No stray strands.

She checked the peephole and saw Bryce, dressed in tailored khaki pants and a button-down shirt under a corduroy jacket. He was also wearing a patient expression.

Though feeling pressed for time, she watched him for a few seconds. After two had ticked by he looked up and scanned the area with a steely gaze, almost like a sentry on duty, then his face resumed the content look.

Hmm… That was …different. She unlocked and swung open the door. "Hey Bryce."

"Good morning, sunshine." He winked at her. "This is your friendly neighborhood travel agent, ready for takeoff, ma'am." He made a show of consulting his wristwatch. "Luggage ready?"

She turned and waved to the suitcase waiting against the wall.

"We are very relieved to see that you managed to fit your supplies in one case, Miss Stephenson." Bryce grinned. "It makes it easier on our transport crew."

Cara laughed, amused by his little charade. "Would the *transport crew* like anything to drink before we leave?"

"Sorry ma'am, no time, but they'd be happy to take a rain check on that offer." Bryce stepped inside and wheeled the suitcase to the doorway.

~*~

In the brief glimpse he'd seen of Cara's apartment, he got the feeling of peace, order, style, and creativity. Her interior décor was simple but dynamic, in a color palette of grey, mint, berry, and pale avocado. The furniture ranged from the glass-topped coffee table to the plush plum sofa.

He turned back to see Cara turn to reach for her purse, her braid swinging behind her. Her *four-foot-long* braid! The end of the golden rope of hair thumped against the back of her thigh.

"Whoa!"

She looked up at him in surprise. "What?"

He stared, forgetting himself. "Your hair is so *long*."

Cara stuck her fist on her hip. "Yeah. And?"

"And..." He broke off, laughing. "You must get that a lot."

Cara didn't snort, but the noise she made came perilously close to it. *"Don't* tell me about it. I never hear "You have great hair," "Your hair is beautiful" "What lovely hair"... I only hear "Girl, your hair is *so* long."

There's another one of those moments I wish I could just rewind a few seconds and re-try. I'd tell her that her hair is amazing instead of staring like a dunce.

Bryce shrugged as Cara locked the door behind them and they descended the steps. *Oh well.* "It's probably the first thing people think. The length impresses them."

She looked at him and he held her gaze for a long moment. There was a tinge of sadness, disappointment even, in her face.

"But it *is* beautiful." *Really, really beautiful.*

Cara looked away. "Thank you." It came out quietly, but she sounded pleased.

Bryce felt like he'd dodged a bullet. Make that a cannonball. Obviously, her hair was a sensitive point. He would keep that in mind.

They reached the parking lot and he headed for the green sedan.

"What is this?" Cara asked as they walked up to the car. "I thought you drove a black Mustang."

He stared, shoulders tensing. "How did you know that?"

Her face froze, and then she turned red. "I saw you getting into one in the parking garage at work."

You mean you watched *me in the parking garage.* Otherwise, why the blush? "Oh, is that all?" He laughed. "Some friends are loaning it to me. They'll pick it up at the airport later after they get off work."

He loaded her suitcase into the trunk, nestling it next to his luggage.

Cara's eyebrows rose. "Okay." She seemed all right with letting that go without further questioning, for which he was grateful.

What Cara didn't know was that he didn't want his Mustang sitting in the airport, open to being sabotaged. He had a long list of enemies.

~*~

Cara wouldn't have admitted it, but she was very glad for Bryce's arm around her as he escorted her through the crowds of people in the airport. Atlanta had the busiest airport in the country, and right now it was packed.

It was odd, how she could feel claustrophobic in such a large area. The press of people around her felt stifling. Bryce was busy working a path through the people and didn't seem to notice her discomfiture, something she was glad of. It would have been embarrassing to admit she was scared of crowds.

~*~

They checked their luggage. Cara's black suit case glided down the conveyor belt. Bryce calmly laid his cases on the belt and watched them slide away from him. He had called ahead for security clearance to explain why his modest faded blue suitcase was loaded for bear with some seriously high-tech weapons. Attached was a government-issue tag with his agency identification that would be scanned and waved through.

And the airport had been alerted that Special Agent 50938QD, approximately six feet, two inches tall, with light brown hair and hazel eyes, would be passing through – and carrying a Colt M1911 in a shoulder holster underneath his corduroy jacket.

So when they entered the special security checkpoint before boarding the plane, he gave the staff member a discreet nod. The man eyed him up and down, taking note of the corduroy jacket, and asked "May I see your ID, please, Sir?"

"Cara, is that Mr. Gungerson's secretary?" Bryce pointed vaguely into the middle distance.

"Matilda? Where? She never travels."

"Over there." Bryce pointed again with one hand and pulled out his wallet with the other. With a purposefully bored air, he flashed his Agency identification. Cara was staring in the direction he had indicated and didn't see the card he showed the airport worker.

The man nodded. "Have a nice day, Mr. Reynolds."

"Thank you." Bryce ushered Cara towards the gate and they walked along for a few minutes. "It must not have been her."

"No, I don't think so." Cara replied. Then she looked up. And gasped.

~*~

"A private jet?"

Bryce smiled. "Now *this* is traveling in style."

Cara was still reeling in shock when they sank into the cushy, padded leather seats. She could not believe Mr. Gungerson was sending them in one of his private jets. Every nerve felt raw. Mr. Gungerson never treated anybody this well besides himself – and his son, who was spoiled rotten. She gripped the arms of her seat and held on tightly.

~*~

"Ca-ra." Bryce made his singsong whisper teasing. "We haven't even lifted off the ground yet. You don't have to crush the chair arms."

She jerked her head in his direction and stared at him. "Not. Funny."

He sat back and studied her. *She's terrified.* "What's wrong?"

"This feels like a bribe." Cara snapped. "Look around. Nobody gets treated this well without giving something huge back in return. I don't want to do this."

Bryce was torn. Cara probably wouldn't have decided to accept this mission if he hadn't encouraged her to… and it could, *potentially*, be dangerous. But he couldn't do it without her, because his cover with Silver Strand was acting as her assistant. He had to calm her down.

He reached over and clasped her hand. "I'll take care of you. I promise. I'll be your handy-dandy assistant, and coordinate everything. I'll keep a lookout. If I smell a rat, you'll be the first to know."

He looked into her eyes, willing her to trust him. He needed her to trust in him.

Cara sighed softly. Her hand tightened around his. "First, you have to tell me something."

He knew what she was going to say before the words left her lips. Sure enough…

"Why didn't you say goodbye?" Hurt pooled in her eyes, and in a flash he glimpsed the same devastation he'd felt at being left. His father had left him, but he had left Cara.

"Cara… I'm so, so sorry."

"I don't want an apology, I want an answer." Her tone was grim, and her hand was trembling. Wide eyes waited to see if he'd follow through.

They had told no one in Alvaton where they were headed or why they left, but rumor had surely spread nonetheless, for his mother had received several phone calls from women who had called her their friend, but only hungered for the latest shred of fresh gossip like predatory sharks.

He'd never gone to Cara's house to say goodbye. He couldn't tell her his Dad had dumped them... would have been unable to bear the sharp shards of grief and loss in her moonlight-gray eyes, mirroring his own hurt. Never looked for her, years later, dreading the awkwardness he feared would be there – when they'd hardly had to speak to know each other's thoughts before.

"My dad left us."

She gasped softly and closed her eyes. She looked like she was walling herself off from attack.

Oh, dear Lord, I can't believe I forgot. Cara's father, a dedicated police officer, had been shot in a gas station hold-up when she was five years old. That was when she and her mother moved in with her Nana to the house on Burberry Street. He hadn't met Cara until she was nine, but knew the missing presence of her father was still keenly felt in the all-female household.

"He didn't die like your father. He deliberately left us, with only a note to explain it."

Cara snapped out of it and opened her eyes. "What did the note say?"

"Mom never showed it to me. She just told me he said he had to leave." He had to look away. The plane window provided an escape for his gaze.

"I couldn't tell you. I felt such... shame, at his leaving us. Like we were trash that could be thrown aside."

"Oh, no! No." Cara bit her lip and shook her head vehemently. "You weren't trash."

"I felt like it. Not the smartest thing to think, but I was young. I should have known better." He still held her hand in his, like a lifeline. She seemed to have forgotten about it. "And after that it just seemed awkward. What would I say to you?"

Cara drew back a little. "I don't know. 'Hi', maybe?" She sighed, rolling her eyes. "I suppose communication seems much simpler to girls than it does to guys."

Not going there. If she wanted to play the guy-girl card, let her. He had work to do.

"So." He probed her face with his gaze, searching for a sign. "Will you trust me?"

A long, long, *long* moment passed before her hesitant nod. "All right."

He smiled. *Yes! Atta girl.*

~*~

Cara awoke feeling groggy. She picked up her head and rubbed her eyes.

"Hungry? It's lunch time." Bryce smiled down at her.

Hmmph. Why did he have to be the suave one and stay awake?

"How long have I been sleeping?" Cara looked at her watch. 11:58.

"Long enough. I turned off your iPod for you when you fell asleep, to save the battery."

How thoughtful of him. "Thanks."

Bryce handed her a menu.

A *menu*? "No. Way."

He grinned. "Yes way. We have a choice of Chicken Cordon Bleu, or Hamburgers with Angus beef."

"They both sound great. What are you having?"

He rubbed his chin with a lean hand and looked thoughtful. "I think I could go for a burger."

"Then I'll get the chicken, if I can beg a little bite of your hamburger. You can have a taste of my lunch."

Bryce smiled. "Sounds like a good plan to me."

Cara felt like giggling, but held it in. She wasn't quite ready to freely express her every emotion around him. "My mom and I usually order that way. We taste each other's entrees and sometimes even trade if we each like the other's choice better."

Bryce leaned his head on his hand and studied her openly.

"What?"

"I think I'm going to enjoy getting to know you all over again."

"You're impossible!" She rolled her eyes and bit the inside of her cheek to hold in her flattered smile.

"No, just honest."

~*~

"Please fasten your seat belts, we are about to begin our descent." The captain's voice warned over the intercom.

"That was a long flight." Cara stretched, and then massaged one of the kinks out of her shoulder.

"Yes, Miss Understatement. Ten hours, fifty-five minutes. You slept for most of it." Bryce growled, rubbing his face and eyes.

"You poor baby. I should have stayed awake to keep you company." Cara teased. She began unbraiding her hair, which had become mussed during the flight.

One of Bryce's eyes glinted with amusement from behind his hands, and then he dropped them and tipped his head back in the chair, closing his eyes again. "Wake me when we get on the ground."

Cara pulled out a brush and ran it through her hair. "Oh, now that I'm awake, you can sleep?"

The slow smile that spread across Bryce's face was the only answer.

Exasperating man. Was he asleep or not? Cara turned her attention to her hair, working out every last tangle as the plane slowly coasted down towards the ground. Once finished, she looked up to see Bryce staring at her.

"Hasn't anyone ever told you that staring is rude?" Cara asked, feeling heat rise to her cheeks.

"Sorry." Bryce said, but he didn't look away, as if his wide-open eyes were glued to her.

Cara shifted her gaze away from him and decided to look out at the scenery instead. She soon forgot about Bryce... well, almost... as she beheld her first glimpse of Italy. The colors were marvelous, vibrant. She had never seen such blues and greens.

~*~

Cara had the most gorgeous hair he had ever seen. Freed from the braid, it flowed down in front of her over her lap all the way to her knees in shimmering golden waves. She gazed out the window down to the beautiful landscape, completely ignoring him.

He didn't mind missing the scenery. He'd seen Italy from the air before. Come to think of it... he had seen a lot of places, period.

He finally tore his gaze from Cara and started readying for their departure from the jet. Montrose hadn't been kidding when he warned him about distractions, and the guy didn't even know Cara. Bryce ran a comb through his hair and tossed his Bible into his carry-on bag.

"Cara, I hate to ask, but would you mind putting up your hair?"

She glared at him. "Why?"

"It attracts too much attention."

"*Your* attention?" She sent him a pointed glance.

He gave her a slightly apologetic look. "*Everyone's* attention. We're here to investigate, not become the object of everyone's interest. The little girls will all be screaming "It's RAPUNZEL!" and pointing at you."

"Hmmph." Cara frowned, but meekly retrieved a clip from her bag and did something incredible – wrapping her hair around her hand, twisting, a coil, and suddenly all the hair had vanished into a modest bun, secured with a clip.

He tried not to look too fascinated as he zipped his bag shut. Then his head snapped upright as he remembered something.

"Oh, and I might as well tell you, Italian men have a thing for blondes."

"A *thing* for *blondes*!?" Her smooth voice became squeaky.

He also tried *not* to laugh at her look of utter horror, but this time did not succeed. "Ha! Don't worry. I'll keep them away from you."

~*~

"*Bryce*, ease-play oo-day omething-say!" Cara hissed in his direction. The words came out so fast that it sounded like she was speaking gibberish.

"*What?*" he whispered back.

"Do Italians speak Pig Latin?" she murmured, keeping an eye on the desk clerk in the Marco Polo airport, who was definitely turning on his charm.

Bryce's ribs hurt from suppressed laughter. He dealt with the clerk and then took her arm to lead her through the airport. They moved through the ground floor, the first floor above being reserved for departures. He guided her towards the luggage claim. They'd pick up their bags and head for the water terminal.

"I'll buy you a scarf or something."

"A what?" She looked shocked.

"...To tie over your head."

"NEVER." She pressed her lips into a firm line.

A dark-haired man walking towards them suddenly smiled at Cara. "*Sei molto carina! Ti amo!*"

"I don't want to know what he just said." Cara gritted her teeth as they walked away from the man, who was blowing kisses in their direction.

"He said that he thinks you're so cute, and he loves you." He winked. "I speak some Italian."

"Bryce?"

"Yeah?"

"Please buy me a scarf."

He hooted with laughter. He was only human, after all.

After he bought an overpriced scarf at the airport gift shop and Cara covered her golden head, they collected their bags, and continued on their way.

"This way to Venice, Milady!" He guided her in the right direction with a hand on her elbow.

"So, we're not in Venice yet?" Cara looked confused. "But this is the Venice Airport."

"I know. Venice is actually built on an archipelago of islands formed by canals in a shallow lagoon, and it's connected by 409 bridges."

Cara listened in silence. "Go on, Mr. Tour Guide."

He hoped his smile wasn't too smug. "In the 19th century a causeway to the mainland brought the *Venezia Santa Lucia* railway station to Venice, and the *Ponte della Libertà* road causeway was built during the twentieth century. That's how we'll travel into the old heart of Venice – the railway. From there we'll need to go by boat."

Cara eyed him accusingly. "Bryce. You've been here before."

He raised both hands as if she was holding a gun on him. *Ugh, perish the thought.* He hated being held at gunpoint. "Guilty as charged."

She smiled briefly before her frown returned. "When have you been here before?"

Bryce thought fast. "In college. School trip."

"Really. Care to elaborate?" her eyes narrowed.

The last thing he needed was a suspicious female on his case. "Nope."

Cara sighed. She suddenly looked weary as she trudged along beside him, her head wrapped in the colorful scarf. "I need a good, long soak in a hot bubble-bath."

Sympathy shot through him like a dart. "You'll get one when we reach the hotel."

"And when might that be?"

"Soon. Be patient. I've got the directions. From the Santa Lucia railway station, we'll take line 1 on the *vaporetto* – that's the public water bus – and get off at the *Ponte di Rialto* stop."

Cara nodded, but he got the feeling that she wasn't really listening. He grinned and wrapped his arm around her shoulder. "Come on. Let's find our bus."

~*~

Cara felt dazed, as if she was in a dream. They were taking a water 'bus' to the hotel and riding down the Grand Canal – a long, wide 'street' of sparkling water lined by buildings that exuded age and elegance. Brightly colored striped poles lined the wooden docks, and little boats of every shape and size floated alongside. Bryce's grin looked permanently pasted on his face as he watched her looking around, drinking everything in.

"There it is." Bryce told her as they passed in front of a modest building tucked between two larger ones. "We'll have to get off over there," He pointed to the water bus stop, "and cross the bridge on foot and go to the hotel through the back."

Cara kept turning her head from side to side, trying to soak in the splendor. *This place is incredible!*

They arrived at the bus stop and disembarked from the boat. He managed his bags while she rolled her own suitcase along. They reached the bridge, and a shiver of delight raced down her spine as they stepped onto the old stone.

"Bryce, we have to take a picture. Now." She stopped him at the crest of the bridge.

~*~

Bryce held back a sigh. His arms were aching from hefting his luggage, and he was really looking forward to putting them down. "Now? We could come back later after we drop off our bags..."

"Now! I don't want to forget this moment." Her beautiful eyes beseeched him. At this moment, they were shining with a green hue instead of their usual soft gray. It nearly took his breath away.

He found himself unable to refuse. She was right, it was a perfect moment for a photo – the light glowed golden and sparkled on the water as the sunset unfolded.

"Oh, all right." He set down his suitcases against the edge of the bridge and waited as she pulled out her camera from her carry-on bag.

She snapped several photos in each direction, and then stopped a middle-aged Italian lady walking past. "Please, would you take our picture?" Cara asked her, motioning to herself and Bryce.

"*Sì!*" The lady smiled and took the camera. Cara showed her which button to push, and then stepped back to Bryce's side.

"Uh... Cara..." It wasn't the best of ideas for them to be photographed together. If it became public, his enemies might find a copy and be able to identify Cara, and get to him through her. Or worse, get to *her* through him!

She looked up at him with those innocent eyes again.

"Never mind." *Hang the risk!* He wrapped his arm around her and smiled for the camera as they stood against the side of the bridge.

The lady returned the camera with another smile. "*Spero che vi divertiate!*"

"She said she hopes we have fun." Bryce translated for Cara.

A soft smile curved her mouth.

He eyed the top of her head. "You do realize you just got photographed, *scarf* and all?"

For an instant her smile dropped, but then she laughed. "Mom will enjoy the story behind it."

~*~

Cara was stunned. Entering the little hotel, checking in, and walking up to their rooms had been like walking through a dream. Everything from the gorgeous chandeliers in the ceiling down to the beautiful patterned rugs here and there on the flecked stone floor was ornately stunning. The furniture looked like it belonged in an antique store… a pricey one.

Then she walked into her room. Italian damask-patterned wallpaper embellished the walls and matched perfectly with the damask bedding and canopy over the bed. Fresh flowers graced the top of the chest of drawers and permeated the room with their fragrance.

There might as well have been dollar signs stamped on everything inside the four walls.

She looked back over her shoulder at Bryce, who stood in the doorway. "No. No – Bryce, this is too much." Cara scanned the gorgeously furnished room in one quick sweep and turned her eyes to his face. "It must cost a small fortune to stay here."

"Cara, please, reserve your judgment for one second while I stick my luggage in my room, okay? I will be *right* back. Don't go anywhere." He pleaded.

"Fine." Her voice was sprinkled with ice.

~*~

Bryce chucked his luggage into his room as fast as he could, hardly looking at the room in his haste, and dashed back to Cara's suite. She let him in, her face a tight mask of apprehension.

"Okay. Now where were we?" He took a seat on the edge of the bed and tucked his hands into his jacket pockets, attempting to look right at home… though in truth, he was impressed by the hotel's grandeur. Most of the time, his digs weren't quite this ritzy.

Cara began pacing on the intricately designed carpet. "I feel like I'm in way over my head. I am highly uncomfortable with this whole thing, and we don't even know where to start looking for the missing man… all we know is that he was last seen in this hotel! We have no informants, no contacts, and no help whatsoever. We're on our own, and I'm not sure it's even legal for us to be investigating here in Italy!"

He was impressed that she had managed all that on one breath. "Cara, come here."

She turned, obviously bristling.

"Please?" He turned the order into a request.

She perched cautiously on the other corner of the bed, wary, alert.

He sighed. "Cara… everything's okay."

She folded her arms across her chest. "You know what, it's starting to bug me when you say that because you *don't* really know that everything's okay."

"But Cara, I do." He wanted to take one of her hands, but they were tightly pressed against her midsection.

"How?" It was a soft challenge.

It looked like he was going to have to explain a few things. Hopefully it would *only* have to be a few.

"Well, for starters, you don't have to worry about us not being 'legal'."

She quirked an eyebrow at him.

"I did some part-time investigating for – a private detection agency. I kept my license current just for the fun of it." All true. Well, sort of. It wasn't a *private* agency. It was a top-secret *international* counterintelligence agency.

And sometimes it wasn't fun at all.

"Is your license good in *Italy*?"

"Yep." She still looked unconvinced. "*Yes.* I know for sure. I'm cleared for investigation here." He insisted, at last.

She gave him a strange look. "You are a very unusual person, Bryce Reynolds."

Time to change the subject. "And you are a very pretty one, Cara Stephenson, even when you're wearing a scarf on your head."

"Aaaaagh!" She yelled, ripping the scarf off her head, "I hate this thing!" And then she started laughing.

Bingo.

"Then don't wear it." He laughed along with her. "I'll tell you what. When we're out in public, we'll act like a – couple. You know... you hang on my arm. Then the Italian guys will be less likely to bother you."

Cara brushed a strand of hair off her forehead. "Well, okay. It's either that or buy a dark wig."

He coughed. "I don't think you could fit all of your hair underneath a wig."

"This is true." She sighed. Then looked at him. "Bryce? Will you do something for me?"

"Name it." A little reckless of him, but he was willing to do almost anything for her at this point. He had to keep her working with him.

"*I* want to be *your* assistant. You're the investigator, for Pete's sake! I'm an artist. You should be the one leading this 'investigation', not me. But I'll help you."

Relief washed over him. She could not have asked anything of him that he would more willingly do.

"Sounds like a plan to me." He grinned.

She smiled, her whole face relaxing.

"Now go take your bubble bath. And that's an order." He winked. "I'll do some asking around, and then I'll take you out for that dinner I mentioned."

"Yes, *Sir*!" Her huge grin brought adorable dimples out of hiding.

~*~

Bryce didn't bother to unpack, but he opened his weapon case and checked his guns as he dialed up Monty on his Bluetooth earpiece.

"Montrose speaking."

"Hey, Monty. It's Ashburn."

"Bryce! How was the trip?"

"Uneventful, which is good. Cara felt nervous about the whole deal, so I told her I had some previous "investigation experience" and that I had a current license. She thought we might be acting illegally, I had to reassure her."

His boss grunted. "Well, don't tell her any more. Any leads yet?"

"I just got here. Give me five seconds to catch my breath. This is only the check-in."

"Well, I'm glad you made it through your trip on the private jet and arrived at your five-star hotel unscathed." Typical Montrose dry humor.

It was only a four-star hotel, but he didn't attempt to correct his boss. "Thanks. I'm taking Cara out to dinner in a little bit, but I'm going to do some asking around first."

"What is Cara doing at the moment?"

Bryce cleared his throat. "Taking a bubble bath."

"Aha." His boss evidently decided to let that slide by without comment. "Well – let me know how it goes. Be careful. I'll keep you posted on the fresh information from our end."

"*Grazie.*"

Montrose chuckled. "You're welcome." The line went dead.

Bryce turned off his earpiece. His weapons were all in order, so he closed and locked the case again. He slipped his M1911 handgun back into the shoulder holster and donned a blazer. He ran a comb through his hair, which finished off his preparations for dinner out. He'd start with the hotel staff. It was surprising how a little charm could coax information from a cleaning lady, and a few dollars – or euros, in this case – could pry details from a bellhop.

~*~

Cara brushed a touch of mascara onto her eyelashes, added a hint of gloss to her lips, and stood back to survey the result. She didn't look like a stick-thin fashion model, but one would have to admit she was attractive… especially all dressed up.

She wore the 'nice dress' Bryce had told her to pack. It fell down past her knees in a satiny pink swirl, with sheer cap sleeves and seed pearls sprinkled across the draped neckline.

Not quite daring yet to leave her hair down, she had coiled it into three flat 'shell' buns clustered on the back of her head, pinning Penny's gray silk flower to one side. The result was an intricate hairstyle resembling a golden bouquet.

Penny would have approved.

She had just slipped in a pair of dainty pearl earrings when a knock sounded at the outer door. Leaving the bathroom, she ran through her room, ducking down from her full height to look into the peephole before opening the door.

"Hi." She said softly.

He went completely still at the sight of her, except for his eyes, which traveled all the way down to her shoes, then snapped back to her face.

"You —" His voice cracked. "You look great." He cleared his throat.

Bryce looked pretty great himself, having changed into a blazer in a coppery shade of brown that brought out the golden glints in his nut-brown hair.

"You do too." She gave him a warm smile, hoping he'd snap out of what she thought was probably the old shyness resurfacing.

"I'll just get my purse." Cara left him in the doorway.

~*~

Wow.

Bryce leaned against the door frame, trying to collect his thoughts, which had been completely scattered when Cara appeared like a heavenly vision just a moment before. He forced himself to check the hallway for any danger. Nothing.

"So how did it go?" Cara reappeared, purse in hand.

He caught a light whiff of a tantalizing fragrance as she passed him in the doorway.

"Uh... I'm sorry. What?" He shook his head.

Get a grip, Bryce!

"How did the questioning go? You said you were going to ask around about Freddie. Any results to report?"

How she moved down the hallway so gracefully in those high heels was a mystery to him.

"Well... not much. I had a few bites when I mentioned him, but most of them were dead ends. I found out which room he stayed in, though."

"How does that help?"

"We'll have to go in and search it later."

"*What?*" Her whisper was shocked. "*Search* the room?"

"He might have left something of value in the room, some clue as to where he was headed. I don't plan on missing out on anything that points to his current location."

He looked at her, one eyebrow raised. "It's what investigators *do*, Cara. They investigate."

She looked away. "I'm sorry. You're right."

Relieved, he opened the door for her, and then they were on the foot-streets of Venice once more.

"So where are we going? We could have just eaten at the hotel, you know. I'm sure the food there is fantastic."

"I'm taking you to a great place I visited the last time I was here, *Fiaschetteria Toscana.* They only serve fresh local fish." He answered, "And it's a nice walk over there from the hotel."

"All right. Sounds lovely." Cara smiled at him and slipped her hand into his as an Italian man swiveled his head in her direction. The man looked away, regret etched on his face.

Bryce grinned. He'd almost forgotten about their pact to play a charade. "I'm sorry, *darling*. I nearly forgot to pay attention to you."

She laughed, eyes dancing. "It's all right, *honey*, I'm fine." She was irresistible when she laughed.

She might be fine, but *he* was definitely in for it now.

~*~

He watched Cara lift a delicate forkful of rice to her mouth, then pat her lips with the linen napkin. "This is delicious."

"I'll say." The flavors danced and mingled with the perfect texture of the grilled *Dorade*. "Even better than I remembered." He forked another bite, relishing it.

What ambience. Candles in ornate candelabra holders glowed on every wall, and fine china plates on shelves lined the top of the walls. Wooden rafters crossed the ceiling overhead, stone pillars reached down to the checkered floor, and fresh floral arrangements graced every white tablecloth.

They were seated with two other couples at a table in the middle of the room, most of them being full when they arrived. There was a Mr. and Mrs. Totteridge, a staid middle-aged English couple on an anniversary vacation, and a young boyfriend and girlfriend from Belgium, who spoke very broken English.

"And what are you visiting Venice for, my dears? You know, it's so fascinating to speak with Americans." Mrs. Totteridge beamed at them over her glass of water as the meal drew to a close.

"We're on vacation." – "It's a business trip."

He and Cara looked at each other in horror, having both spoken at once.

Mr. Totteridge broke into a hearty chuckle, while the Belgians merely smiled at their expressions.

"You didn't tell me it was a business trip!" Cara was quick to say in false-but-convincing annoyance, salvaging the situation.

Bryce plopped an uncomfortable look on his face, staying in character. "I... ah... didn't see the need."

Cara stood up, grasping her purse with both hands. "I think it's time we left." She pressed her lips into a thin line.

"Yes, of course, honey. Anything you say." Bryce jumped up and called for the check.

"That young man is definitely in hot water." Mr. Totteridge's voice rumbled as they moved away from the table.

Cara waited with an impatient look on her face as Bryce settled the bill and then stalked out the door ahead of him.

They waited until they rounded a street corner to burst into uproarious laughter.

"Oh, Cara, that was priceless. You were awesome. Great save." Bryce could have taken care of it but was secretly very pleased that she'd come up with a solution. *Smart girl.*

"I can't believe we did that. You get to answer all the questions from here on out, okay? That way, the answers will all line up!" She shook her head, still laughing.

"Deal." He took a deep breath. "Well. Back to the hotel?"

"First, I'd like to find a small souvenir for my mom, and my grandma. Any ideas?"

"Yep. I remember a small curio shop that sells authentic handcrafted Venetian jewelry. How does that sound?"

"Perfect. Lead the way." She fell into step beside him.

He looked ahead up the street to see three young Italian men heading in their direction.

He slipped his arm around her waist and pulled her close as they walked along. It worked. The three young Italians only smiled at Cara, passing them without remark.

A tiny sigh of relief escaped her as they disappeared. "Thanks."

"Don't mention it." *Please don't mention it. Ever. Or I'll want to do it again.*

They walked around until they found some pretty necklaces and bracelets for Cara's mother and grandma, featuring handmade millefiori glass beads with tiny floral designs. The shopkeeper told Cara that "Millefiori" meant "thousand flowers."

They reached their hotel without further mishap. Bryce escorted Cara to her door.

"If you need me, knock three times on the wall adjoining my room, wait, then knock three times." He told her. "I'll hear it."

"Okay. And if you're snoring like a grizzly bear and *don't* hear it, I'll just call the desk and ask them to ring your room." Cara fired back coyly, eyes flashing.

"I don't snore." He protested, but felt one corner of his mouth tipping up in a half-smile.

"All guys over twenty-two snore. It's practically a mark of manhood." Cara persisted, leaning against the doorframe.

Well, he was twenty-five, but that didn't mean he snored.

He put his hand on the wall above her shoulder and leaned on his arm. "Not this man."

Cara eyed him as if she still didn't quite believe it, but then covered her mouth with one hand and yawned. She looked like a cute, sleepy kitten.

"It's been a long day." She apologized.

"You've got that right." He was looking forward to a few hours of sleep.

"Thanks for taking me to dinner." She actually *winked* at him. "I enjoyed myself."

"Me too." *More than you know.* "Goodnight."

"Goodnight." She whispered, then edged back and closed the door with a soft 'click'.

The hallway felt cold and empty without her. Bryce did a quick security check, and then slipped into his own room.

After a shower, he set his wristwatch to go off in five hours, when he would again do a security check. As he settled between the sheets, visions of Cara in the pink dress began to intrude on his mind. He groaned and rolled over.

"God, you're going to have to help me do this. I need a clear head and concentration for this assignment. If it's right for me to be attracted to Cara in this way, show me, but if not, slam that door shut hard, Lord."

He ran a hand through his hair. "*I don't even know if she's a believer, Father. I don't know if marriage is right for me at this stage in my life, when I'm serving my country in this dangerous job. Please show me your hand in this. Keep us both safe from harm. And please... help this mission to be one of the successful ones."*

His last conscious thought was of whispering an "Amen" after his silent prayer ended.

~*~

Cara awoke at 6:00 AM with the vague feeling that someone needed her. Then a knock came at her door, and she realized who.

She quickly slipped on her robe and darted to the door. The peephole afforded her a fishbowl-shaped view of Bryce waiting in the hall, tapping his foot. She cracked open the door a quarter-inch.

"What is it?" She cringed. Goodness, her voice sounded rough this morning. She felt positively parched.

"Quick, get dressed. I need your help."

Her mind was foggy. "What?"

"It's time to earch-say a certain oom-ray."

The mental light bulb clicked on. "Oh! I'll be right out, give me three minutes."

~*~

"Have you found anything yet?" Cara's cautious whisper echoed through the room.

Bryce had finished searching all the obvious places and switched to the more clever hiding spots.

"Not yet. But we will. I know it. There's got to be something here. Because if there isn't, we are back to square zero."

She watched him crawling around, inspecting the undersides of the furniture. He'd looked behind the pictures hanging on the wall, inspected the folds of the draperies, searched through every drawer, and practically combed the carpet with a fine-tooth comb.

"This would be a lot easier if we had a forensic evidence team working with us." Bryce grunted as he slid underneath the bed.

Cara walked into the bathroom. Perhaps they had missed something. She looked again in the cabinet under the sink. There had been nothing floating in the tank behind the commode. The trash can was empty except for a used Kleenex.

"Well, at least they haven't cleaned the bathroom yet." Cara called, "or this tissue wouldn't be here."

Bryce suddenly appeared in the doorway, his face alive with excitement. "I just remembered something."

"What?"

He closed the bathroom door. "Let's work up a little steam." He turned on the bathtub faucet full blast, and hot water began to pour out in a steady stream.

"What are you *doing*?"

"You'll see. Why don't you stand at the outer door and keep a lookout?" He suggested.

Cara nodded and slipped out the door. It seemed like it took ages, but then he quietly called her back.

"Cara, come here, quick."

She peeked into the bathroom. He tugged her inside the steamy room and closed the door.

She slapped away his hand from her elbow. "Bryce-!"

"Look!" He pointed to the mirror.

Amid the condensation forming on the glass, a message had appeared.

"Oh my word." Cara breathed.

It was an address. And a request.

**18 Place du Pont Neuf
PARIS, FRANCE
HELP!**

Cara turned to Bryce. "How in the world…"

He grinned sheepishly. "My brother and I used to draw funny faces and write messages on the mirror to each other. It disappears when the room dries out, but when the glass gets steamed up again, you can read it."

She shook her head. "Boys..."

He entered the address into his phone, and snapped a picture of the mirror with it. Then he grabbed a towel and wiped the mirror, erasing the message. "Pack your bags, Cara."

She looked up at him.

"It looks like we're headed to Paris."

Chapter Four

Shall We Dance?

Bryce led Cara back along the hallway as they silently snuck back to their own hotel rooms.

"I need to call my mother to tell her about this change in plans. She thought I was staying in Venice for a week." Cara pitched her voice at a whisper as they reached her hotel room door.

"First, you need to call your boss. Then you can call your mom." He disliked having to order her to do that, but it was imperative that they gave the man an update. And soon.

Cara winced, but nodded. "Will Mr. Gungerson be pleased with the lead we discovered, do you think?"

"He'll be more pleased than if you were calling to say we had zip."

"Good point." She conceded. "I'll call him and then pack up my suitcase."

"Brave girl." He smiled at her.

She smiled back. Then she went off to dial Mr. Gungerson.

~*~

He found her just hanging up the call after he collected his belongings from his room.

"Well, that was about as nice as swallowing a whole bottle of Robitussin." Cara rolled her eyes as she walked along beside him, headed for the front desk to check out.

Bryce chuckled. "Mr. Gungerson has the same effect as bitter cough syrup?"

"Yup." Cara nodded once, her gaze drifting to the opulent surroundings.

"You poor thing. But at least now you can call your mother."

Cara's face brightened. "*That* will be like sipping strawberry lemonade."

She liked strawberry lemonade. *I'll have to remember that.*

~*~

Cara stepped out of the taxi, laughing. "I will, mom. Thank you. I'll have quite a story to tell you when I get back. Love you too. Bye." They'd chatted all the way from the hotel until they had reached the Marco Polo airport. *It felt so good to reconnect with her.*

Bryce closed the taxi door he'd opened for her. "Did she understand about you being 'transferred' to Paris?" He asked.

Cara eyed him. "My mother *always* understands."

He winked. "Good to know."

She opened her mouth, but before she could speak, he stopped her. "Shh! Don't create a disturbance in the middle of the airport. I'll quit teasing you."

She settled for sticking her tongue out at him, and immediately felt silly. Which he capitalized on.

"I can't believe it."

She refused to look at him.

"The elegant Cara Stephenson actually just stuck out her tongue at me."

"I couldn't help it. You bring out my inner preschooler." She retorted in her own defense.

"Your *inner preschooler*? Oh, this is too good."

"Just get us a plane, Bryce." She inserted the remark before he could continue. "And I thought you were going to stop torturing me with your *ceaseless* heckling!"

"Oh, come now, I know you actually like it behind that façade of annoyance."

"*Whatever* gave you that impression?"

"Oh... maybe the blushing and the twinkle in your eye..."

I blush when he teases me?

"*Bryce!*" She was mad now, and thoroughly embarrassed, which was worse.

He backpedaled. "You know, that idea of getting us a plane might be worth following up on. Wait here." He turned to head towards the airline counter, but she grabbed his sleeve.

"Oh no, you don't! I'm not going to be left out to dry in plain sight of any Italian guys. We're still in Italy, in case you haven't noticed. I'm going with you."

"Suit yourself." He winked. "I pity the poor 'Angelo's and 'Roberto's whose hopes I'm dashing."

That was too much.

~*~

Teasing her was addicting. But had he gone too far?

They'd managed to book two second-class seats on a flight taking off in an hour, leaving them with a little time to kill before they lifted off. They'd eaten a huge, delicious breakfast in the cozy hotel lounge, so neither of them was hungry.

"So… what shall we do for an hour?" He asked as they strolled along.

"I don't know." She said tonelessly, like a robot.

He looked at her. "Hey… what's wrong?"

"Nothing." Her face was turned away from him.

"Cara?" He stopped and tried to turn her to face him but she pushed him away.

"Not here, okay? There are billions of people watching us." The sprinkles of ice returned to her voice.

Uh-oh. He had stepped in it.

"What-"

"Just stop." She marched away like a drill sergeant, trailing her suitcase behind her.

"Come on, let's go outside." He suggested.

She sighed, but at least she accompanied him until they were out the door and walking along the sidewalk. Once they followed the walkway for a little while and reached a line of trees, there was almost no one around but the two of them.

He parked his suitcase against the edge of the sidewalk and set down his weapons case.

She stopped with one hand on her suitcase, the other tucked through the shoulder strap of her carryon bag. They stood an uncomfortable distance apart, until Bryce crossed it tentatively in two slow steps.

She looked up at him. "I'm sorry – this is stupid. I'm being oversensitive." Her words still sounded cold. She was shutting him out.

"No." He shook his head. "I crossed a line I shouldn't have."

Her face softened, lines smoothing on her brow.

"Look, Cara… I love to tease. And I especially like teasing my friends." He risked a smile. "And I consider you one of my friends."

She was listening, her expression now open.

"But I never meant to make you mad. Will you please forgive me?" *Please.*

She smiled, which was all the forgiveness he needed right there. "Yes."

Breathing was suddenly a lot easier. "Thanks."

"But we need a signal, or something, for when your teasing is getting to be too much!" Cara looked adorable when she wore a serious expression. "In case we're out in public, and I can't just say 'Bryce, if you go any farther you'll be making me uncomfortable'!"

"Okay…" He rubbed his chin. "How about a code word… "Caviar"?"

"Yuck. I hate caviar." She wrinkled her nose.

"Perfect."

Cara laughed. "If you say so."

There. The normal Cara was back. He checked his watch. And just in time, too. "Well, we used up our waiting time. We'd better go."

"To Paris, then! *Vive la France*!" Cara exclaimed, linking her free arm through his as they headed back into the airport.

It felt wonderful to have harmony restored.

~*~

Mitchell Gungerson, Sr. rested his head on his hands, seated at his desk, alone in the office.

This was not … really …supposed to happen.

He'd sent Cara to Italy to get her out of his son's way for a while. It was the only time he had ever denied his only child anything. But Cara was not a sports car, a mansion, or a private island. She was a human being. And, doting parent though he was, he realized that Mitch would not be good for her. Mitch was selfish… spoiled. It hurt to admit it, but there it was.

Cara... a beautiful, accomplished, bright young woman. Pairing her with Mitch would crush her spirit. She was not 'trophy-wife' material. He knew it was best that they be separated. But his son claimed a different opinion.

He hoped that by forcing them apart, he had not inadvertently created an obsession for his son. Would Mitch desire this girl just because he was told he could not have her? It seemed likely.

What have I done?

He had another team working on the disappearance of Freddie Nigel McDonald. But the original search team had come up with zilch, and it was Cara and her assistant who had discovered a scrawled message on a mirror from the missing field operative. So he'd had to give them the go-ahead and send them on to Paris.

"Good morning, Sir." Mitch entered the room with his usual jaunty strut.

Mitch only called him "sir" when he wanted something. A fact that had taken him years to realize. But what could it be this time?

"Hello, son."

"How are you today?" Mitch asked, seating himself across from the desk and settling back in the chair with a comfortable air.

"Oh, can't complain." He studied his son's face, hunting for clues.

Mitch leaned forward. "So. Enough small talk. How's the investigation coming?"

So that was it.

"That information is classified at present, Junior."

"Not for me, it isn't. Come on, I'm your son. You really don't trust me?" Hurt sprang into Mitch's eyes. "I miss Cara. Can't you even tell me how she's doing?"

He relented. "The investigation is going well. They have a lead on Freddie."

"*Really?*" Mitch's voice raised a few notches. "I knew she was smart. What is it? Do they know where he is?"

"They have reason to believe that he's in Paris." Mr. Gungerson told his son, "And that is all I am able to share at present."

"Well." Mitch cleared his throat. "I hope they have good luck. Seems like they're gonna need it." He popped up from his chair. "See you later, Dad."

After his son exited the room, Mr. Gungerson sighed heavily. There was something about Mitch's attitude that unsettled him.

~*~

"I'm missing the private jet." She whispered in his ear.

He wasn't. Not if it meant being squeezed next to Cara. But he wasn't about to tell her that.

"There is a little less leg room, now that you mention it." He pitched his voice low, although that didn't mean the people in the seats around them couldn't still hear it. "But it's only for one hour."

That was one thing he did miss, the option of talking freely without being overheard.

Cara shifted in her seat between him and the window. He'd taken the aisle seat – thankful, at least, that there were only two seats across in their row.

"I suppose, for one hour, I can stand it." She whispered jokingly.

"If you feel like a nap, feel free to use my shoulder for a pillow." He offered.

Her response was to rest her head on his shoulder and close her eyes. "Thanks."

He hadn't dreamed she would actually take him up on it.

~*~

The Paris-Charles de Gaulle Airport was a far cry from the Marco Polo Airport. It felt harried and rushed and extremely modern to Cara. Bryce told her it was the second busiest airport in Europe, and it was easy for her to believe. Also, they really needed to hire new cleaning ladies, as the state of the bathrooms was atrocious.

"Welcome to Paris." The security staff person appeared to be a chatty mademoiselle. "Will you be touring here for long?" She asked, as Cara stepped through the security checkpoint.

Cara shifted her gaze to Bryce, a subtle reminder that he should be handling all the answers.

"We'll see how it goes. We definitely want to stop by the Eiffel Tower while we're here." He blasted the lady with a charming smile.

~*~

As Cara looked around, Bryce slipped his Agent ID out and flashed it at the girl. Again, everything had been arranged ahead of time.

"Oh. Oui, of course." She waved him through. "Well, have a good time!" The girl smiled, obviously taken with him.

So far, so good. He had ceased to be surprised at how Montrose managed the airports, to send an explanation ahead of him about the faded blue suitcase... and its contents.

As Bryce shepherded Cara through the crowded terminal, she bumped against his shoulder right where he was wearing his Colt M1911.

"What was that?" She turned and stared at him.

"What?"

"That... *lump*, under your jacket?"

"Uh, can we talk about this later?"

She gasped. "It's a *gun!*" She hissed, "Why are you carrying a *gun*? In an *airport*!? You could get *arrested*!"

"It's okay, I promise." He noticed that an elderly man nearby was giving them an odd look.

She gasped again. "Is *that* why they keep waving you through those checkpoints?"

"Caviar." He said softly as she took another breath in preparation for another remark.

"You –" She stopped mid-sentence, but her eyes were full of fire.

Vastly relieved, he took her elbow and continued through the airport, putting some distance between them and the elderly man.

She'd buttoned her lip, but she was sure giving him some exasperated looks as they collected their luggage and left the airport.

Chalk one up for Cara – when it came down to it, the girl could hold her tongue.

As they stood waiting for a taxi, she spoke again, all the while studying the sky, the asphalt, anything but him. "That's supposed to be my code word for *you* to stop teasing."

"I know. But I figured it might get you to stop talking... thankfully, it did. Let's use it both ways."

"And now I can guess why a man of simple tastes had to bring two suitcases. One of them is probably stuffed with bombs." Her voice sparked with sarcasm, and he wasn't sure if she was upset or teasing.

He *didn't* want to talk about the suitcases. "I will explain the gun. Just let me get somewhere I can talk to you without being overheard."

"What's wrong with here? You could whisper in my ear – it would look perfectly natural. Once we get into the taxi the driver would overhear us."

"Hmm." He had to admit, she had a point. "All right."

~*~

What is he hiding? Cara felt fear and anger boiling up inside, and didn't like it.

Bryce dragged her and the luggage over to a black iron bench, plopped down beside her, casually dropped his arm around her shoulders, and leaned close.

"Well…" he began slowly, pitching his voice at a whisper, "…I've made some enemies in my past work experience. The gun is for protection only. I'm highly qualified to use it, and it's saved my life in the past. I thought it would be best to be ready for anything on this trip."

Her thoughts raced. What kind of enemies could you make doing part-time investigation work for a private agency? How much of this was gobbledygook?

Some people walked by, and Cara pasted a smile on her face, gazing into Bryce's eyes as if moonstruck by his whispering.

He sent her an admiring look. "You're pretty good at playing a cover."

"Keep talking, buster." She ground out between gritted teeth, though the smile remained.

"Man. You're also good at interrogation. Where did you learn this tough-girl act?"

Her gaze was glued on his face. "You've just run into my streak of granite. I suggest you continue the explanation."

He ran a hand through his hair, ruffling it backwards. "I'm afraid that's all there is. I am carrying a gun for my own safety, and also, should the need arise, to protect you."

Protect you. *Protect you.*

The words rang in her mind, echoing, clanging.

~*~

Cara's eyes had left his face and were staring into the middle distance at nothing in particular. Very unsettling.

"Cara?"

"Daddy." She whispered, closing her eyes as a tear slipped out and began a mad dash down her high cheekbones.

He pulled her closer, arm around her shoulder. "What about your dad?" The dad who had been dead for... quick mental calculation told him *seventeen years.*

He knew all the particulars from looking her up in the Agency files with a touch more than just professional curiosity.

With a shuddering gasp, she opened her eyes again. "He used to promise that." He only got a brief glimpse of her eyes, for she dropped her head and hid her face in her hands, elbows on her knees.

"Did we ever tell you about him?" Her voice drifted up in a choked murmur.

"Tell me." He urged, keeping his voice soft. She should talk, to release some of the long-buried grief.

She trembled. "My dad always said he'd protect me. But he was killed." She picked up her head.

He held his breath. The abandoned look in her eyes was tearing him apart.

"You know he was a police officer… well… he was shot in the chest during a gas station holdup. He was the bravest man I've ever known!" She started slowly, but finished in a rush.

He squeezed her shoulder. "Cara. I'm so sorry."

"I was five. I -" She sniffed, wiping her wet cheek with one hand. "…I barely remember him."

He was beginning to wish he was the kind of guy that carried a monogrammed handkerchief to offer to weeping ladies.

"Well… I'm glad you can be so proud of him. He died bravely. My dad…" he trailed off.

Cara looked at him.

"My dad disappeared. Just up and left." There it was. That hardness inside of him that he hated, had tried to get rid of, but wouldn't go.

The grief in her eyes melted into sympathy. "Oh, Bryce."

"I don't feel like talking about it." He looked away. *Where are the taxis, anyway? Hiding?*

"Let me know if that changes." She offered.

He swallowed around the squirrel-sized lump in his throat. "Thanks." He stood up. "I give up. Let's see if we can find a bus. It must be "French taxi-driver's national day off"."

~*~

"This is it. 18 Place du Pont Neuf." They had traveled through beautiful Parisian streets and seen some lovely scenery, only to arrive at a dingy building with peeling paint scrunched next to a *Laverie Automatique*... a Laundromat.

Hôtel du Bonheur. The sign perched precariously on the building read. "Hotel of Happiness." Bryce translated.

Apparently he also spoke French.

They opened the creaky door and gingerly crept in.

"Good grief, if this is happiness, I'd hate to see despair." Bryce quipped.

Cara stared at the dusty carpet, dingy walls, and the dim lighting. It was either laugh or cry.

She giggled. "Oh well. Who cares? We're not really on vacation anyway. We have some dirty work ahead of us... might as well do it in a grungy hotel." She pitched her voice at a whisper, even though nobody was there except the desk clerk, who was snoring in his chair.

"I appreciate your optimism." Bryce sauntered over to the counter and dinged the rusty bell twice. "Hey, buddy. Would you mind waking up and giving us some service here?"

The man awoke with a snort. "Oui, yes, what can I do for you?" He owned a thick French accent. And thinning hair, which he put some effort into combing over the bald, greasy dome of his head.

"We're supposed to have reservations. Two rooms."

The man grunted and opened a tattered book, running his finger down the page. "Name?"

"Well, it would have been a Mr. Gungerson who made the arrangements." Cara interjected.

The man read his list. "Ah, yes. A Monsieur Gungerson has booked you a room for two nights."

"A room? Not two rooms?" Bryce demanded.

"Everysing else iz already booked." The man stated dully.

Like, no, it isn't. She didn't know how this dump stayed in business... nobody in their right mind would lodge here if they had other options.

Bryce pulled a roll of bills from his pocket and casually began counting them. "Are you sure?"

The man's eyes bugged out and he hastily said "Well, ah, that ees, there might be somesing I can do."

Bryce slapped a stack of euros on the counter. "Two rooms. Adjoining each other."

"Very good, sir. Your rooms are on second floor. Numbers... 14, 15. Here ees keys." He handed the room keys over. They were made of tarnished brass, not plastic.

Bryce slipped them in his pocket and turned to go, but then looked at the man again. "I suppose it would be useless to ask if you have Wi-Fi."

The man shook his head. "Sorry sir, no internet. Nice internet café down ze street, just a few steps."

"Of course." Bryce's voice was full of irony. He looked at her. "Come on, let's go."

ASHBURN — Julia Erickson

They lugged their suitcases up an extremely narrow flight of stairs. She followed Bryce as they reached their rooms, indicated by the metal numbers tacked to the rickety doors.

"Bryce, I don't feel good about this."

He gave a short laugh. "My sentiments exactly. Don't say anything once we get in there."

"What?"

"Caviar. Ok?"

She held her silence behind him as he slipped his handgun from the holster and unlocked the door with the brass key. He flattened himself against the wall and pushed the door open, then glanced inside.

Silence.

He walked in and inspected the room before motioning for her to come inside. He put a finger to his lips, silently rolled their luggage in and closed the door.

She watched, curious, as he unlocked his faded blue case. He sent her a warning look before opening the lid.

Oh my word! She clapped her hand over her mouth to muffle a shriek.

Bryce was armed to the teeth. She didn't know what most of the ominous-looking stuff in that case was, but there were several guns, one of which looked like an automatic. There were gizmos and gadgets and strange devices. And that was just the top layer.

Bryce pulled out an odd little device from the second layer and closed the case. He plugged a pair of earbuds into it, which he slipped into his ears. He pushed a button and the moved soundlessly around the room.

It looked to her like he was sweeping for bugs. And not the cockroach variety, although she was sure if he looked he would find dead specimens of those in most of the corners.

What is going on?!

~*~

Bryce listened. Nothing as of yet, but he wasn't done looking. He waved the device over the room, moving in a clockwise circuit. It was when he got to the cracked mirror over the bureau that he hit pay dirt.

Beep. *Beep.* BEEP.

He ran his fingers behind the edge of the mirror and discovered a small electronic device wedged between it and the wall. He carefully dislodged the bug from its hiding place, and held it up for Cara's inspection. Her eyes grew huge and she covered her mouth with one hand again.

He found a cup in the bathroom, filled it with brackish water from the sink and dropped the bug into it with a 'plop'. It was the old-fashioned way to dispose of a bug, but it still worked. It was just a cheap one, or he would have popped it into a soundproof box so they could later trace back the signal.

"Oh." Cara breathed softly, "Someone bugged our room." She appeared to have forgotten his array of weapons in the blue case in the shock of finding that someone had been listening to them.

"Mmmm-hmm." He nodded. "That's probably it for here. But I'll check the bathroom and the other room too."

~*~

The second room harbored no bugs. Well, the electronic kind. But in the first room's bathroom, another bug hid behind the stem of the pedestal-style sink. It joined its counterpart in the glass of water.

Cara stood in the first room, wrapping her arms around herself. *This is so disgusting.* "I don't even feel like I can sit down in here. And now I'm afraid to talk."

Bryce shook his head. "You can talk now. I've found all the bugs."

A cockroach chose that moment to crawl out from behind a framed still-life of some tired-looking pears.

"Ugh." She gulped as Bryce grabbed a moldy stuffed pillow off the chair and whacked the insect, squashing it against the dusty wallpaper. "Look, I'm trying to be brave, but I *cannot* stay here."

"Under normal circumstances, I would never ask you to." He tossed the pillow back to its place in the chair. "But for the purposes of this investigation, we have to get into this building. Easiest way is to pretend to stay here. But I've got an idea."

"Anything." She begged. *I sound like a wimp… but I don't care!*

"We'll check into a different hotel and sneak out our luggage. But we'll pretend to come back here as if we were actually staying."

"Okay." *Wait. Hold the phone.* "Why did you suspect the room had been bugged?"

Bryce shrugged his broad shoulders. "I just had this gut feeling. A healthy dose of suspicion is a good quality for an... investigator."

"Who did it?" She rubbed her arms, still feeling creeped out.

"I don't know. But I intend to find out." His face was set resolutely.

"All right, but how in the world are we going to sneak out our luggage? There's only one flight of stairs."

He thought for a moment. "Well, the fire escape won't work... somebody outside might spot us. We could get arrested for being cat burglars. One of us is going to have to distract the desk clerk." He pointed at her.

"*Me?* Why can't you talk to him while I sneak out the bags?" *This is not sounding like a good idea!*

"You can't manage all three of them at once, and I wouldn't want you setting off one of my *bombs*." He gave her a roguish grin.

She gasped. *The gadgets!* "I nearly forgot. What in heaven's name are you doing with all of that STUFF in your case?"

Bryce didn't even blink. "It's investigative equipment. Things to help me listen through walls, tracking devices, the bug scanner..." He winked. "Even a couple of harmless smoke bombs, in case I need to create a distraction."

That wasn't all. You can't fool me like that. "And guns."

Bryce tilted his head to one side. "Yeah. For *protection*." He reached for her hand and grasped it with one of his own. "Can I ask you to trust me?"

She studied him for a long moment. His eyes were innocent, no guile or deceit lurking in their honest hazel depths.

Finally, she nodded. *For now.*

"Atta girl. Come on, let's go distract one middle-aged, balding hotel clerk."

~*~

Bryce watched from his hiding spot in the janitor's closet with the luggage as Cara walked up to the desk.

"Sir?"

The clerk looked up as she spoke to him. "Ah, mademoiselle. What can I do for you?"

Cara smiled engagingly. "I'm afraid I have a little problem... would you be so kind as to assist me?" Her voice was sugary-sweet.

The man sat up straighter. "*Oui*, of course, but what about your, ah, boyfriend? Can he not help you?"

Bryce just barely controlled the guffaw that threatened to erupt. *Her boyfriend? Only in my dreams.*

"Bryce? Oh, he's my cousin. And he's indisposed... so I really, really need your help."

The man rose from his chair so quickly he sent it tipping over backwards. Blushing a blotchy red, he righted it. "Of course, I would be happy to help. What is it?"

"Come with me, I'll show you. There's a... some kind of *animal* in my room!" She was really laying the dumb-blonde act on thick.

The man followed her like a puppy up the stairs, past the janitor's closet. As soon as they went into Cara's room, Bryce slipped out of the closet and thumped down the stairs with their luggage and was out the front door.

He hailed a taxi, stuffed the bags into the back seat, and gave the man a 20-euro bill to wait. "There's a lot more where that bill came from, buddy, so I'd wait there if I was you. I'll be back in a couple minutes."

~*~

"What kind of animal did you say it was?" The man looked a little unsure of himself.

"It looked like a ... rat. Maybe a squirrel. It was right in there!" Cara pointed in the bathroom, "Sitting in the shower!"

The man cautiously peered into the bathroom, discovering that it was, of course, empty. "Your, ah, *animal*... seems to be gone." He grinned. "Now, what is the real reason you came to *moi, ma petite chérie*?"

"I'm telling you, it was an animal. Maybe it got out!" She suggested innocently, waving to the open window.

He took a step closer. "Ah, I see. Mademoiselle is in strange country – she is lonely."

Oh boy. He thinks I'm coming on to him?! Help!

"*What's going on here*?!" Bryce thundered from the doorway.

The man jumped and whirled to face him, going several shades paler. Relief splashed through Cara at the sight of her partner, who made quite a threatening figure with his muscles flexed.

Bryce speared her with an accusing look. "Lonely, are you?!" But was that a wink?

"Bryce…. Wait…" She infused her tone with weak placation.

"I'll show you *lonely*! Come on, we're taking a walk." Bryce crossed the room and grasped her by the arm. His touch was actually gentle, but didn't look it.

He scowled fiercely at the desk clerk, who was wringing his hands. "And you had better not be here when we get back." He threatened, pulling Cara out the door.

"I assure you, sir, nothing could tempt me to –" the clerk started to say, but Bryce ignored him and stomped down the stairs, and she trailed meekly behind him.

As they exited the hotel, they heard a muttered "Cousin! *Bah!*" from the clerk's direction.

~*~

The cabbie grinned at his passengers, who appeared to be slightly sloshed as they sat squeezed between their luggage in his backseat. They certainly were laughing enough to be a wee bit drunk. And it was only noon! "Enjoying our trip to Paris, are we?"

The pretty blonde wiped her eyes, still giggling slightly. "Oh yes."

The handsome young man cleared his throat. "We're having a fine time. Not *lonely* at all."

For some reason, this sent his lovely companion into a fit of more giggling. "Did you see his *face* when you walked in?" She whispered, which set the young man laughing again.

"Cousin! *Bah!*" The young man's next odd remark *really* brought on the laughter.

The cabbie shook his head. One certainly met all sorts of people when driving around in Paris.

~*~

"*L'Hôtel Diamant Blanc*.The White Diamond Hotel." Bryce knew Cara would like this much better than their last excuse for a hotel. Crystal chandeliers sparkled overhead and the scents of fresh lilac and wildflowers laced the air.

"Now this is more like it." Cara explored the well-furnished lobby with her gaze as they waited in line behind the other guests waiting to check in. "I just have one question."

"Which is?"

"Who's footing the bill? Because I can't afford to stay here!" She confided in a whisper.

Actually, the Agency would, via his expense account. But what to tell Cara?

"I'll take care of it."

She looked at him, mouth open. "*Bryce*. How sweet. But I can't take your money."

Now it was awkward. "Tell you what, I'll call Mr. Gungerson – think private jet. If he doesn't fund our stay here, it'll be my treat."

She sighed. "Oh, all right. But I may end up owing you you a big one."

He grinned. He was okay with her owing him a favor. "Seems to me like I got the better end of this deal."

Her face told him she wanted to retaliate but didn't dare, in the middle of this ritzy lobby.

"You're a rascal, you know that?" She exclaimed.

He nodded in agreement. "True. But a charming one, I hope." He noticed she hadn't said 'caviar' yet.

"Rascal, yes. Charming? Debatable."

"Ouch. That was harsh." He pretended to wince.

"I'm not harsh!" She denied earnestly with a shake of her blonde head.

"Then am I charming?"

"Maybe. Am I harsh?

"Maybe." *I really should stop flirting with her like this.*

She pouted playfully. "You're exasperating."

"Ahem. May I help you?"

They both looked up to see the hotel clerk waiting for their attention. Everybody in line ahead of them had finished and gone on.

Cara blushed becomingly.

"Sorry." Bryce apologized, then quickly paid for two rooms, glad that they were on the same hallway.

"That was embarrassing." Cara murmured as they walked deeper into the hotel, luggage in tow.

Bryce decided not to say anything. But he worried that his mind wasn't on his job.

They deposited their luggage into their rooms and then met back in the hallway.

"How about some lunch? I could eat an elephant." He suggested.

"Sounds good to me. Lunch, that is. Not the elephant." She wrinkled her nose.

"I'm sure we can find something else to eat besides poached pachyderm."

"Poached pachyderm? Where do you come up with these things?" She asked as they walked down the beautifully-wallpapered hall.

"I have no idea. They just float into my mind."

~*~

La Rose de France. It was a delicious place to eat, an outdoor café, which did *not* have elephant on the menu. They *did* have "*6 Escargots de Bourgogne*" -six large burgundy snails marinated in Chablis wine with rich herbed butter... and "*Cuisses de grenouilles en persillade*"- Frogs' legs in a parsley sauce. Thankfully, there were lots of other options.

Cara shivered as she read the menu. "Mitch loves escargot."
And thinks everyone else should too.

"Why am I not surprised?" Bryce rolled his eyes.

She shook her head. "I don't want to think about him. Besides, he's halfway around the world, practically. I'm almost never this far away from him."

"Then... why are you thinking about him?" He looked a little miffed.

"Well, the snails reminded me. And actually... this is going to sound completely nuts... but..."

Bryce watched her. "But?"

Should I tell him? I have to. "I feel... like I'm being stalked, almost. A sense of... foreboding." She looked up at the puffy clouds sailing above the street. "Like an unseen piano about to be dropped on my head."

Thankfully, Bryce seemed to take her seriously. He folded one hand over the other and rested his chin on them, leaning against the table. "Really?"

"Mmm-hmm."

"You could be on to something. I'm not one that scoffs at women's intuition. We'll check up on him."

He studied the menu. "I think I'll get the *Tartare de bœuf* – steak. With fries. I could go for some actual 'French' French-fries."

She smiled at him. "Hate to burst your bubble, but French fries are actually American."

Bryce shrugged. "Oh well. Whoever invented them, I'm grateful."

She laughed. "I'll get the *Magret de canard aux piments d'Espelette, gratin Dauphinois* . What a mouthful to say 'grilled duck with peppers and potatoes'. I'm glad the menu includes the English translation!"

"That sounds good. I hope I get a taste."

She tapped her chin with one finger. "Hmm. I seem to recall you've been pretty nice to me lately. Paying for my hotel room and all. I think I can share."

"Hey, works for me. What goes around, comes around."

~*~

Forty-five minutes and two empty plates later, their delicious lunch was done. Bryce liked this, eating with Cara. Pity it wouldn't last after this mission was over…

Cara sighed dreamily. "That was lovely." She twirled her straw around in her water glass.

"Indeed, it was." He sat back and studied the scenery. Something ducked out of sight as he turned his head to the left.

Instantly, every nerve buzzed with tension and his senses went on high alert.

"Well, are you about done? I think it's time we get moving." He tossed a few bills on the table and smoothly rose from his chair.

"All right." And they were on the move.

Bryce glanced into the only shop window on the street as they passed, checking the reflection. There. One man slipped around the corner of a building and walked along twenty feet behind them. Bryce stopped for a moment, pretending to study the display of paintings. Tall buildings stretched up to the sky, walling each side of the v-shaped road.

Sure enough, the man stopped too, leaning against the concrete wall of a library building.

Bryce felt boxed in, and he didn't like it. The little move with the shop window had uncovered another person who was following their movements at the other end of the sidewalk. They had halted when he did.

They were good. But he was better. If they had been more skilled, they would never have tried to duck out of sight, which was what had alerted him to their presence in the first place. He just had to keep his cool. And hope that Cara could keep up.

"I need to tell you something." He slipped his arm around her waist as they walked along, increasing their pace by a hair.

Cara looked up at him in surprise. "We're not in Venice anymore."

She thinks I'm faking the boyfriend act again. "I know. Listen carefully. Please remain calm. We're being followed." He smiled as if in light, casual conversation.

Her only response was to stiffen slightly. "Followed." She repeated, somehow managing the word without moving her lips. She was good at this! "First bugs. Now we're being followed."

"Yeah." He whispered. "Just do what I tell you to, and please don't ask unnecessary questions."

"Okay." She didn't seem to be scared, but she might just be hiding it under that composed face.

"At the end of the street, once we turn the corner, we're going to start running. Hang onto me."

She half-smiled. "I guess I picked the right day to wear jeans and flats."

"Right on." They were almost to the corner. "Here we go."

They rounded the corner and Bryce broke into a sprint, Cara matching her pace with his. They were a good fifty feet down the sidewalk when shouts rang out behind them. Bryce dared to glance over his shoulder and saw the men who had been following them also running. One of them was speaking into a walkie-talkie.

Not good.

"In here!" He leaped down an alley between a café and a bookstore, Cara racing by his side.

He felt like they were going to make it. Cara wasn't even breathing hard as they reached the end of the alley and turned onto a larger side-street.

Suddenly, she screamed, and he felt her hand ripped away from his hold. He turned and in a split-second blur saw her struggling in the grip of a burly man wearing a denim jacket.

Enemy backup had arrived.

He lunged at the attacker, freeing Cara, and threw a right cross that the man blocked with a forearm, and followed it up with a punch in the gut using his left fist.

Cara shrieked and waved her arms. "Police! Somebody call the police!"

The man nearly hit him with a stiff right jab, but he ducked it and decked the guy with an uppercut that nailed him right under the jaw.

Yells from down the street in the direction of their pursuers spurred him to action. "Come on!" He gripped Cara's hand again and they kept going.

"Through here!" They ducked into an old theater. He slowed and walked up to the counter with a leisurely stroll. Cara followed suit.

"Two please." Bryce said pleasantly, tossing a bill onto the counter. "Keep the change."

Cara smiled, breathless.

The attendant let them through with a shrug. "Movie half through! You wait?"

They ignored him and moved into a dark theater that was playing *Roman Holiday* and had just gotten to the kissing scene. Orchestra music swirled around them as they tiptoed down the side and out through a back exit.

"Good. I think we just bought about fifteen minutes." Bryce huffed.

"There they are!" A deep shout rang out.

"Or not!" Cara yelped.

They pelted down the lane and then through a small park, narrowly avoiding a collision with a baby pram and the gray-haired nanny that was pushing it.

Up ahead, a crowd of people danced as a band played live music near a trickling fountain.

"Well, my dear," Bryce shot a quick look behind them, "Shall we dance?"

"Are you *kidding* me?" She looked at him as if he was insane.

"Nope." Bryce whipped out a pair of dark sunglasses and slid them onto his face. "Put your hood up. Change your appearance. " He rolled up the collar on his jacket.

Cara threw her jacket hood over her head and pushed down her sleeves for good measure as they melted into the crowd. Bryce wrapped his arms around her and they swayed back and forth to the violin and cello music.

"They're good." Cara remarked, sliding her arms around his neck. "Is that Canon in D?"

"With a little percussion thrown in. Unique." He could feel the pounding of her heart against him.

A light sweat glistened on her forehead. But other than that, she seemed okay. Her stamina was impressive, for a civilian.

Bryce kept his back turned towards the direction they'd come from, sheltering Cara in front of him. Using the mirrors built into the sides of his sunglasses, he scanned through the people emerging from the alleys and streets behind him.

ASHBURN — Julia Erickson

Two men popped out of an alley, jerking their heads back and forth, clearly in search of them.

"I see them. Keep your head down."

Cara took him literally, and buried her face in his chest. With the hood over her head, her face was completely hidden.

The musicians sounded like they were winding down towards the end of the song. *No!*

He needed them to keep on playing for just a few more seconds. They had to keep dancing.

The men looked around, swiveling their heads back and forth, and then argued with each other.

He looked into the magnified little circle of mirror in the left corner of the glasses frame. It offered a zoomed-in view. The men both wore jackets with a funny insignia on them. It was a capital R with two peculiar swirls, one on each side. He turned his head towards the guys, winked twice to capture an image with the computerized glasses. Slowly turned away.

The seconds ticked by. Measure by measure, the song drew closer to the end.

After what seemed like forever, the men shrugged, turned, and left, slinking back into the alley.

The violinist drew the bow across the strings one last time, and then bowed amid the scattered applause.

He sighed with relief. *Thank you, Lord.* Yet another miraculous escape. "They're gone."

She picked her head up. "They are?"

"Yeah." He noted that her gray eyes matched the light-gray jacket she was wearing. "Thanks for not wearing any bold colors today."

Cara shuddered. "To think, I almost wore my bright coral cardigan."

His stomach felt queasy at the thought. "Who knew wardrobe choices could be so life-changing?"

She smiled for the first time since lunch. "Wardrobe choices are *always* life-changing."

"I had no idea."

The musicians struck up another lilting song as she shook her head in disapproval. "Classic symptom of bachelorhood. Not caring about one's apparel."

He would have liked to pursue that topic, but now was not the time. "We'd better get while the getting's good."

Her breath caught in her throat. "Oh my, you're right, we can't just stand here chatting!" She followed as he strode towards a street at the opposite end of the park.

"Oh, wait." He dug in his pocket and then tossed coins into the open violin case lying on the cobblestone ground as they passed by. The musicians nodded and smiled.

Bryce winked at Cara. "It was the least I could do." He whispered to her as they left the shady park.

Chapter Five

Who Are You?

Bryce led them back via a circuitous route to *L'Hôtel Diamant Blanc*, where they sneaked in through a side exit, then retired to their respective rooms. He said he had a phone call to make. Suspicious, much?

"If you need me, don't use your phone, I've noticed the cell service is sketchy… use this."

He slipped a device from his pocket that looked like a plain silver wristwatch. "If you push this button, the watch face lights up." He showed her.

Cara frowned. "I have one of these already."

He shook his head. "Not one of *these*. If you tap the watch face three times while it's lit up, it sends a distress signal to the watch I'm wearing." He held up his hand, exhibiting what looked like a regular, albeit costly, man's wristwatch, "…triggering an electromagnetic pulse, which will make my hand throb. Trust me, I'll notice, and come for you."

She looked up at him with a curious, puzzled expression. "Bryce… this is like, spy gear. What normal person has something like this in their possession?"

"I'm not *that* weird, am I? I'm pretty normal." His voice was purposefully light-hearted.

She pierced him with a burning stare. "Are you a spy?"

~*~

Granite again. This was getting old.

"You know, I've never liked that word, "spy"."

Her mouth dropped open in astonishment. *Oops.*

Hastily, he jabbered "I'm not a spy, Cara. I'm just your average dude serving his country in a somewhat anonymous, slightly unusual fashion. I investigate things, collect information, verify facts, and report it. It's not a big deal." Lame, lame, lame. *Time for a quick exit.*

He zipped to the door. "...And I really could use a shower. See ya."

~*~

Click. He was gone.

Lies. She hated lies. Half-truths were ten times more inexcusable, and Cara felt like that was what Bryce was feeding her. On a silver platter, no less!

She looked around at the expensive hotel room. It really was nice... everything was of the finest material. The bedspread was silk, probably Duponi, with a designer floral print that matched the chairs.

She pulled her camera out of her purse, remembering her mother's request that she take lots of pictures. She shot a few of the view from her balcony window, pleased that they included the Eiffel Tower on the horizon. Only a few buildings in Paris could boast a view of the tower, due to the strict height restrictions.

Oh Bryce... What do I really know about you? Handsome, an air of innocence and sweetness about him. A gentleman.

Chivalrous. That was certainly rare these days. Homeschooled, like her. Christian. *Definitely* Christian, from the way he prayed over their food like God was actually listening to him talk.

Hah. She knew better. Whipping off her grey jacket, she hurled it at one of the chairs, where it landed limply.

God took my father from me.

It was the continual refrain that had echoed in her head, her whole life. If God was so loving, so merciful, why would he tear away a little five-year old girl's father from her? Her mother had nearly died from grief. Thankfully they had been able to move in with her sweet Nana. But without that, they wouldn't have made ends meet.

She kicked off her leather flats and they banged against the gold wallpaper.

My daddy loved me. But he died. While countless fathers abandoned their children without a second thought, every day. And lived.

Just look at Bryce's absentee father.

She shook herself and walked into the bathroom to freshen up. "Back on topic, girl. Focus. We were evaluating what we know about him."

Bryce. He called himself an "investigator." Yeah, right. What did he really do? He was carrying enough weaponry and who knows what else to start a terrorist operation! What was his game?

Cara washed her face and arms and reapplied fresh makeup as her thoughts continued to burn through her brain.

Why had Bryce come along on *her* mission to find some stupid missing technology tester? He was obviously way more qualified to run an investigation than she, but he had gladly gone along with the plan to be her assistant, until she offered a role reversal.

Who is *he?* She stroked the silver watch he'd given her, clasped about her slim wrist.

He handled himself on the streets of Paris like a *pro.* Keen sense of danger. Incredible street fighter. Of course, the dancing in a crowd was a little off-the-wall.

A rogue smile softened her lips in remembrance of their dance - but she straightened them back to a hard line. *Stop it! It wasn't* that *romantic.*

Cara left the bathroom, flopped backwards on the bed and blew out an exasperated sigh. She couldn't take it any longer.

She *had* to know.

~*~

After a quick shower that rinsed off the grime from the chase, he had to deliver another uncomfortable report. He dialed up his boss, knowing he wouldn't like what Bryce had to say.

"Montrose."

"We had a tail. Three guys. Cara almost got nabbed."

"Good grief. What happened?" Monty's voice grew grave.

Bryce walked into the bathroom and began unpacking his toothbrush and toiletries. "Well, it started at the café. But I think they had a line on us from sooner than that."

ASHBURN

He filled his boss in on everything that had transpired, giving him a detailed description of the men that had chased them.

"Ashburn! That was risky, hiding out in the open like that." His boss scolded him after hearing the account of the dancing.

"Maybe, but it worked. Sometimes a thing is hardest to find when it's right under your nose."

"Besides..." Montrose sounded like he was sipping his afternoon mug of coffee. "I didn't know you could dance."

"Me either. But you gotta do what you gotta do. I pulled it off."

"I'm sure you did. How is she doing after that ordeal?"

"Cara's okay. But starting to ask a lot of questions. I'm fielding them as best as I can, but it's getting harder."

"Your job is a secret, Bryce. She can't know. She doesn't have security clearance. She's only a civilian. You make sure you don't tell her anything, and keep her safe." The words fell hard and fast like bullets.

"Yes sir. I won't tell her anything. And I'll take care of her."

"One more thing. That R with the curlicues? From the description and photos you gave us, we've identified it as the logo for the Ravenmeister "special force". We're looking into it. Be careful. Those guys mean business."

Bryce laughed. "Yeah. Well, *I* mean business. Nothing's going to get in my way."

His boss chuckled. "I know. You're the best. And I don't say that lightly. So take care of yourself, and keep me posted."

ASHBURN   Julia Erickson

The line went dead. Bryce hung up.

~*~

Cara used the extra key to Bryce's room to open his door, and oh-so-cautiously popped her head inside. *Clues. Looking for clues.*

The room was empty, so she slipped inside the door, engulfed in guilt. This deception thing didn't come naturally.

"Me either." Bryce's voice echoed in the bathroom, and she realized he was on the phone.

"...You gotta do what you gotta do. I pulled it off." A few seconds of silence. A jingling zipper being pulled. The sound of bottles being set on a countertop.

"Cara's okay. But she's starting to ask a lot of questions. I'm fielding them as best as I can, but it's getting harder." Silence again, a little longer this time. A few unidentifiable clicks and thumps.

"Yes sir. I won't tell her anything. And I'll take care of her."

A shiver ran down Cara's spine. *What is* that *supposed to mean?!* She froze in fear.

A dry laugh crackled. "Yeah. Well, *I* mean business. *Nothing's going to get in my way.*" There was a forceful emphasis in his voice.

Her heart skipped a beat. She backed towards the front door, but the door to the bathroom flew open and Bryce appeared with wet hair, shirtless, wearing jeans. He was holding a Bluetooth phone attachment in his hand.

His eyes widened as he caught sight of her.

Oh my God. If only she could just melt into the carpet.

~*~

"*Cara!* What are you doing in my room? Is something wrong?"

What did she hear? And how did she catch me off guard – ME, the secret agent? Oh right. Shouldn't have given her that key.

Her eyes were fearful, as she stammered "No. I mean yes! I... uh..." Apparently, Cara couldn't lie to him with any success. And she had heard enough to be scared of him.

He stalked to his suitcase and yanked out a white cotton T-shirt, which he pulled on with a quick jerk while his mind raced. What did he do *now*? He replayed his end of the conversation in his mind, and it wasn't good.

She folded her arms across her midsection. "I came in to ask you something."

He sat on the bed. "Well?"

She looked back up at his face. Her large, beautiful eyes were now narrow, suspicious slits.

"Why are you lying to me?"

Oh boy.

~*~

Cara braced herself.

"All right. Fine. You got me." Bryce snapped. "I haven't told you everything."

"I think I kinda figured that out by now. What I would like to know is *what* you haven't told me. Like that you're a terrorist. Are you?"

"NO!" It was a cry, like he'd been deeply wounded. Then he curled his hand into a fist as if controlling himself, and spoke quietly.

"No. I *am not* a terrorist. I would never wreak havoc on the lives of innocent people, not even if my own life depended on it."

She felt ashamed that she had to question him like this. It was so hard asking somebody like him these questions. But the way things looked...

"Please, forgive me for having to ask that. But look at it from my viewpoint."

She counted on her fingers. "First, your gun in the shoulder holster. Then the case full of weapons and who-knows-what-else. The surprising revelation of your astonishing street-smarts. That terribly bad-sounding telephone conversation." She ticked the items off one by one, counting on her fingers.

"I don't blame you, but that conversation would sound completely different if you had heard the other end of it."

He rose and walked to her, taking her hand in his. "I was promising to take *good* care of you, not 'take care' of you as in *hurt* you! I would *die* before I hurt you."

Wow. Either he's the best actor ever, or he really means it. "Okay. I can believe that. But the rest of it?"

"I *know* how bad it looks. How bad *I* look. But Cara, you've got to believe me. I'm on the right side of this fight." He was pleading with her now.

She hoisted up those stone walls around herself that had served so well in the past, and pulled her hand away.

"Who are you? Who do you work for? What is this all about, Bryce?!"

"I am not at liberty to answer that." He murmured.

It sounded like a knee-jerk response to Cara. It must have showed on her face, because his eyes grew slightly wild.

"I can't tell you what I really do. I *can't*. Or I would!" He insisted.

"Then, I'm sorry, I can't trust you."

He recoiled as if her quiet words were a shock wave. "Cara."

"If you could just tell me that you're F.B.I, or C.I.A, or even NSA, this would be so much simpler. Are you?" *Please say yes. Tell me you're working for the good guys.*

He swallowed. "No." He choked on the word.

Cara walked over to the window and stared out at the Paris skyline. People dreamed about coming here. She was in Paris, but the only thing she wanted was to go home as if this whole thing had never happened.

She turned to face him. "Bryce, I'm still going to work for you."

He lifted his head to look at her.

"Until you give me an undeniable reason *not* to trust you, I'm going to hold off on deciding whether to trust you or not. Let's finish this senseless investigation, and then we'll sort everything out."

He looked grateful. "Okay. That works for me. I promise, I'll earn your trust." He sighed. "And if we're patient, maybe I'll get clearance to tell you *everything* about me."

She took a deep breath. "Now. What do we do next?"

~*~

Cara melted a little when Bryce extended a hand to help her out of the taxi. She couldn't help it. If he was up to something unsavory… at least he was terribly sweet.

"Back at the Happiness Hotel." Bryce announced as they exited the taxi.

"Oh joy." Cara rolled her eyes.

They walked through the door together, the musty air of the lobby assaulting their noses.

The balding clerk remained at his post, and blanched when he saw Bryce come in.

"Oh yeah? Well I don't even LIKE potato chips!" Bryce exclaimed, as if continuing an argument.

"You don't *like* much of the stuff I do, do ya?" She retorted, putting more than a little southern twang into her voice. "Maybe you should just *leave me alone*." She gave him a saucy little jab with her forefinger, right in his chest.

"*Get sassy.*" Bryce had told her. *"It'll be more convincing."*

She hoped it was, because it made her feel downright ridiculous. Not to mention that the last thing she wanted to do right now was argue with him. She' had enough of that.

Bryce folded his muscular arms tight across his chest. "Well, maybe I will, and we'll see how you *like* it." He stomped up the narrow steps.

She bit her lip thoughtfully, and then turned to see the hotel clerk watching her. She smiled and ambled over to him.

"He's all bark and no bite." She drawled, leaning against the counter.

His eyes shifted nervously to the stairwell, but he smiled back. "I am sure mademoiselle is right."

"Hey, maybe you could help me find a friend. He was stayin' here. But I don't have a room number, just a name." She aimed for sweet, but tried to keep the twang clear enough so that he could understand her.

"A friend of yours, oh, how nice. What was heez name?" He was already opening the register.

"Freddie. Freddie Donaldson. Ya know, kinda like Mcdonald's?"

"Oh yes, *oui*, I know it." He didn't have to search far. "Ah, yes, heez room was on fourth floor. Number 45. But I am so sorry, he checked out, and there is no forwarding addresses or telephone number."

She pouted as if greatly disappointed, the sighed. "Shoot. I hate to git this far and miss him by just a leetle bit."

"I do apologize. Would mademoiselle like to leave a phone number in case her friend returns? I will pass eet on for her."

Oh, smooth, buddy. No way would I give you my phone number.

"Sure! It's 1-800," She watched him scramble for a pencil. "...G-E-T-, L-O-S-T."

He wrote down the letters eagerly, then stared at them, befuddled. "One eight hundred, *get lost*?"

But Cara was already skipping towards the stairs. "Bah-bye, nayow!" She waved over her shoulder as she danced up the steps, long, blond ponytail swinging behind her.

Bryce met her in the hallway. "Thanks a lot. I nearly *died* trying not to laugh. You should have your own comedy show." He grinned, face alive with amusement.

"Hey, you wanted a room number; I got you a room number. Don't complain about my methods." She teased. Her heart felt light and unfettered. She hoped the feeling wouldn't go away anytime soon.

~*~

Room number 45 was deserted.

Trash littered the room and dirty scraps of clothing were scattered across the floor. Cara looked around in dismay. *Ugh. So gross.*

"Oh, great." Bryce muttered as he stepped inside the room and surveyed the debris. "I *really* wanted to search through a pile of garbage today. Not."

"Let's think uplifting thoughts. Maybe we'll find Freddie from something we discover in here." Cara suggested, tiptoeing across the room.

Bryce rolled up his sleeves. "Let's get to work."

The very first thing they did was to check the bathroom mirror. It was so little that Bryce thought they should just breathe on it to form a layer of condensation, rather than steaming up the whole room with the shower.

Cara and Bryce huffed warm breaths at the mirror in tandem, but suddenly Cara burst into giggles. They looked like a pair of goldfish in an aquarium, wide, gasping mouths close to the glass.

"What's so funny? Quit laughing and start blowing!"

"We look like goldfish!" She squeaked, still laughing.

Bryce shook his head as if perplexed. "I don't think I want an explanation for that." He stopped breathing on the mirror. "We've fogged that thing up. There's nothing on it but a few fingerprints. Remind me to lift them and send them in for identification, though."

Send them in? Where? Cara shrugged the thought away.

They began a systematic search. Bryce tackled the bedroom while she stayed in the miniscule bathroom.

On the cluttered counter, a tube of lipstick stood upright. But something was wrong with it. The waxen stick resembled a piece of worn sidewalk chalk.

That's been written with. But where? She scanned the filthy room, then grabbed a handful of toilet paper and lifted the toilet seat. *Jackpot!*

Just as she opened her mouth to call Bryce, he yelled. "Come here!"

She walked into the bedroom, holding her discovery behind her back.

"Look at *this*." Bryce held up a plastic pen. "I found it dropped behind the end table next to the bed." He turned it in his hands until the printing showed on the plastic side. "It's monogramed."

Frederick N. McDonald.

Cara felt her mouth drop open. "It was really him – he was here!"

"We're on the right track." He agreed.

She held up her free hand. "Not so fast, though. There's more." She pulled her other hand from behind her back to display a tube of lipstick.

Bryce eyed it. "Trust a girl to find the lipstick."

She shook her head. "Trust *you* to not know I never wear lipstick. I wear lip *gloss*."

"Same difference!"

"I hate to tell you this, but you are sadly misinformed. They're very different."

"Whatever you say. What about this lipstick is so amazing, anyway?" His brow wrinkled.

She popped off the cap and twisted the tube, expanding the red point. "Look how roughed-up it is!"

Bryce stared at her. "So?"

"So, a woman's lips are smooth and soft. Whoever used this has been rubbing it on something that was *not* a pair of lips."

At last, it clicked for him. "Like writing a message?"

"Mmmm-hmm." She nodded. "I found the message, too."

He leaped to his feet. "Show me."

~*~

Bryce hadn't expected this. Once one lifted the hinged toilet seat from the base, the message appeared, smeared in thick letters with the bold red lipstick.

Moving to a Ravenmeister office.

Rue Amelie. Hurry!

Whew. Watch out? Freddie was trying to warn them. And finally, a tangible link to Ravenmeister, Incorporated, They even knew the road it was on. *Rue Amélie.*

"I have a bad feeling about this." Cara whispered.

"You and me both." Bryce looked for anything of value they might have missed. As far as he could tell, it was just junk. And the edgy feeling he was getting meant that they didn't have time to stick around and sort through every soiled T-shirt and empty soda can.

"Come on, let's get out of here." After Bryce collected the fingerprints using a strip of tape, they left room 45. Next stop, Rue Amélie.

"What made you zero in on that tube of lipstick anyway?" He led her back down the hall, on their way to the front door.

"It just seemed so... out of place. It makes me think a woman is involved somehow. And what woman would step foot in that room without trying to tidy it up? It makes me think she's either a sloppy hag or a high-maintenance chick that never cleans up after herself."

She looked thoughtful. "I'm leaning towards the latter. It wasn't cheap lipstick."

"Interesting theory." *And that was kind of... brilliant.* He studied her face, noticing that her eyes were sparkling with a green tint. She looked excited... and gorgeous.

"So, shall we pretend to go get some dinner, but really search that place for Freddie?" Cara suggested.

"Well, you can pretend. I'm starving!! But let's go check out that office first. If we can find it. It might *not* have a big neon sign on the front blinking "The Ravenmeister Badguys are **IN HERE**."

Cara chortled. "That would be nice!"

Bryce smiled as he started to descend the stairs down to the shabby lobby, but she stopped him with a hand on his elbow.

"Wait. Should we have another argument on our way past that guy? Or would we have made up by now?"

Bryce shrugged. "I think we can skip the arguing. I don't want the clerk to think I'm some kind of grump."

"Good. I hate playing the dumb blonde with the brute of a boyfriend. I mean, cousin." She smirked.

~*~

Rue Amélie. Cara was expecting a shady alley lined with trash cans and tramps. But it was a sunny street with a good metro vibe, just a little ways from the Eiffel Tower. The sidewalk was scattered with people carrying everything from shopping bags to briefcases.

A quick walk down the street proved that Bryce's assumption was correct. Nowhere did it say "Ravenmeister Incorporated", much less "FIND BADGUYS HERE."

Bryce and Cara turned around and began walking back up the street.

Cara looked intently at everything they passed. First, a toy shop with bright displays placed at a child's eye-level. Then, a plumber's office. Above, wrought iron balconies and windows studded the sides of the four-story buildings. Flower boxes with bright red geraniums. A shoe store, with ladies' pumps on a chic shelf. *Chez Maman...* what looked like a barbeque joint, with delicious smoky aromas wafting from it. A Best Western hotel ...sandwiched between a Laundromat and a T-Shirt shop featuring a design that said "I Heart Paris". Another hotel. A fashion boutique.

Cara felt anxious. What if they were on the wrong track?

A nondescript beige building with a title stamped above the tiny doorway in etched letters. *Maître Corbeau Société de Sécurité.*

A funny tickle traveled down her spine as they passed it, and the fine hair at the base of her neck stood up. "Bryce, hang on a sec."

She leaned against a wall of a bright green building that looked like it might be a thrift store and pulled out her smartphone, opening up the Google Translate app.

She entered the weird name, and instantly it revealed the translation, sending a tingle through her hands.

"That's it." She whispered under her breath.

Bryce looked over his shoulder at the doorway to the beige building. "That's it?"

"That's it." She turned the screen towards him and his eyes focused as he read the words.

Master Crow Security Company.

"Oh. Wow. You're right."

"Master Crow is a pretty simple change from Ravenmeister." Cara observed.

Bryce chuckled. "If it were me, I would have picked something like "Little Bird Catering". I mean, Crow? That's so obvious."

"Well, it is if you can translate *'Corbeau'*." Cara waved the phone at him.

~*~

Bryce took a look around. Very little cover. Lots of people. A parking area nearby. He'd need more help, and a vehicle.

"We need a van." He announced. "Come on." He took Cara's elbow in his hand and walked her down the street.

"A van for what?" She looked up at him as she slid her iPhone back into her pocket.

He leaned close to her for an instant to grin and whisper "Surveillance technology."

A veil dropped over her features and her eyes dulled. "I see. And just where are we going to get one of those... the local car dealership?"

He straightened his shoulders. "I'll make a call."

"He'll make a call, he says, just like that." Cara informed a lamppost as they passed.

After they returned to the hotel and he connected with Monty, the van was delivered to *L'Hôtel Diamant Blanc*. The operatives driving it left before Cara had even seen them.

A Ford Transit, white with dark windows. The trim, European-style exterior would blend right in on *Rue Amelie*.

It was on the inside that things got interesting.

Once past the false back that opened up to reveal a small compartment lined with handyman tools and a coil of rope, the van morphed into something worthy of a Mission Impossible movie. Radar and TV screens and a maze of glowing lights, switches, microphones and other technology coated the walls. Not to mention the hidden weapons cache.

Cara groaned at the sight. "Good grief. Don't even tell me what all this stuff does, I don't want to know."

Time to take charge. "I'm afraid you'll have to, because you'll be staying in the van when I go in."

She looked at him as if he'd grown a second head.

"No, I'm not kidding."

"*Bryce!* I can't run this thing! What if I set something off or trigger an alert?"

"I'll show you everything you need to know. Cara, I know you can do this. The same girl that whizzes around with those intricate graphic design programs can run this simple surveillance van. Besides, it's mostly ...automatic."

Because there are agents remotely operating it and standing by. But I can't say that part.

"I spent months learning to use those diabolical graphics programs." She stared blankly. "And if you think this is a 'simple' surveillance van..."

"Then speed it up a little this time, because we move in at 7:00."

Cara looked at her wristwatch. "One hour?!"

"Yup."

At her frustrated glance, he reminded her "We don't have a lot of time. Freddie told us to hurry."

She sighed. "All right. Tell me what to do."

~*~

"Diamond, this is Ashburn, do you copy?"

"I hear you, Bryce." Cara watched the glowing screen that had a blue dot for Bryce's location. "I see you, too."

"Ahem. Use our code names, okay? Let's keep this professional."

"I still don't know why you gave me that 'code name'. And besides, why does it matter? It's just you and I talking to each other. Nobody else can hear us."

"That's what you think."

Cara sat in the dark, silent depths of the techno-van, alone, and reluctant to decipher that last remark. Who could be listening to them? The Badguys? Or Bryce's ... people, whoever they were?

"Who?" She broke the silence of a few minutes with the short question.

"Not sure. I'm hoping our "Crow" friends won't pick up on our frequency." Bryce's deep, distinctive voice was coming in clearly over her headphones. "M'kay. Let's cut the chatter. I'm moving in."

Cara felt a clench in her gut as the blue dot approached the front entrance to the Ravenmeister office. "Be careful." She whispered.

"Shh. You know I will." Bryce murmured, before the line went silent.

~*~

Bryce didn't like the fact that he would have to walk right in the front door of the enemy's office. But they had scoped the place out, and aside from landing on the roof with a helicopter, which would immediately tip them off, there was nothing else to do. He figured that they might have a subterranean exit underground, but there wasn't a way they could find it in time. It would have to be dash-in, dash-out.

He was so proud of Cara. She jumped right in, after her initial resistance. Now that she had the go-ahead, Cara seemed right at home among all the technology.

He hoped he'd shown her everything she might need to know for today. Cara was unaware, but he had backup waiting in the wings should things go sour. Two fellow agents placed in Paris were on standby in nearby streets, while a third was watching the Happiness Hotel a few neighborhoods over. Sticking Cara in the bulletproof van was a good way to keep her out of trouble.

He reached for the knob and opened the creaking front door. The stink of mold surrounded him as he stepped inside the room onto the ancient carpet. Harsh fluorescent lighting emitted a faint buzzing noise on the ceiling. A receptionist's desk sat plunked against the wall at an awkward angle, with a heavy middle-aged woman seated behind it. Doors led to separate offices and a flight of stairs was tucked in the back corner of the room. An artificial potted plant against the wall looked like it survived World War II.

"May Ah help you?" The woman slurred in a French accent as he moseyed over to the desk. She looked tired, with puffy dark circles underneath her bleary eyes, and her mauve lipstick was smudged.

Time to ham it up. "I believe I have an appointment."

"Ees dat so? Vith whom do you have an appointment?" A spark of interest lit her face

Bryce gave the woman a pleading look. "I'd like to talk to the boss, if you don't mind." He smiled.

Cara's pretty voice suddenly sounded in his head from the tiny earpiece he wore. "Seriously? Trim off some of that goody-goody. She'll be more likely to believe your act if it's believable."

As the woman looked down at the notepad on her desk, he winked at the one lobby security camera that they had tapped into. Cara would see it. How was it possible to be annoyed at somebody, yet grateful at the same time? She was right.

ASHBURN   Julia Erickson

Another remark like that and he would come off as cheesy as a plate of nachos.

The woman shook her head. "I am sorry, he ees not een today. He ees out." She rolled the 'r's in 'sorry'.

Sure. "Then may I talk to one of the supervisors or the managers? I've got a contract they'll be ...*interested* in seeing." He leaned closer with a husky whisper, glancing around the office.

The woman's eyebrows rose. "Very well." She nodded, and then waved him toward the stairway. "First door at the top of the stairs."

"Thanks."

~*~

Mitch could definitely take a few pointers from Bryce's husky whisper. Cara felt a warm glow on her cheeks from only hearing it secondhand.

Cara watched in awe as Bryce's blue dot moved deeper into the building. The woman had believed him. "I can't believe you just nailed that." She whispered into her microphone.

A soft chuckle. "Okay. Which door?" His voice was pitched low enough to be caught by the microphone in his jacket collar, but not loud enough to attract attention.

"Not the first one. That probably takes you to the bigwig's office." Cara told him, "At least that's what I'm guessing."

"I'll go with your woman's intuition on that one." Bryce answered. "What about the door at the end of the hallway?"

~*~

"I will ask you again, you slimy vorm of a technology developer. HOW do ve get that piece of metal out of your skinny arm vithout destroying it!?" The harsh voice of the man standing above Freddie echoed through the bare room.

Freddie blinked up into the one garish light bulb trained on his face. "The chip will self-destruct if not removed properly, as-as I'm sh-sure you kn-know." He was stuttering, terrified of this interrogator. "This will, ah, of course, cause m-me and any th-thing within t-ten f-feet of me to ... be, ah, blown up when it explodes. And the Personal ID chip would be destroyed... y-you'd lose your chance to s-steal it."

The man cursed and stomped around the room.

"Easy, Armand. There's no need to get excited."

While Freddie was scared of the burly half-German, half-French interrogator with the fiery temper, he was twice as frightened by the dark, silent personage sitting in the corner of the room. He couldn't see the man's face, but his voice was cold, low, and American.

Just then a beep sounded, and the man in the shadows picked up a phone. "What is it, Giselle?"

The grating voice of receptionist could be heard throughout the still room.

"There ees a man here to see a supervisor about somesing *interesting*, or so he say. I thought you would like to know."

"Who is he?"

"He said he has a *contract*. I sent him upstairs to Monsieur Franco's office."

"What did he look like?" The man demanded. There was an unsettling energy that had crept into his cool voice.

"Oh, he was young, good-looking, maybe 25 years old. Tall." Giselle's giggle floated out of the phone.

"Thank you." There was a satisfied ring in the man's tone as he hung up. "Looks like we've got a little company."

Freddie's adrenaline skyrocketed. They found his note written in lipstick. They'd come for him. But now their man would get caught. He *must* do something.

The shadow man and Armand left through the only door.

"Do not go anywhere, you scrawny freak." Armand fired over his shoulder as he closed the door behind him.

The sound of the deadbolt sliding into place made Freddie's nerves tingle. He couldn't believe his good luck. They had left him alone.

All right... I can do this. He reached for the remote control, paper-thin and about the size of a dime, which he had hidden in the secret pocket of his vest.

~*~

Cara's jaw dropped. *That dirty receptionist!* "Bryce. They're on to you. Look out!"

"What?" Bryce's voice rose higher in alarm, like a bow climbing violin strings.

"The receptionist smelled a rat. I heard her call somebody and they're on their way to find out who you are!"

"Where are they?" He demanded.

"I don't know! I only heard her end of the conversation. The call went to somewhere above the first floor."

"Okay." Bryce's voice was calm again. "Keep your eyes out for suspicious activity."

A green light started to blink on a small device that was docked into the side of the van in a special holder, and it began emitting a series of soft "beeps". Cara sprang up to examine it, and nearly choked on her gasp when she realized she was getting a transmission from none other than *Freddie Nigel Donaldson's Personal ID Chip.*

~*~

Bryce jogged down the hallway and dropped to the ground to look around the corner, only showing one eye and the tip of his nose around the edge of the wall. Clear. And there was a service elevator at the end of the hall. He could get trapped like a sardine in a can, or it could be his escape route. Muffled voices coming from behind him made the decision an easy one.

He streaked for the elevator and pushed the button for the fourth floor. As the doors slid closed, he murmured "God... please get me out of here."

"Bryce!" Cara hissed in his earpiece, "I'm getting a transmission from *Freddie!*"

He gasped, stunned at this development. "Where?"

"Third floor, in the north corner of the building."

Blast. "I'm in the elevator, heading up to the fourth floor." He hastily punched the button marked '3' as the machine drew near the fourth floor landing.

"He must have reactivated his signal somehow!" Cara's voice trembled in amazement.

Bryce held his breath as the doors opened. No guys with guns… yet. He looked out. The three hallways, right, left, and straight ahead, seemed to be empty. He bit his lip, thinking about his next move.

A door cracked open to his left and in an instant he had dived and rolled once, landing on his hands and heels, safely out of view for the moment in the hallway that had been directly in front of him. He pushed to his feet and padded silently down the hall, looking for the right door to duck into.

"Concierge" the plaque read on what looked like a small closet door. *Janitor.* Bryce opened the door, only to be greeted with the startled eyes of two people in white lab coats and face masks.

Secret lab, anyone? This day was full of surprises.

One of the workers whacked a button on the wall that started red lights flashing and a siren wailing throughout the entire building.

"Bryce?!" Cara sounded panicked.

He slammed the stupid "closet" door shut and raced back down the hallway. "I think they're definitely on to me now."

"Get out of there. I'm coming in." Her voice was determined.

What? "No! Please! Stay where you are!" He shouted into his microphone.

"We've *got* to get to Freddie!" Her words rang with conviction.

"*Je le vois!*" The shout echoed from his left. He whirled around and leaped for a small man who was screaming at the top of his lungs into a walkie-talkie. One punch from Bryce knocked him out.

"Cara, just sit tight while I fight my way out of here!"

Silence.

"*Cara?!*"

More silence. Cara had left the van. Or been discovered.

Oh God. Help.

~*~

Cara took a deep breath, poised on the windowsill of the boutique, and then leapt across the tiny alley. Intense relief sang through her body as her hands caught the wrought iron mini-balcony and she hoisted herself inside. The window was locked, but she'd already thought of that.

She pulled out a sharp tool that she found in Bryce's case and used it to slice out one of the panes of glass. Reaching her gloved hand inside, she unlatched the window. Easing herself inside, she landed on the tile floor of an empty bathroom.

Freddie's signal was still reading strong, on the screen of the handheld device she'd taken from the van. And now there was a red dot on the screen marking her position.

ASHBURN

Julia Erickson

She looked up at herself in the bathroom mirror and tucked a loose wisp of hair behind her ear. "Let's do this, girl."

~*~

"Angelwing, Markdown, do you copy? I need backup. Shadowchaser? Somebody get over here!" Bryce managed to send his request for help as he dashed down yet another hallway with two French men tearing after him.

"We're on our way." The voice crackled. He recognized Markdown.

Well, that was of some relief. Maybe he would make it out of this alive.

He ran down another flight of stairs, trying not to get twisted around in his mind, feeling like a lab rat looking for the peanut butter. Now that Cara wasn't responding, he had her to worry about as well as himself. He had to find her first. Then he could concentrate on saving his own hide.

"Cara, where are you?"

Still no answer.

~*~

Freddie's head jerked as the deadbolt was slid open and a figure appeared in the doorway. A tall, gorgeous woman rushed into the room, wearing khaki jeans, a denim jacket, and gloves. In one hand was a steadily beeping tracking device and in the other was a small backpack.

"Are you Freddie?" She asked, sweeping him with one glance from her huge gray eyes.

He nodded nonstop like a bobblehead. "Yes! Who are you?"

"That's not important. One of the good guys. We've got to get you out of here."

"Well, good luck with that." He jerked his left hand to reveal that it was handcuffed to the metal chair, which appeared to be bolted to the floor. "How did you find me?"

Her gaze darted around the room and then returned to his face. "We picked up your trail in Venice at the hotel. Nice job with the mirror message." She pulled what looked like an extended edition of a Swiss army knife out of her bag. "Let's see... maybe there's something on this that will unlock you."

She knelt next to him and began working the tools against the cold metal of the handcuff. "I was the one who found your lipstick scrawl, which led us here."

"I was hoping somebody would! They're getting ready to move me again. They seem terrified that ... uh, somebody might snatch me back." He smiled at his lovely rescuer. "You're beautiful."

She looked up in surprise. "Um, thanks. But save the guy-girl thing 'till later, okay? You and I have to get out of here *now*. And we have to help Bryce." She returned her attention to his handcuffs.

"Who's Bryce? And who do you guys work for, anyway?" *Who is this woman? She moves like a secret agent!*

"I work for Silver Strand Technologies. Believe it or not, I'm a graphic designer." She tried yet another tool. "Bryce is ... a friend of mine. And I'm not exactly sure who he works for. But he's a good man. He'll help you."

"What's your name?" He studied her face through his horn-rimmed glasses.

She sighed, still working on the handcuffs. "Cara Stephenson."

It's her?! No way! "*The* Cara Stephenson? The brainchild-top-wonder-designer? The pride-and-joy-of-Silver-Strand-Technologies Cara Stephenson?"

She laughed incredulously. "I guess so. I never heard of myself in that light."

I sure have. "You ought to hear them sing your praises over in the development side of things. Everybody loves your work."

Click.

He was free.

"*YES!*" She high-fived him as the handcuffs slipped from his wrist. "Come on. Let's go."

"Are you *sure* you're not a secret agent?" He asked as she led him out the door.

"Very sure. Now move it!"

~*~

Bryce had shed the original two French guys and dealt with three others, but he knew the time was rapidly drawing to a close. Every second brought him closer to death if he didn't find Cara. He'd somehow made it back up to the fourth floor and was navigating the hallways, trying to reach the north corner of the building. He had a hunch that she might have escaped notice in all the confusion centered on him and made it to Freddie.

He slammed against the wall as he heard a familiar voice. "...This way."

Cara. She spun around the corner with a geeky-looking man in tow.

Bryce reached out and grabbed her, one arm around her middle, the other thrown across her mouth, silencing the scream before it could come out. "Cara! It's me."

The skinny young man, who must be Freddie, stared at him in shock, mouth gaping, as Cara struggled for a split second, and then went so limp that Bryce thought she might have fainted. He jerked his arm away, afraid he'd cut off her air.

"Bryce." She gasped, the instant he removed his arm from her mouth.

"I'm sorry. *Are you okay?!* What were you thinking, leaving the van?"

She glared at him. "Caviar! Now let's get out of here!"

Freddie looked completely puzzled. "Is that some kind of code word?" He asked as they snuck down the hallway at high speed.

"Later, dude. It's a long story and we don't have a second to waste." Bryce's clipped words came out like bullets. "Cara, how did you get into this building?"

"I jumped across the alley from a boutique window next door." Cara answered calmly.

"O-*kay*. That was creative." Bryce rolled his eyes.

"I am nothing if not creative." Cara declared, smiling at him.

"That's true! You have to be creative if you're the top designer for Silver Strand. She's definitely creative." Freddie chimed in.

Bryce eyed him. *He's like a little nervous, yapping terrier.* "Freddie, will you please stop babbling?" He peeked around the next corner. Men with machine guns were coming down the hall.

He pushed Cara and Freddie back against the wall behind him. "No good." He whispered through his teeth.

"What do we do?" Cara breathed in his ear.

All three of them looked up as the door directly across the narrow hall from them swung wide open.

~*~

Freddie gulped. In front of them stood Armand with the man that must be the shadowy figure who sat in his room. He was muscled and lean at the same time, with a shocking paleness to his skin and absolutely black hair above striking facial features. His eyes glittered cold and steely as he lovingly stroked the huge, menacing gun he held against his chest, with the barrel pointed straight at them.

~*~

Bryce recognized the gun instantly. It was an Uzi-Pro automatic submachine gun, which was accessible only to military personnel... or illegal dealers. But it was the sight of the man holding the machine that made the hair prickle on the back of his neck in sheer terror.

Ryan Black.

"RUN!" Bryce roared in the same instant that he flung the lower half of his body into the air in a kickflip, popping the gun from his enemy's grasp with a blow from his leg. The hot sting of a bullet grazed his left shoulder as he collided with the rock-hard form of his greatest enemy.

~*~

Freddie wished that this was all a bad dream.

Cara screamed. Bryce and the shadow-man fell to the floor together in a heap, while at the same time Armand lunged for Cara and Freddie.

He was thrown off-balance as Cara shoved him out of the way. She leaped in the opposite direction but Armand got a hand on her right heel and pulled, knocking her to the floor.

No! You can't have her! Freddie righted himself and launched a kick at Armand's head that miraculously connected and momentarily stunned the man. Something in his ankle snapped painfully, and he sank to the ground, unable to bear the weight of his body on his foot.

A whimper from Cara captured Freddie's attention. Her eyes glazed over and she curled into a ball, gripping her wrist with her other hand.

Bryce wrestled with the shadow man, locked in a battle for the Uzi. But then Bryce slipped the gun from the man's grasp and leaped to his feet. For a brief moment, he had complete control of the situation, with the gun aimed at his opponent.

But then Freddie looked up and saw fifteen men running towards them.

"Take Cara and go!" He shouted hoarsely.

Bryce responded, moving carefully out of the doorway into the hall and pulling the limp Cara to her feet with an arm around her waist.

"Freddie, remember this." Cara murmured a phone number through her obvious pain, still clutching her wrist.

The number might as well have been seared on his mind with fire. He wouldn't forget it.

And then his new friends were gone. Freddie watched the fifteen men approach, determining to hold out until Bryce and Cara came for him again.

"After them!" Ryan Black howled in rage.

Chapter Six

Broken but Beautiful

Someone had bolted the front door, but a powerful kick from Bryce fixed that issue. Evading the receptionist's pistol bullets had been more of a challenge. Especially with Cara hurt.

She struggled visibly, in great pain, but managing to stay on her feet. He helped support her weight with one arm around her.

They exploded from the door and into the street. Dusk blanketed Paris and lights flickered as they blinked on all over the city.

Bryce had never been so glad to see an overcast sky. But he wouldn't be able to sit there savoring the sight.

"After them!" The cry was the voice of Ryan Black. He sounded like he could be as close as the front office.

Which meant the task of escaping was far from done.

"Come on!" He clasped Cara's uninjured elbow and pulled her towards a motorcycle parking area, where the backup plan awaited.

She stumbled behind him as they ran towards a red Ducati Streetfighter motorcycle.

Good ol' Monty. Gotta love how he plans for the unexpected.

He whipped out a key and started the motor. "Get on! Hang on to me!" He pulled Cara onto the back of the bike behind him and they roared off.

ASHBURN — Julia Erickson

Cara circled her arms around his torso, and held on tightly with her good arm, weakly with the injured one.

"We'll be okay. Just hold on and let me do the balancing. You take it easy back there."

"We left Freddie." Cara moaned as they hit a main street. "And we've just stolen a motorcycle."

Bryce wished he could stop and wrap his arms around her. The poor girl had just suffered a very traumatic experience, and was nowhere near as jaded to it as he.

"I'm really sorry about Freddie, but his ankle was in bad shape. There was no way all *three* of us were getting out of there alive. They won't kill him. He's holding the chip." Shouting over his shoulder was the only way to make himself heard over the growl of the bike's engine.

"I hope you're right." Cara's tearful voice was scarcely audible over the cacophony of noise surrounding them.

Then she gasped. "Your jacket has a rip... you're bleeding!"

His left shoulder stung from the bullet graze, but it wasn't serious, ugly though it might look. He knew what a dangerous gun wound felt like, and this did not compare. "It's just a scratch. I'm okay."

He swerved around a delivery truck. "Look back. Are they following us?" Looking into the rearview mirror afforded him only a limited view.

He felt Cara shift slightly, and then she leaned to talk in his ear. "That dark-haired man – he's right behind us!"

Bryce bit back a groan. "Hang on. This could get rough."

ASHBURN   Julia Erickson

~*~

Cara wanted to faint. But if she fainted and fell off the bike, then she'd die, because she wasn't wearing a helmet and she *was* riding on a motorcycle that had to be going at least 80 miles an hour. So she focused on keeping her arms locked around Bryce's lean midsection. The blur of buildings and streets raced past, clogged with honking cars, buses, people, but somehow they didn't collide with anything.

It was almost miraculous, if there were such things as miracles.

~*~

Bryce was starting to actually get scared. He had done everything he could to lose Ryan Black and the guy was still right on his tail, and getting closer. He'd also fired some shots from a handgun with a silencer on it.

Just then, ahead of him, loomed the icon of Paris. The tall iron structure that everybody recognized and visited when they came to this city. It was glowing against the darkening sky, lit by hundreds of tiny lights.

The Eiffel Tower.

A dip in the road jostled them, extracting a moan from Cara.

"Come on, honey, I need you to stay with me!" Bryce encouraged her.

Because I'm about to do something crazy.

Lord, help!

Bryce drove the motorcycle straight for the tower. A second's glance in the mirror showed Black following, leaning low over his machine in hot pursuit. Could they even get through without crashing into something? The space underneath the tower was crammed with things to run into.

One heartbeat. Two.

They hopped the curb and shot underneath the tower base, a network of wrought iron overhead. Dodged the screaming people. Cara pressed her cheek tightly against his back. Tourists scrambled to safety as he struggled to drive through. Almost there. Another three agonizing seconds ticked past, and they were out on the other side. He swung the vehicle to the left, hard. They nearly tipped, but he righted their balance, heaving his body to the right, just as his knee was about to collide with the concrete. Cara screamed, with an impressive range of high notes.

A sharp crash behind them did another number on his eardrums as the tires slid, leaving black streaks in their wake. They skidded out onto the main road, just missing a taxi that slammed on the brakes. He looked back and glimpsed Ryan Black's motorcycle lying on its side, with the driver spread-eagled on the pavement.

He caught a nanosecond-long look of Cara's pale face. She had her eyes squeezed closed... probably a good thing.

Hearing sirens in the distance, Bryce slowed to a safer speed and set his course for the nearest hospital.

~*~

Cara's stomach churned. *I think I'm gonna throw up.* A building only a few blocks away from the Eiffel tower sported signs indicating that they had an ER. Bryce parked the bike and jumped off, standing next to it.

"Cara, are you all right?" His whisper was full of worry.

The blurry surroundings were making her dizzy. "I don't know about my wrist, but the rest of me is okay… I think."

"Come on, let's get you checked out." Bryce reached his arm around her and helped her off the bike. "If anybody asks, you nearly got mugged, all right?" He led her towards the door.

She nodded weakly in response.

The sweet, heady scent of the rosebushes planted outside the hospital entrance extended healing welcome. Cara tried to ignore the sharp ache in her wrist. Touching the injured area sent a jolt of pain shooting all the way up to her shoulder.

Cara couldn't see the interior of the hospital clearly, but it was very white and bright and quiet compared to the world of gleaming yellow lights and busy traffic outside.

Bryce sat her in a chair against the wall and then went to the desk. She waited while he talked to the lady on duty, with her injured wrist held against her chest, above her heart, which seemed to ease the throbbing some.

She didn't realize that she'd closed her eyes until Bryce spoke from right beside her.

"Hey, sweet girl."

Her eyes flew open. "Mmm?"

"They're going to X-ray your wrist now. Come on."

"Stay with me." She pleaded, wincing as she stood.

"I will."

After the mercifully quick X-ray, a nurse ushered them into an examination room to wait for the results. He hoped, for Cara's sake, that they would be fast.

A print of a Monet painting hung on the wall next to a clock with the hands pointing to 8:31. Cara waited on the crinkly-papered examination bench while he sat across from her in a metal chair.

I've gotta take her mind off this. "You know, my brother broke his leg once."

Cara's eyebrows rose. "He did?"

"Yeah. He fell out of a tree. I think it happened when he was fifteen." He shook his head. "The little scamp… he was always getting into trouble." *Still does. Ah, Blake.*

Cara tilted her head. "And you were the responsible one."

Bryce nodded. "I had to be. I was the oldest."

The door opened and in stepped the doctor, a portly man with a fringe of silvered hair. Kindly eyes looked at them from behind small square glasses.

"Well, Miss Stephenson, I have some good news, and some bad news." He announced in excellent English.

"Hit me with the bad news first." Cara told him, straightening her shoulders.

Bryce grinned. *She's so cute when she's brave.*

The doctor chuckled. "Very well. The bad news is that, yes, you have fractured your wrist. It's a typical broken wrist, with a fracture of the radius bone. It's not shattered, and the broken edges of the bone are close enough together that all I will have to do is a simple manipulation to move them back into proper alignment."

Cara winced, then nodded, a sober expression on her face.

"The good news, young lady, is that you do not need surgery." The doctor consulted his clipboard. "I will put your wrist in a cast after the reduction of the fracture."

"Reduction...?" Cara's brow wrinkled.

"I put you under light sedation and carefully move the bones back into place. It's a very simple process."

Cara shivered, then sighed. "All right. And after that?"

"In a cast, it should heal within six weeks."

Six weeks?! Oh great. The heaviness of guilt slammed him. *It was my fault. I put her in danger.*

~*~

Bryce yawned, feeling fatigue beginning to creep in. *Whew. Glad that's over.*

Cara had regained complete consciousness now and sipped a protein shake from the hospital cafeteria. 9:00pm, and they hadn't eaten since noon. He wasn't hungry... ravenous was the word for it.

Cara's wrist bore a white cast that stretched from her knuckles to her elbow. The doctor had given them a list of exercises to practice so that her fingers and arm wouldn't become stiff while the wrist healed, and informed them they would need to keep the cast dry at all times, and elevated for at least the first week.

"This tastes like stale peanuts and old armadillo." Cara remarked with a blithe toss of her head. It was the first bit of humor he'd seen from her since they had moved on the Ravenmeister building. Good. She would need to keep laughing.

"When did you ever taste armadillo?" He smiled into her eyes. At the moment they were tinted a soft blue-gray, which seemed to match her mood now that she felt calmer.

Fascinating.

"Come to think of it, never, but this is what it must taste like. Want some?" She tilted the straw towards him.

"Uh, I'll pass, thanks."

"When do we get to leave? I want to go home... um, that is, back to the hotel... and order room service."

Before he could reply, the door opened and a nurse peeked into the room. "You may leave now, Miss Stephenson."

Cara shot Bryce a relieved smile. "Thank you."

~*~

On the way back to *L'Hôtel Diamant Blanc* they ended up with an awful taxi driver that jerked back and forth all over the road in a style that would have made a sidewinder viper envious.

Bryce walked Cara to her hotel room door and they entered the comfortable apartment. Cara sighed wearily and sat down on a tufted chair, rubbing her forehead with her left hand.

"Do you want to eat first or change clothes?" *Poor thing, she looks completely worn out.* Her denim jacket was coated in a thin film of road dust and her hair was falling out of the bun she'd coiled it in.

"I'm not very hungry, but a nice hot shower–" She halted, and looked up at him.

Shower… uh-oh.

Obviously, they had some thinking to do. How would she manage with only one hand, and her left one at that?

"Ah, well, let's talk about that. First, we need to keep your cast dry." He forced himself to remain matter-of-fact. Acting awkward would only make Cara feel embarrassed. "A plastic bag and some rubber bands will do the trick."

Cara relaxed visibly, expression softening. "I've got ponytail holders, for rubber bands, but what about a bag?"

He looked around the hotel room, spied an empty trash can under the desk and lifted the plastic bag from it. Cara found some elastic ponytail holders in her suitcase.

She tried to shrug off her jacket but it caught on her cast. He moved closer to help, but she waved him away. "I'm fine." Her voice was cool and her shoulders tense as she slowly peeled the jacket off her injured arm.

"Cara, I have a mom and a younger sister. I know that 'I'm fine' in that tone is really just girl talk for "I'm *not* fine"."

ASHBURN

Julia Erickson

A smile dimpled her cheek. "Yeah. That's pretty much true."

"Here, let me help." He carefully slid the plastic bag over the white cast and gently secured it with two elastic hairbands, one near her elbow and one around the palm of her hand.

"Thank you." She seemed to have softened a trifle. Then she dug in her suitcase with her left hand and pulled out a plastic shower cap with red hearts printed all over it.

"Caviar!" She warned him, eyes narrowed, "Do. Not. Say. A. Word, just help me get this on my head."

He bit his lip in an effort to keep from smiling, took the shower cap from her and stretched it over her head and lopsided bun, tucking the bits of stray blonde hair inside the edge.

"There you go. All set?" He asked.

"I think so. Leave for a few minutes and I'll call you on the hotel room phone when I'm done." She stopped pulling clothes from her suitcase for a second to yawn, and then found a pair of pajama pants and a long-sleeved knit shirt.

"All right." He paused at the door and turned back for a moment. "I'll call Mr. Gungerson for you and give him an update."

She closed her eyes and moaned. "Oh... I'd forgotten. I am so getting fired after today."

"Never mind. Don't think about it, I'll take care of everything. And Cara... I was calling all the shots. I'll take the heat on this one."

She sighed softly, opened her eyes, and regarded him for a few minutes. "Thank you." There was a resigned acceptance in her tone.

He reluctantly left her and crossed the hall to his own suite, taking a quick security survey on his way.

All clear.

The shower called to his tired body in a most inviting way, and his stomach was growling like a caged grizzly, but he knew what he had to do first, and that was phone Montrose. And then Mr. Gungerson. A hot shower and dinner would have to wait a little longer.

He waited about five seconds for Monty to answer his call before his boss picked up.

"ASHBURN! What in blazes went wrong?" He was definitely riled. "Markdown reported a hullabaloo-"

"-Two words. Ryan Black."

Silence. Then a few words that Monty only used when extremely provoked.

"I know."

"And you're still alive?" Montrose's tone altered slightly as he seemed to realize this fact.

"I seem to be." Though not without a few scratches and a bruised hand from all the punches he'd thrown.

"Thank God. You know that guy has an agenda to put you six feet under. And how fares Miss Stephenson?"

"It turns out she has a broken wrist. One of Black's goons knocked her down and she landed right on it."

"And how did *that* happen?" Monty sounded irate.

"It wouldn't have, had she stayed in the van, and had I not been busy wrestling with Black for control of his Uzi."

Stunned silence.

His boss had a right to be shocked. He'd been out of his mind to attack a man holding that kind of weapon. Even if he had mad skills in street fighting. It had literally been insane – a move that was 95% likely to get him killed. The only reason it worked was because Ryan Black hadn't seen it coming.

He'd also been nuts to drive through the Eiffel tower. They could have died in a motorcycle crash, or killed someone else running over them. But he shook off Ryan black, thereby saving their lives.

"By the way, I'm not sure Black made it after the end of that little game of motorcycle tag we played through the streets of Paris. He crashed after we drove through the Eiffel Tower."

"Agent Markdown reported that the driver walked away from that wreck and vanished. Although we didn't know it was Black."

Bryce noted that his boss's tone didn't even react at the mention of the tower.

"Oh yes, and Angelwing secured the van and brought it back to the France operations warehouse… after you abandoned it to go hot-rodding on your Ducati."

"He was breathing down my neck. The bike – which, I might add, was *your* idea for a backup plan – was the only viable option."

Montrose huffed. "At least we didn't lose any agents, meaning you. Next time, play it safer."

"Yeah. Ok." Then an important fact floated to the surface of his memory. "Also – I almost forgot. Cara gave Freddie Donaldson her number."

"Her cell?"

"Yeah. Do you think he might be able to contact us?"

"I doubt it, but there's always hope. In the meantime, keep sniffing around. The Ravenmeister building is deserted… they've moved Donaldson again."

Now Bryce felt like using some choice words, but resisted the urge at the last moment, instead releasing a heavy sigh. "Here we go 'round the mulberry bush, again."

"Just watch your back. With Ryan Black on their task force, this is a whole different ball game. I almost feel like pulling you in, but can't bring myself to do it. We *need* this mission to succeed, and your track record speaks for itself."

"I'll try to live up to it. In the meantime, what should I tell Gungerson? We're supposed to call him with an update."

"Give him a brief account and tell him you're still looking for Freddie. I don't have to tell you to omit sundry details like how you got into the building or the reappearance of your greatest nemesis."

Montrose coughed, then spoke again. "And, Ashburn, keep your ear to the ground for two things. One – proof that Ravenmeister is the front for the illegal arms dealing. And two – a connection between Ravenmeister and Silver Strand. We got an anonymous tip that the two companies might be connected in some way."

"Got it."

"Good." *Beeeeep.* The line went dead.

One conversation down, one to go.

…But first, a 2-minute shower.

~*~

Mr. Gungerson sat reclining in an office chair that was so tall it towered over his head, completely alone in the gloom of his private study. The only light came from the banker's lamp on his desk, a dim glow emanating from the green shade. He had given the servants the night off, needing quiet.

He stroked his forehead with his hand, hoping to ease some of the tension headache. It didn't help. He tried to ponder out a solution to his dilemma, but found his thoughts drifting nowhere. That was when he realized he was drumming the fingers on the right arm of his chair, while his other hand was crushing a chair arm in a death grip that whitened his knuckles.

Ring! The mobile phone vibrated on the smooth wood of his desk. He grabbed it and punched the button. "Hello?"

"Hello sir, this is Bryce Reynolds." A smooth masculine voice responded.

"Reynolds." He acknowledged his new employee. "How did it go today?" *Cara. Is she well?*

"I have both good news and bad news for you, sir. We made brief contact with Donaldson, but I'm afraid the Ravenmeister people still hold him in their grasp."

He sat in stony silence while Bryce gave him a recap of the day's events. A bubble of rage roiled up inside him when he heard that Cara's wrist had been broken, but he managed to keep it in check without bursting out at young Reynolds.

"Well." His thoughts were racing. Did he dare demand that they quit, when so close to getting Freddie back?

"I assure you, Sir, that we are taking every precaution and will be very careful in our maneuvers from here on out. We hope to hear from Freddie again soon."

Yes... It had been sheer brilliance on Cara's part to give Freddie her number. *She is so bright! If only I had such a child of my own.* He wished he could give her the enormous raise she deserved without causing his whole arts department to throw back their heads and howl with indignation.

By thunder, if this investigation was successful, he would raise her pay, no matter the backlash.

"Carry on, then, and keep me informed." He caved in. The investigation would continue. They had to recover Freddie and the chip, at all costs!

"We will. Goodbye."

"Goodbye."

~*~

Mitch smiled slowly and turned off his signal-interception, rolled back from his laptop and propped his feet on the desk.

There were distinct advantages to being a techno-whiz. His daddy would never find out that he had been eavesdropping on the signal to his cell phone – having cracked the encryption code and tapped into the frequency.

So Cara had broken her wrist in all that brouhaha at the undercover Ravenmeister district building. It served her right! And whatever she saw in that Bryce Reynolds was more than he could understand. The guy was a complete neophyte in the world of graphics and technology. Whereas he, Mitch Gungerson Jr., was highly experienced. Some would say brilliant.

The sting of rejection embittered him with its poison. *Why couldn't she love* me? The better question was – how would he retaliate?

~*~

Cara wasn't looking forward to dressing herself in real clothes tomorrow. Getting into the comfy clothes had been hard enough without the complication of buttons or zippers. She called Bryce's room, waiting for him to answer, when a knock came at the door.

A quick look showed her Bryce making a silly face and gazing straight at the peephole from the outside. She swallowed her giggle as she opened the door.

"You're so goofy." Her voice came out warm and fuzzy-sounding, which had not been intentional.

He gave her a wink. "Anything to win a smile from you, Milady." His gaze dropped to her wrist, which was cradled in her other hand. "How are you doing?"

She let out a sigh. "I'm glad it's not any worse." Her voice quavered on a few of the words. *I sound like a sissy.* She bit her lip in annoyance.

"Awww." He murmured in sympathy. Bryce closed the door behind them, and then moved to take her into his arms in a brotherly hug. A deep rumbling growl sounded somewhere within him and she leaned back to look up into his face in alarm.

He grinned, shamefaced. "I'm afraid my stomach clock has just gone off. Shall we order room service?"

"Please." She nodded. "Do you think they have something simple, like soup? I'm not in the mood for anything elaborate."

"I'll see what the kitchen can whip up." Bryce let go of her and hunted around for the room service menu, finally locating it on top of the bureau. "I took a shower, then called your boss and filled him in."

"You angel. Thank you." Cara felt as if a great weight had been dragged from her shoulders now that she didn't have to talk to Mr. Gungerson and tell him how badly she'd failed.

Bryce chuckled. "You're welcome." His eyes locked on one spot of the menu. "Aha. They have steak."

"Of which, I gather, you are *most* fond."

"Why yes, I am." He responded to her bantering with his own as he dialed the hotel phone. He ordered steak for him and soup for her.

Cara tidied up a little as he finished the phone call, tucking things back into her suitcase, one-handed. Her hair kept getting in her way, sweeping around to the front in a tangled golden stream that was longer than her arms.

~*~

Bryce rose and went to her. "Here, let's do something about your hair."

She looked at him in disbelief. Then shook her head. "I already tried. I can't do anything with it, with only my left hand."

He held up his hands and wiggled his fingers. "Mine still work. Where's your hairbrush?"

Cara waved towards the bathroom. "In there." Her expression was a mixture of surprise and apprehension.

He found it quickly and walked back, brush in hand. She sat cross-legged on top of the bed. Good grief. Her hair nearly reached the floor. "Rapunzel, Rapunzel, let down your hair."

"Ha-ha. It's down." Her voice chided him dryly. "Start near the ends and work up." She still seemed a little edgy… nervous. Maybe she thought he would pull her hair.

He would never have thought of brushing hair that way but she was right – it worked. The tangles smoothed out easily as the free hair near the ends was brushed. Her fine hair was silky-soft in his hands. He reached the crown of her head and felt an immense satisfaction at being able to pull the brush all the way down her hair, unhindered by any snags.

He could feel her relaxing, bit-by-bit. Eventually no more tangles remained.

"All done. Do you want me to braid it or something?" Come to think of it, that would take forever – and he didn't know how.

Cara shook her head, causing the golden river to swish back and forth. "No… I'd rather put it in a shell bun, but you wouldn't know how to do that and I can't show you how with my left hand."

"What *is* a shell bun? That thing you did on the plane with the twists and the hairclip?"

She stared at him, wide-eyed. "Yes! That's it. I can't believe you remember."

"Hmm." He gathered her hair into one long ponytail. "Let's see… you did something like this, and then this… and then wound it around like that…" And suddenly there was a nice, neat coil on her head underneath his hands. His earlier shameless scrutiny paid off.

She surveyed it in the mirror's reflection on the wall and gave a shocked gasp. "Bryce! How did you…? That's a shell bun. Of course, it's really very simple once you know how to do it."

He looked around. "Pity there isn't a clip within reach!"

Cara smiled. "Here, I'll hold it. You'll find a clip in the satin drawstring bag in my suitcase."

Her hair secured, dinner arrived, and they curled up in their respective seats to eat their food. He polished off his thick, juicy steak and savored the taste of the creamy mashed potatoes seasoned with garlic. Cara sipped delicately at her chicken soup, using her left hand quite deftly to transport the spoon to her rosebud mouth.

The meal over with, he asked if they should call it a day. But Cara leaned forward with a scared look in her eyes.

"No… please. Don't go. Not yet." She settled back into the chair. "What about a movie?"

He was wired from the day they'd spent in high-adrenaline situations. If he tried to go to sleep now, he would only make a wadded mess out of his sheets, tossing and turning. A movie sounded great.

"I'll pick something out from the vending machine I spotted earlier. Any requests?" He would offer the ultimate sacrifice. "...A chick-flick, maybe?" *Please don't say yes.*

Cara wrinkled her nose. "Not unless they have anything based on the works of Jane Austen."

Bryce pantomimed wiping his brow in relief, which earned a smile from her. "I'll find something good."

Finding something good proved to be a greater challenge than he'd thought. He finally selected a movie filmed in their own home state of Georgia, even though the plot line about four fathers made him feel uneasy. He didn't know if he could stomach a whole movie about fatherhood. But none of the other options were remotely acceptable. He was choosy with the media material he inserted in his brain.

He saw enough violence, danger and filth in his line of work.

Bryce returned to Cara's room, and victoriously brandished the DVD. "Ta-Da!"

She was curled up in a corner of the little couch, wrapped in blankets pulled up to her chin, with her broken wrist elevated on a pillow with a bag of ice cubes. That accounted for the rest of her being warmly wrapped up. "Ooooh! *Courageous*. I've wanted to see that. Great choice."

"I hope so." He popped it into the TV, and then tried to decide where to sit. None of the chairs were in a good place to view the TV, which was directly opposite the couch. Everything was smaller in France than in America, including the hotel rooms.

"Here." Cara thumped the expanse of unoccupied couch next to her. "There's plenty of room."

Sure, if you're a toothpick.

He hesitated for a second, then gingerly sat next to her. She didn't seem to care about the close proximity, and he eventually relaxed.

The movie opened with a bang, with someone's truck nearly getting stolen with their baby in the backseat. From there on it segued into the lives of four fathers who all worked for the Albany sheriff's department. Bryce was enjoying the story line when tragedy struck.

"No!" Cara gasped as two tears fell down her cheeks. "She was such a sweet little thing!"

Bryce actually felt like crying himself, which shocked him so thoroughly that all notion of it fled from his mind.

Scenes from the little girl's funeral played, with the grieving parents in the forefront. Bryce tucked an arm around Cara as she sniffled, dabbing her tears away with her left hand.

"Wow. This is an emotional movie. Maybe I should have gotten something else." His voice sounded thick.

"No, it's ok." Cara shook her head, gaze never wavering from the screen. She was completely engrossed.

Oh man. Earlier in the film, the father had refused to dance with his daughter in a parking lot. Now, he drove back to the same place, got out of the car, and did 'his part' of the dance.

ASHBURN Julia Erickson

Cara buried her face in his shoulder and wept. He hugged her close with one arm, careful of her wrist. Perhaps Cara needed this emotional release after the day they'd had.

"I'm sorry," she whispered at last, returning her gaze to the movie, "It's just that *my* daddy will never dance with me again. He used to, before he died. He'd twirl me around the kitchen. I remember."

He was wordless. "I'm so sorry, Cara." It didn't seem a fitting response, but it was all he could think of. "One day, the right guy will come into your life, and he'll twirl you around the kitchen, again." *I'd like to be that guy.*

Cara dried her tears. "Thanks, Bryce."

Boy, what a roller-coaster. They laughed like loons at the hilarious scene with 'Javier' in the back of the patrol car, where the harmless man frightened the living daylights out of a young gangster.

And then it came. The moment that made his heart sink like lead. One of the fathers betrayed his family and his God. It came out that he had been illegally dealing drugs on the side, stealing here and there from the evidence they'd collected.

Betrayed.

No! There it came, trying to overcome his senses. That black fog that had enveloped him for weeks after his father had left them. He would not let it overpower him again.

He rose stiffly and marched into the bathroom without a word to Cara. He heard the sound cease. She must have paused the movie. He stared into his own eyes in the bathroom mirror. For an instant, he saw the frightened hazel eyes of a skinny fourteen-year-old, who suddenly had to be the man of the house, caring for his bereft mother and younger brother and baby sister.

The silence lingered.

He flushed the toilet for no reason and opened the door to return to the hotel room.

Cara was waiting patiently on the couch. She looked at him solemnly. "You are *not* okay."

He ran a hand through his hair. "No. I'm not." He wasn't okay, he was falling apart in a million tiny pieces for the millionth time.

She watched him with her large gray eyes. "But you *will* be okay."

"Yeah." His voice shook. *Drat.*

She tipped her head to one side. "Come here." She stretched out her unbroken arm.

He sat on the couch again, and this time it was Cara who wrapped an arm around him. He rested his head against hers.

Silence again. But the peace flooded in, and he felt the hand of God heal him once more. *Thank you, Father.*

He sat up straighter and reached for the remote. "What do you say? Shall we finish it?"

Cara nodded. "I want to see how it ends." Her eyes were still full of sympathy.

She was right. Finishing it had been the best thing to do. The movie ended with a stirring call for fathers to stand up and be courageous in their generation, here and now.

Bryce had already resolved within himself to be a better father than his dad had been. That is, if he ever had the chance. But he felt the firm conviction strengthen deep inside.

"That was a great movie. I don't know if I would have chosen to watch it tonight if I'd known what a tear-jerker it was, though." Cara stretched and sighed.

Bryce glanced at his watch. 12:42. "Let's try to get some sleep now, so we can face the world again tomorrow."

Cara smiled. "All right."

He got up. "Anything I can get for you before I head to bed?"

"No... I'll be fine." She yawned, covering her mouth left-handed.

"Okay. Call me if you need me." He walked to the door, opened it, and then stood there in the doorway. "Goodnight."

~*~

Chapter Seven

Not a Sparrow Falls...

His body wasn't thanking him for rising before dawn. But it was essential. He spent half an hour reading his Bible and praying, pouring himself out before his Maker in earnest supplication. He needed to feel God's hand in this, needed help. Because he and Cara were not going to make it on their own.

Bryce loaded up for the day, donning his shoulder holster and throwing a couple of unusual devices into his pockets. *What will I need to protect her?*

Cara. His mouth formed a smile just thinking of her name.

He'd met a lot of women in his line of work. Many of them were drop-dead gorgeous, or wealthy, or witty, or winsome. Many were a combination of all of that. But nobody had slipped past his defenses like Cara.

There was something about her that begged him to shelter her... an innocent purity that he felt compelled to defend from this ugly world. She was so beautiful, and had a sweet sense of humor. A hint of mystery about her made him, the spy, desire to discover all her secrets.

But until he knew for sure that they served the same Lord, he could move no further down that path.

~*~

Cara huffed in frustration. *Come on.* She tried again, this time with success, to fasten the last button on her blouse with her left hand. *Whew. Finally.* It was so strange that movements that were so familiar with one hand were completely foreign when using the other.

It was simple to pull on the elastic-waisted flouncy chiffon skirt. She was beyond grateful that she'd thrown it into her suitcase at the last moment.

Her cell phone rang as she was slipping on her ballet flats, playing the bouncy song she'd set for Penny's number. *Penny!*

Cara dived for the phone with her left hand and managed only to knock it to the floor. She pounced on it and lifted it to her ear as she kneeled on the carpet.

"Oh Penny!" Cara gasped. "You'll never believe what's happened to me! And we're in Paris!"

Penny's wonderful voice turned instantly sympathetic, picking up on Cara's mood. "What is it about being that close to the Eiffel tower that upsets you, Hon?"

"I broke my wrist!" Cara's voice also broke with the words, and a sob erupted.

"Oh, babydoll! You poor lamb! Ohhhhh." Penny crooned from the other side of the phone. "I wish I was there to brush your glorious hair and give you a hug!"

Cara sniffed, standing up. "Well, Bryce did that for me."

Penny's voice went a few notes higher. "He hugged you?"

Cara laughed through her tears. "No..." *Wait, did he?*

ASHBURN

Julia Erickson

He did.

"...well, not like that, but he brushed my hair."

"A nice perk, considering." Penny's tone was full of mischief, even filtered through a mechanical device like a cell phone. "Is it your right wrist?"

"Yes." Cara moaned.

"Oh, darlin'. I am *so* sorry."

"I need to wash my hair, and there's no way I can manage without my right hand."

"I know!" Penny sounded excited. "You just find yourself a chic lil' French salon and ask them for just a wash and blow-dry. I know you hate beauty salons like you hate collard greens, but it'll be a lot easier than washing your own hair."

"Penny! You're brilliant. I would never have thought of that."

"But don't you *dare* let them whack off that beautiful hair of yours, or I will personally swim across the ocean and whop them upside their foofy French heads."

Cara giggled while stepping into the bathroom to find a towel. She dried her tears, noting that her nose had turned red. Oh, the hardships of having very fair skin.

"Don't you worry. If they even pick up a scissors within five feet of me, I'll be out that door so fast you'll hear a sonic boom."

Penny chortled. "Good!"

A knock sounded at the door.

"I think Bryce is here. Want to say hello to him?" Cara asked Penny over the phone as she padded to the door.

"I'd better not. I might tell him something about you that you'd rather I didn't."

Cara felt herself blushing. "Like what?" She looked through the peephole. Yep, it was Bryce. She reached for the door handle with her left hand and swung open the door, then quickly returned the phone to her ear in time to catch Penny's reply.

"Like that you're perfect wife material and if he lets you slip through his fingers he's a complete nincompoop."

She bent double as an uncontrollable laugh spurted out from her.

Bryce eyed her with a curious glance.

"You're outrageous." Cara motioned with her head for Bryce to come in.

"Life is so much more fun, that way." Penny retorted saucily. "But I'll try not to make you blush if he's standing right there."

"Mm-hmm. He is."

Bryce's gaze snapped back to her again. His eyes narrowed as if in suspicion.

"Well, I'll let you go." Cara could just hear the teasing smile in Penny's voice.

"Have fun with the rest of your trip, and do get well soon!"

"Thanks. Love you." Her best friend really was sweet.

Bryce's eyes popped wide.

"Love you too, sweet thing. Bye!" Penny hung up.

"Bye." Cara turned her phone off.

"So…" Bryce looked at the cell phone. "I'm assuming that wasn't Freddie?"

"No. That was Penny."

Was it just her… or did his face relax? "Oh. I see. And who is Penny?"

A soft smile spread across her face. "My dearest friend."

Bryce smiled in return. "I'm glad you got to talk to her. She sounds like quite a character."

You have no idea. "Oh, she is."

"Are you ready for some breakfast yet? You look nice."

I look nice? Without a speck of makeup on, and unwashed hair? She took a deep breath. "Thank you. You have no idea how much I appreciate that."

He grinned. "No problem."

"Actually… I think I'd like to visit a salon first for a wash and blow-dry. Unless you're starving."

His eyebrows rose. "Hey… that's a brilliant idea. They'll do that? Just wash your hair without cutting it?"

He's obviously not spent much time at hair salons. Something mischievous inside inspired her next words. "Well, no, they'll probably insist on cutting off a few feet. Oh well." She sighed.

The look of alarm on his face was priceless. Also his expression of relief when she laughed.

"I'm sorry. I don't know where that came from." *Probably Penny's influence.* "Yes, they'll just wash and blow-dry if you ask for that."

"Sounds like a plan to me." He frowned, but his hazel eyes twinkled. "And you had me nervous there for a minute, Rapunzel."

She shook her head, grabbing her purse. It felt odd wearing it on her left shoulder. "No worries. I only trim an inch off, once a year."

He held the door for her as they left her room. "Then I'll protect you from any villains brandishing scissors."

~*~

The chic salon smelled of wet hair and strong hairspray, masked by the overbearing aroma of French perfume. It was like a cloud of chemicals resting on a field of blossoming flowers. He didn't know whether to gag or to breathe deeply.

Bryce had to stifle a chuckle at Cara's panicked look as three hairdressers swarmed around them, cooing like pigeons. Two ladies, one plump, one thin, and a man with a well-trimmed moustache, dazzled by Cara's hair. The plump lady had left a woman sitting unattended in a haircutting chair, with half her hair neatly cut, the other half shaggy.

"What hair! It is *magnifique!*" 'Monsieur Moustache' exclaimed.

"Ooh-la-la!" The thin woman's hands were pressed to her cheeks.

The plump lady remained in stunned silence, but reached out a tentative hand to gently finger the ends of Cara's golden tresses.

"She's just here for a wash and dry, folks. Let's not get too excited." Bryce stated in a firm tone, striving to keep a serious expression on his face.

Cara sidled away from the plump lady and found her voice. "I broke my wrist, and can't wash my hair with one hand." She held up the white cast for their inspection.

Sympathy sprang to their three faces. "Ah! *Oui!* We understand." Monsieur Moustache answered for everybody.

The bereft customer rattled off a long line of complaint in French and the plump lady hurried away, jiggling as she went. The thin woman turned to Monsieur Moustache with a pleading expression, but he held up his hand. "*Non*! For this lovely mademoiselle, I will attend her myself."

Cara turned to Bryce with huge deer-in-the-headlights eyes. It was either say something now or let Cara squirm.

He cleared his throat.

"Ahem. While we are flattered by the attention, I believe mademoiselle would rather have a female attendant. She's demure like that, you see."

Cara nodded, her head bobbing several times for good measure.

"Of course." Monsieur Moustache gave a gracious smile and a half-bow. He turned to the thin woman, who still hovered nearby. "Chloe will wash your hair. She does not speak English well herself, but she understands it."

Bryce nodded. "I understand some French, but my accent is awful."

Chloe giggled. "You, come wiz *moi?*" She pointed to Cara and then herself.

Cara nodded again with a grateful smile.

Bryce thanked the man and Chloe led Cara to a sink, having her sit and tip her head back. In case they needed a translator, Bryce waited in a nearby chair against the wall. Cara's hair was pooled in the sink and gently washed with salon-quality shampoo. Cara closed her eyes as Chloe began to hum a French lullaby.

~*~

Having fresh, clean hair again was delightful. Chloe had even braided it and coiled it on top of Cara's head.

Leaving the salon, they'd gone in search of breakfast. One of the hundreds of charming cafés fit the bill nicely.

Bryce smiled at her across the tiny table, his hazel eyes dancing.

"Thank you." Her words were simple, but weighted with sincere gratitude.

"Feel better?"

"Much." Cara took a sip of her coffee-with-extra-cream. Her useless right wrist lay in her lap under the table, out of sight. If it weren't for the dull throb, she could almost pretend the injury had never happened. "So, what's the plan for today?"

Bryce looked completely at ease, a talent for a tall guy sitting in a miniscule chair. "Well, I've got feelers out for the

Ravenmeister people... who, by the way, have disappeared from the building we found yesterday."

Cara rolled her eyes. "Wonderful."

"Yeah. So, for right now, the ball is in Freddie's court. We're trying our best, but the clues are spread thin. I'm hoping he'll contact us again, if he can. He's done a pretty good job of it so far... And let's hope he remembers your cell phone number."

She patted her purse, which was sitting on her lap next to her right hand. "The phone is right here, fully charged, if he should call us."

"Good."

She looked around the interior of the warm, cozy café, glad to be indoors. It was too bad that their last outdoor eating experience had ended in such chaos. Now she felt nervous about the idea of eating out where everybody passing by could see them... like sitting ducks.

Bryce wrapped his hands around his mug and leaned slightly forward. "Can I ask you a personal question?" His voice was low and quiet.

She froze and stared at him, stunned.

What in the world? Why would he need to ask me *a personal question? Well, it's not like I can say 'No' now, I'm too curious.*

"Sure." She did mean it, although the word came out more hesitant than she had wanted it to.

He stared into his coffee for a moment, and then lifted his gaze to her face. "How do you feel about God?"

The cozy feeling shattered. She leaned back as far as possible in her café chair until the iron pressed into her back.

How dare he? What business is it of his, what I feel about some spiritual being up there in the heavens?

She laughed, although no humor graced it. "So. What gave me away? The fact that I didn't bring a Bible with me and spend an hour reading it every morning?"

His eyebrows rose, but her biting words elicited no other reaction.

"I'm sorry." What had come over her? "I didn't mean it like that."

He waited. No condemnation stained his face – only patience. It made her feel even guiltier for snapping at him.

"I… that is…" She sighed. She wanted to tell Bryce, felt as if she might be able to trust him with this hidden part of herself. It made no sense… she never revealed anything to anyone. Even Penny didn't know… this. But the tug to confide in him was there, nonetheless.

She surrendered to it. "Sometimes I wonder why God even bothered to make us."

Bryce breathed in, and out, quiet, calm. "Really?"

"Yes. I mean… if he's not even going to be involved with our lives, why take the trouble to create… that?" She waved to the café window as she finished her sentence, indicating the bright world outside. Sunlight sparkled through the rich lime-green leaves of the tree planted outside the window.

"So... you do believe in God, but you think he's detached from us." Bryce sipped his coffee, and took a bite of his croissant.

She hesitated, staring down into the black well of her coffee mug. "Well... yeah. It's the only way I can explain away what he did to me."

"Your father?"

She looked up at him. "God took my father from me." Her voice was low, shaking with anger.

He stole a little five-year-old girl's father from her. He made a good man die, while bad men live and breathe and kidnap people like Freddie. The chant echoed, with a new, added note.

"Cara..." He gripped his coffee mug tighter. "God did not kill your father. A bullet from a sinning man killed your father. God only allowed it to happen, for a reason we don't know right now."

She pointed her finger at him. "That's it, right there. God allowed it to happen, and for that, I cannot forgive him."

~*~

Oh, Lord. She's hurting. Her heart is broken. She's a wounded sparrow.

The scripture from somewhere in the middle of Matthew flashed through his mind like a bolt of lightning. *"Are not two sparrows sold for a farthing? Not one of them shall fall to the ground without your Father knowing it. The very hairs of your head are all numbered. Fear ye not, ye are worth more than many sparrows."*

Give me the words, Father.

"That cast under the table. Why are you wearing it?" His mouth formed the words before his mind really knew where he was going with the remark.

Her eyebrows arched higher. "Uhh... because I have a broken wrist."

"Exactly. It's broken. And if you don't wear that cast, your wrist will not heal, right?" *Aha. So that's where it's going. Thanks, God.*

She eyed him as if she thought he might be slightly insane. "Um, yeah."

He reached for her left hand and held it, devoutly hoping she wouldn't take it the wrong way. At this moment he was her brother in Christ, nothing more.

"Cara... your heart is broken."

Two tears spilled from her eyes in unison, trickling down her face, but she made no move to pull her hand away.

"It needs to be healed. Holding unforgiveness against God is hurting your heart. Living without his presence in your life is... scarring you."

She pulled her hand away and fiercely swiped at her eyes with the paper café napkin. He hoped she was still listening to him. At this point, she was avoiding his gaze.

"God loves us, and cares deeply about us. I haven't had a perfect life either. My dad abandoned me, for cryin' out loud. But I still believe in God's goodness. I've felt it, seen it." He paused, waiting for a signal to continue... or stop.

She stared at the wall. "I can't talk about it right now."

It was a resounding *"Stop."* And he felt like his own heart was breaking for her.

~*~

"*How* did they *find* him?!" the angry voice on the phone trumpeted in Ryan Black's ear.

"We don't know." Black's tone remained unruffled. He leaned back in his chair and held the phone a little farther away from his head. "Somehow, he told them his location. Twice."

"Did the wimpy creep signal them, or what?!"

"No. There have been no electronic signals until yesterday, when he reactivated his chip. Our sensors picked up his signal only a few minutes before he was found by them."

"But you have him back, right?" The voice demanded reassurance of this fact.

"Yes, he was recaptured. However, we do not know how he restarted the GPS transmission."

"Let me guess, mental telepathy." The biting words dripped with sarcasm.

He had just about had his fill of this jerk, but there was a nice, hefty paycheck waiting at the end of the yellow brick road. He'd keep walking it for now. "Impossible, as I'm sure you know."

"Don't get fresh with me. He must have a remote. Have you searched him?"

"Of course. We found no remote." His eyes wandered to the clock on the wall, but the time didn't register in his mind.

"He must have swallowed it. Did you pump his stomach?"

"Yes." Even *he* had been disgusted by having to do that to the skinny young man.

"Oh. Well, it may have been damaged by his stomach juices and disintegrated."

"You're the expert. You tell me." He ran a hand through his black hair, enjoying the slick feel of it against his hand.

"I told you not to get fresh! Fine. Move him to the hillside hut near the Ravenmeister compound, for now."

"Hillside hut? Which one? There are three Ravenmeister compounds."

"The one in Munich, you twit. The place we mentioned earlier!"

"Munich. Whatever you say, boss." he placated the tempestuous man on the other side of the line.

"Now, about the girl."

"The girl?"

"Cara Stephenson."

Across the room, the beautiful woman lying on the couch looked at him and arched her black eyebrows, graceful as swallows' wings. He smiled at her and shook his head, letting her know he was not discussing her.

"I want her caught and brought to me, unharmed."

"I can bring her to you. But if I have to get past Reynolds, it will cost you a pretty penny."

"Do it." He hung up.

Ryan stood, letting the phone slip from his hands into the desk drawer. "Don't worry. He's gone." A rakish smile tilted his mouth.

Tatiana arose from her catnap and stretched her silken limbs, limber as any member of the feline tribe. "What a horrible man."

"Well, my darling, at least he has lots of horrible money."

"Mmm." She purred, and crossed the room in a few long, smooth strides. Slipping her arms around him, she tucked her head under his chin. "I am sorry that you have to have dealings with him." She owned a voice that was rich, low, and accented with the tones of Russia. It was one of the many things about her that intrigued him.

"As am I. But with you to console me, what more could I ask for?" The heavy scent of her dark perfume drifted around him.

Tatiana lifted her head and laughed a throaty laugh, teeth gleaming between full, perfectly curved lips. "Money." She opened her eyes wide in pretended innocence. "Is there anything else to live for in this world?"

~*~

Talk about a lucky break!

Freddie was sure that Ryan Black had no idea about the air vent that transmitted faint, but audible sound into the basement where he currently sat in the dark, amid the rustling of what he hoped wasn't rats. At least he wasn't handcuffed this time, although the door wore a heavy padlock.

He knew where he was headed. But Cara was in danger! *If I only had a phone...!*

The door creaked open and Armand entered, yawning. He pulled a chain "My turn to guard you, oh, vat fun."

Freddie avoided eye contact and said nothing.

"So, you don't vant to, how you say, 'chat'? You must not haf anything interesting to say."

He'd keep playing dumb, who knows, it might work. Unless it angered his bad-humored captor. Then he'd chatter away.

Armand unbuckled his belt with all the gadgets hanging from it and tossed it onto the floor, sinking onto a wooden crate and crossing his arms. "Vell, for vonce I am in good mood. I vill not even try to scare you into telling us your secrets about zat device today. I vill be... nice." He laughed, spittle spraying.

Shouts and calls rang out right outside the door. "Armand! *Benachrichtigen! Kommen Sie schnell!*"

Armand jumped up, sending the crate tumbling over. He pulled his pistol from his waistband and lurched out the door, slamming it behind him.

Nearly before the door had closed behind the beefy man, Freddie was all over the belt.

Providence was certainly smiling on him today. Armand had left behind a cell phone.

~*~

Bryce channel-surfed on Cara's hotel room TV. He never watched TV, but there was nothing else to do. There wasn't anything to report to the Agency, and the other agents were out in the field, sorting out the illegal arms dealing mess, while he played nursemaid to their link to Silver Strand.

Cara sat in a stuffed chair wedged into the corner of the room, as far away from him as she could get. Her broken wrist was elevated on a puffy pillow. She pretended to read a mystery, but he knew she couldn't possibly be concentrating on the words. She hadn't turned a page for half an hour.

He would just vamoose and leave her in peace were it not for the fact that he had to stay near her cell phone to talk to Freddie, should he call.

Mechanical birdsong sounded, a 'chirp-chirp-tweetle-lee' that sent adrenaline coursing through his system. Cara's phone was ringing.

He lunged for the phone that sat on the low coffee table. Cara hopped to her feet, tossing the mystery book into her chair.

"I've got it!" He answered the phone. "Hello?"

"Is this Bryce?" *Freddie!*

"Yes. Bryce Reynolds." He spoke fast, matching the harried pace of Freddie's voice. He nodded to Cara, who seated herself again, clutching her broken wrist in the other hand, her face alive with excitement.

"I don't have a second to spare! They're gonna move me to Munich, to a 'hillside hut' near a Ravenmeister compound of some kind. That's all I know about that. But there's something else."

"What?"

"Ryan Black has orders to kidnap Cara."

"*What?!*" Raw anger ripped through his voice.

Cara's head jerked upright and she stared at him. He gazed back at her beautiful, innocent features.

No! He would die before he let Cara fall into Ryan Black's ruthless clutches. *He is not getting to her!*

"You have to keep her safe! These men are bad, very bad." Freddie's voice cracked on the last word.

"I'll do my best, I promise." He tried to get his message across in his tone, speaking as earnestly as he could.

"I should go."

"No, stay on the line as long as possible, Freddie, the agents patched into this frequency will try to pinpoint your location."

Cara glared at him with an expression of complete shock, mouth open, and eyes wide. "*What?!*" She mouthed.

He shook his head and looked away. That explanation would have to wait.

"Well, I think it would be safer to put Armand's phone back, but okay. Is Cara there?"

Oh boy. Freddie is S-M-I-T-T-E-N. The guy was being held by unscrupulous criminals and he wanted to chat with a pretty girl instead of giving them more details? "Just talk to me for a minute. Where are they holding you now?"

"Some kind of basement. I don't know where, I was blindfolded and stuffed into the trunk of a car to get here. My ankle still hurts pretty bad, I think I might have broken it."

Poor Freddie. "Just hang in there, man, we're coming for you."

"Thanks, Bryce." There was a heartbreaking gratitude in Freddie's tone.

"You're welcome."

"*Vat* are you *doing*, you little...!" A roar of rage sounded over the phone, mingled with a cry of pain as the line went dead.

Bryce felt as if he himself had been socked in the gut. *Oh, God, be with him.*

"Well?" Cara stood again.

He got to his feet. "We were cut off."

Cara's left hand went to her mouth. "Oh, no."

"I have to check if they located him."

An icy glare. "Who are *'they'*? And what are 'they' doing, listening in on *my phone*?"

'They' are government counterintelligence special agents, it's their job, and since it's also my job, I can't tell you a thing.

"I'm sorry." It was all he could say.

Cara's eyes could have been emitting sparks, for all the electricity they held in their gray depths. "I should have known."

~*~

Bryce slammed his hotel room door shut, closing himself off from the hallway, and immediately felt a twinge of remorse. His gentle mother called slamming the door 'wooden swearing', and had banned it in their home.

But, dash it all, a guy needed some way to relieve his feelings, especially if they were anything like the ones that were now tearing him apart. Shoving the door shut a little too hard with nobody around beat cursing a blue streak.

He dialed the agency. They were awaiting his call – it was routed right past reception.

"This is Alpha Major." Montrose came on the line.

"Well?" He asked it almost carelessly, the impact of the mission having paled somewhat in the heat of Cara's intense disapproval. And now she was in danger herself.

A heavy sigh, laden with weariness. "Sorry, Ashburn."

What? "Don't tell me…"

"We couldn't pinpoint his *exact* location."

There was still a shred of hope. "Did you get a regional readout?"

"All we know is that he's somewhere in northern Germany." Monty's tone was grim. "They might really be moving him to a compound. Ravenmeister has several in Germany. Including one in Munich, like Freddie mentioned on the call"

"Well, that gives us somewhere to start." Bryce paced to the window and brushed aside the curtain. He couldn't see the Eiffel tower from his window, although it was visible from Cara's.

Cara.

"Monty, what are we doing now that Cara is on Black's hit list?"

"I'm doing the best thing I know to do, and that is to *glue* her to you."

A nervous chill ran down his spine, while his heart leaped for joy. "Are you sure about this?"

"I'm sensing an attachment to her on your part, to put it bluntly, and I have a feeling that nobody would do a better job of protecting her than you."

He felt the same way himself, but what if being near him threw her into greater danger?

"But I'm on this mission. I have to rescue Freddie. I *promised* him I would do it!"

"You will. I need you to. You're a part of the I.C.E. Agency, Bryce, and the I.C.E. Agency will recover him. We'll work together as a team. But I'll need you to be in two places at once, if you don't mind."

"Your jokes just keep getting better."

"It's true, almost. Keep an eye on Cara until you move in for Black, then turn her over to Markdown or one of the other trusted agents. If you do it right, it'll go like clockwork. Or at least that's the plan."

Bryce sighed. He would trust his boss's instincts. "All right. I'll do my best."

"Good." Montrose sounded satisfied. "That's all I can ask for."

"So what's their game, anyway? I want to hear your take on all of this."

As usual, his boss had a theory all spun out. "They've been hiding him in all of these obscure places because if we had the suspicion he was being held at their headquarters, we could order a search warrant and comb the place. They'd be charged with kidnapping, theft, and worse. If they're the front for the illegal arms dealing, they risk complete discovery."

"Now it makes sense."

"But they're getting scared. We're too close. You and Cara are pushing them to hold Freddie more tightly in their grasp – thus, the move to Ravenmeister territory, if not HQ proper."

"Interesting. Very interesting." He was probably right. Monty had the instincts of a bloodhound when sniffing out the movements of the other side.

"Oh, and Cara will have to ditch that phone and get a new number."

Oh no. "She... what?"

"The problem with the signal-sourcing is that it can be done both ways. Those guys can take their end and work back to hers just as easily." Montrose sounded as if he might be walking through the Agency. There was too much noise for him to be seated in his office.

"Monty, she's already furious that we violated her privacy by tapping her phone signal. How am I going to tell her that we have to take her phone completely away?"

"That is your problem." Phones trilled in the background, with undertones of garbled voices. "You don't want them finding her any more than I do, so just do it." His boss sounded like his patience was beginning to run out. "I hope you're keeping a straight head on your shoulders. You never pussyfoot around like this."

"I'm not pussyfooting around!"

"Hmph. Then prove it, and go disable that phone. Call me back in 45 minutes, I have more to discuss with you."

The line went dead.

~*~

Cara sat alone, smarting from the sting of the last clash with Bryce Reynolds.

I like him. I really like him. And that was why it hurt so much.

Why did he have to go and ask me ... that? Anything but this one thing, she would have compromised on. She wouldn't mind a weird taste in food, books, movies, socks... but God? God was forbidden territory. God was the uncaring *thing* that had let her be hurt.

Bryce's smile flashed before her eyes. He was the sweetest guy she'd ever known, with a core of pure, unflinching steel. He had what it took to protect a girl, plus blazing intelligence. How could he believe in God? Did he know something about Him that she didn't?

Knock-knock. Two taps came at the door.

She groaned and arose, wishing she could have just called 'Come in', but self-locking hotel doors willed it otherwise. She checked the peephole. Bryce. With slightly slumped shoulders.

She opened the door, turned, and walked away before it had even fully swung open.

"Cara."

She froze, bare toes sinking into the plush depths of the carpet. "What?"

"Cara, look at me."

She slowly, slowly turned around to face him. His hazel eyes looked dim, as if they'd lost their twinkle. "I have something to tell you."

"So, tell." She perched on the corner of the bed.

He stepped inside and shut the door behind him, leaning his back against it. He was making the smallest dent in her personal space as possible.

He stared straight into her eyes from across the room. "They're after you."

Her breath caught in her throat. "Me?"

"Ryan Black has orders to kidnap you."

"Why *me*? You're the important one!" *Whatever you are.* "I'm just a graphic designer. Why do they want me? And who is Ryan Black?" She peppered him with questions, craving answers.

"I don't know why they want you. Freddie told me that Ryan Black has orders to kidnap you, and that is absolutely everything I know about that."

"And what about Ryan Black?"

A new emotion crept into Bryce's face, but what was it? Something between anxiety and animosity, she decided.

"Ryan Black is my worst enemy, and he's the one who was chasing us on the motorcycle."

Her stomach did a double backflip. "The dark-haired man with the huge gun? *Him*?!"

"The same. He's a professional bounty hunter-slash-kidnapper, and unfortunately, he's really good at it." Tenderness flooded his eyes. "I've been assigned to protect you."

Her heart warmed, but anger pierced at the same time. "*Who* has assigned you to protect me?"

He merely looked back at her with an empty expression. The merry, fun Bryce was gone, and a sober, serious one had taken his place.

Defiance surged inside. "I'm going to keep asking you these questions. Maybe sometime you'll be able to answer one of them!"

He winced. "Well, I can't answer that one."

She groaned, tired of banging her head against his stone wall. "Fine." *As in,* not *fine.*

Bryce cleared his throat. "Where's your phone?"

Cara flicked her eyes to her purse, which sat on the nightstand. "In there."

In one quick movement, he had stepped to the purse and had slipped his hand inside.

"*Hey!* What do you think you're *doing?*" She jumped up, but to no avail. He held her cell phone in his hand and powered it off.

He turned to face her. "I'm sorry. But they can track you through this."

That was the last straw. "But all my contacts are in there! My music, pictures, information... *everything* is saved on that!"

"I'll extract it for you before I disable it."

Some consolation. But hardly enough. "I want my phone!" To her great embarrassment and completely out of her control, she dissolved into tears. She seized a pillow from the bed with her left hand, buried her face in it, and screamed her frustration, crumpling into a chair.

A soft 'click' of a door closing reached her ears a few moments later. Bryce had left the room.

Let him go. I don't care.

Lie of the century.

~*~

It was getting increasingly difficult to protect a girl who wasn't allowed to listen in on his phone conversations. He'd had to resort to video surveillance while he made the call, plugging in a tiny camera on top of the thermostat in Cara's hotel room while she wasn't looking... being occupied with weeping into a cushion.

Bryce didn't think that bout of crying had been all about the phone. It was most likely a combination of fatigue and highly stressful situations.

But he could be wrong. Women were confusing, and not one of them was alike. To help soften the blow, he first made double-sure that the signal was disabled, and then began downloading her contact info, music, photos, and whatnot into a plain spare smartphone he pulled from his faded blue case.

While that was running, he dialed Montrose again, notepad ready to record the details of the upcoming instructions. His boss would be giving him the lowdown of where to move next and what precautions to take.

After the call concluded, he trekked back across the hallway for what felt like the hundredth time. Cara opened the door for him again. Her high cheekbones were stained with tear tracks.

He walked inside her room and shut the door, and was about to calmly relate their plans when Cara stepped closer.

"I'm sorry." More tears spilled over and ran down her cheeks as she looked up into his face. "I know none of this is your fault." Her eyes were glimmering a blue-gray, the hue seeming to reflect her mood.

They were inches away from what could have been a kiss.

"Thank you. And it's okay." He said softly. And he meant it.

He wasn't sure who moved first, but it became a close, tight hug. They stood there for a few minutes, completely still, holding each other.

~*~

The sound of his heartbeat was the most beautiful thing she'd ever heard.

And then he spoke, voice vibrating in his chest. "I'm sorry too."

The silence was broken, and she pulled away, lifting her broken wrist from its safe perch around his neck.

"Bryce, let's just get through this mission, and then sort everything out. We were going to, remember? What happened to that plan?"

He looked down at her. She could see the golden glints in his hazel eyes. "I'm so sorry for everything I've dragged you through in the past four days. If I'd had any idea of what you'd have to-"

"Shh." She stopped him with a shake of her head. "You don't have to apologize for a situation that's out of your control."

He still looked unsure. "I don't know. If you hadn't come, you wouldn't have broken your wrist."

"No." She sent a brief glance to her wrist. "If I hadn't come, I wouldn't have seen Paris. Or Venice-"

"-Or Germany." An almost-back-to-normal smile brightened his face as her jaw dropped. "That's what I came in here to tell you. We're headed to Germany."

Chapter Eight

In The Dark

How many guys would help a girl pack her suitcase and scan the hotel room, ensuring that nothing had been missed? And how many of them would have been *good* at it? How many of those would have cut up a girl's lunch for her into little pieces so they'd be easy to fork with her left hand?

Not many. He's one in a million.

Cara watched the fast-moving French countryside out the window of the Renault Mégane RS that Bryce had rented, and was driving. The compact 2-door car had room for all of their luggage but looked like a hot sports car. The only complaint Cara had with it was the paint job – a weird shade of mustard yellow.

Bryce rolled down his window and the breeze ruffled his hair, bringing with it a fresh scent of spring and wildflowers. He turned his head to look at her, and she held her gaze, smiling.

He looked away.

Well. Guess there's no need to entertain thoughts of him being attracted to me. A cold chill of rejection ran all the way down from the base of Cara's neck to her fingertips.

She went back to watching the scenery.

~*~

God, she's so gorgeous. He gripped the wheel firmly and resisted the temptation to look back at Cara with a heart-melting smile like the one she had offered him.

"Be not unequally yoked together with unbelievers." The reminder clanged through his brain.

I know... I know. I never knew that would be so hard to obey, Lord. So incredibly hard.

Every other man on the planet would think him off his rocker for not pursuing and wooing Cara with all his might. But he couldn't. He was bound. His commitment to God came first, and until he knew that Cara was on the same page as he was... in a relationship with the Lord... they could never become closer. Not one bit.

To distract himself, he recited their new to-do list in his mind.

Head to Munich. Find and settle into the safehouse. Meet up with Markdown and some of the other agents who will be joining us in Germany. Case out the hillside hut Monty wants us to check out. Keep Cara safe.

Cara gasped. "We need to call Mr. Gungerson!"

He *nearly* slammed on the brakes at the sudden exclamation, stopping himself just in time.

"Don't do that!" He caught his breath. "I thought something was wrong."

"Something *is* wrong! We haven't informed my boss of our situation!"

I informed mine, the real boss of this investigation. I forgot about yours.

"Okay... give him a call and say that we're headed to Germany, and that we've got a big break. But don't tell him more than that, just say you'll call him later."

She eyed him with uncertainty, but started dialing on her replacement phone anyway. She waited a few minutes. Then, "Mr. Gungerson?"

She was quiet for a bit, a smile eventually finding its way to her face.

"Yes, sir, I'm okay. It wasn't Bryce's fault." She looked at him and nodded towards her cast.

Oh, brother. I get blamed for the wrist, and no credit for keeping her from getting sprayed with Uzi bullets. Such is the life of a spy.

"The reason I'm calling is to let you know we have a big break... *other* than my wrist, and that we're headed to Germany. We'll call later with more information." Another pause. "Thank you. Yes Sir."

A strange look crossed her face and she narrowed her eyes. "Ah. Well, thank him for me."

She ended the phone call a few moments later. And then stared out the window. Five minutes passed before she spoke again. "Mitch was right there with him, and wanted me to know that he hopes I get well soon, and that I enjoy Germany."

~*~

Cold. Dank. Dark. He was getting really tired of the dark.

ASHBURN   Julia Erickson

Freddie would have known he was in a hut on the side of a hill even if he hadn't found out the destination beforehand. The small building was constructed of stone and crumbling mortar, with a dirt floor that slanted uphill.

He had to take shallow breaths. He thought Armand might have cracked one of his ribs with that thump he'd given him in the basement after discovering that Freddie was using his phone. A definite no-no, it seemed.

The door creaked open and a beautiful woman appeared in the slit of light. For a moment his heart pounded in his chest, but then he saw the raven-black sheen of the woman's hair, instead of Cara's golden head.

"So, you are Freddie?" The woman eyed him as if he was an exhibit at the zoo. "I wondered what you look like."

Could she possibly be Russian? The cold war had been over for decades... she was too young to have played a part in it.

He stared back at her, determined that if possible, she wouldn't discover what he sounded like too. The call of the wild Freddie would not be heard in the land.

"You are so thin and look so young... I would think you a boy, if not for your... beard."

For lack of a razor, his face was sprouting scruffy mouse-brown stubble. *I guess I'm an inferior specimen of Freddie. So sorry to disappoint.*

"I almost feel bad for you. Being moved about so much. But you take the rest of us with you, and this annoys me. So I feel no pity." Her voice had a rhythmic flow and cadence, but the words were laced with scorn.

Freddie glared. This must be the lady whose lipstick he'd found in the hotel room and snitched, using it to write the message on the commode seat. She looked like the type of woman who would wear 'Femme Fatale Red'.

"We are taking you on another trip. Does that interest you? Too bad you do not have phone or signal to tell your friends." She laughed.

What a snob. A dumb one. They still had no clue about the mirror or the lipstick. *Good. They're underestimating me.*

"We go to Berlin. But that does not annoy me. I like Berlin. Berlin have good parties." She dipped herself towards him a bit. "You will have no way to contact those horrible people who want to get you back. So I can tell you all I want."

He scratched his head and yawned as if terribly bored.

Her eyes glittered as if she wasn't buying the indifference. "Our inside informer-man has told us that your friends are coming here. To this hut. But they will not find you, only a clever trap."

He crossed his arms over his chest.

"So. We go to Berlin. You will see the head-quarters of entire Ravenmeister operation. The real one, at the fortress, not one that everybody know about. Maybe I will even give a tour to you." She threw her head back and cackled at her joke.

He stared at the wall.

She grew bored at last with her one-sided conversation, and left. He waited three seconds before scrambling uphill to the darkest corner of the hut and finding a piece of stone. Hurrying, he scratched a message in the dirt floor.

> TO BERLIN- Secret Ravenmeister HQ Fortress! THEY HAVE INSIDE INFO ABOUT YOUR MOVEMENTS! I'm so sorry about the trap.
>
> ~Freddie

~*~

Munich impressed Cara. Old-world history mingled with upbeat technology and architecture. Not sure what she had been expecting... billboards everywhere featuring beer ads, perhaps... but this wasn't it.

"Wait here." Bryce spoke in a stern voice as he turned off the engine. "No more following when you're told to stay in the vehicle, okay? That was *really* dangerous what you did back in Paris."

She frowned. "But it worked. I found Freddie." *Doesn't that count for anything?*

"Yeah, and we almost died." He got out of the car and shut the door behind him, encasing her in a world of stillness, with the outside noise muffled. He locked the car with the remote dangling from the keys, and then tucked his hands in his pockets and sauntered down the street towards a pub teeming with customers.

Cara watched, dumbfounded, as he worked the crowd around the *beergarten*, sending a smile here, a laugh there. He seated himself at a tiny table with an especially warm grin, across from a buxom brunette. They smiled at each other and looked as if they were introducing themselves.

No. Way. He knows I can see him right now and he's just talking to that babe like it's no big deal? I don't believe this.

~*~

"Where have you been all my life, Angel?" –*wing*. He mentally added. *Angelwing.*

His fellow agent flashed a dazzling smile. "Oh, here and there. Paris, for example. Glad to see you found me safely."

He glanced around. They could probably cut the small talk now. "Yeah, me too." He lowered his voice.

"How's Cara?" She lowered hers, but gave him a slow wink, in case anybody was still watching.

"Watching us."

Her eyelids flew wide open. "Is that so?" A grin appeared. A mischievous one.

Yeah, I know, she's probably jealous, right this second... "Yup. I'm on task to keep her safe, now that Ryan Black wants her."

"So it's true." Her smile stayed in place, but her eyes showed fear… and her voice was barely above a whisper.

"The man called Ryan Black, whose real last name is unknown, whom nobody can even *identify* face-to-face except for you and several dead people, is stalking your girlfriend." She blew out a puff of air. "Talk about revenging himself on his greatest enemy."

Girlfriend? I wish... "I wouldn't call myself his greatest *enemy*."

"What else? You're basically the only thing stopping him from having a total monopoly on the mercenary man-hunter market. And getting away every time."

"I'd say I'm an annoyance to him. A gnat flying around his face that distracts him just enough so that he steers the ship off course, compromising his trip."

"Poetic analogy." Angelwing's face looked as though she knew better, but she let that topic go and got down to business. "Here."

She slid a small card towards him across the table.

"That should be everything you need to know about this job. Markdown and I and the rest of the team will be ready when you are. Monty wants you to call the shots." She nailed him with her gaze. *Direct hit!* "He trusts you."

Talk about pressure. "I know."

"Be careful, Ashburn." Her hand darted across the table and squeezed his in an almost motherly gesture, even though he knew for a fact that she was younger than him.

"Thanks. I'll try." He looked up at her as she turned to go.

"Call me!" She called over her shoulder with a flirty wave, solidifying their cover.

Now to rejoin Cara.

He eased himself into the car, bracing for the barrage of accusation. He was surprised when none came, and dared a look across to the passenger seat.

Cara sat with her slim arms folded across her chest – no small feat with one broken wrist – silently seething.

He knew she would never, ever believe the 'she was a co-worker' explanation unless he could give more details, which he couldn't. So he didn't even try to explain as he navigated the streets of Munich. He reached the outskirts of the city, Cara still simmering.

He parked outside what looked like an ordinary bed-and-breakfast, but was an Agency Safehouse. The married proprietors were agents with over 30 years of experience.

"What is this place?" Cara looked around, a curious light in her eye.

"Um… I know the owners."

"Oh."

"We'll be safe here." He assured her, popping the trunk to pull out his suitcases.

"If you say so." Her voice was cool.

He was staring at her, waiting for her to look at him, when a cheery voice called from the doorway. "Come in, come in! You must be hungry!" Myra Bachmeier stood smiling, her plump cheeks red as apples.

~*~

Dinner proved to be a delicious Bavarian soup with a name Bryce couldn't pronounce, and throughout the meal, Myra and her husband Matthias kept Cara entertained with several ancient German folk tales. Cara laughed, smiled, ate her soup, nodded, and avoided his gaze the entire time.

He finished every bite of his meal even though his appetite had deserted him, knowing he'd need the energy later. Myra showed them to their rooms and Cara disappeared into hers like a turtle slipping into its shell.

~*~

"Bryce?" It was Matthias's crusty voice.

He rolled off the bed and onto his feet on the scarred wooden floor, opening the door to his small bedroom. "What is it?"

He'd been taking a power nap, trying to rest up before the night's activities began.

"The house is being watched. You should go."

A cold, leaden feeling settled in his middle. "Right. Okay. How should we leave?"

"Through the underground passage. Get Cara ready, and then I will show you the way."

~*~

Cara sat on the side of the bed, studying a small painting that hung on the wall of a shepherd with two lambs, when a hurried tap came at the door.

"Cara!" Bryce's voice sounded rushed.

"Yes?"

The door opened. She had been about to exclaim that she hadn't said he could come in, when she saw the tension in his face. The words died on her lips.

"Come on, we've got to get out of here."

She sprang up and grabbed her suitcase with her left hand. "Ready."

"No, leave it. Myra and Matthias will send our things on later."

She hesitated, and he reached for her hand. "I wish I had more time to talk, but I don't. The house is being watched, and we have to leave. Now come on!"

Luggage abandoned, he led her out of the room and down the miniscule hall. Matthias was waiting for them near a closet door. He opened it to expose stairs that led down to a basement. So… it wasn't a closet.

"Come." Matthias waved down the stairs, and clambered ahead, leading her and Bryce to the bottom.

Their footsteps clattered with a hollow ring down the wooden boards that served as stairs, then thumped softly as they hit the dirt floor.

Matthias pointed his sausage-like finger at a tiny European front-loader washing machine along the far wall. "There."

"Nice." Bryce shot an admiring glance at Matthias, and tugged her forward. "Come on, sweetie-pie, you're first." He swung open the circular door.

If the ridiculous endearment was supposed to soften her, it failed miserably.

"If you expect me to crawl in *there-*"

"Yep! In you go." He gave her a gentle nudge with a hand to the small of her back. A butterfly awoke from its nap in her stomach.

"All right..." She folded herself as small as possible and crawled into the hole. The metal tub turned beneath her and she landed on her side, half-in, half-out. Her long legs and waist remained in the basement for all to gaze upon. She could feel her face burning.

"Just open hatch in back of machine, there, Miss." Matthias's helpful voice drifted into her chamber of embarrassment.

Hoisting her functional left arm from beneath her, she managed to turn the small lever and open the secret door in the back of the machine. Popping her head through, all she saw was complete darkness, but her nose picked up a dusty, earthy smell.

"Okay!" She crawled forward, and with a rapid tumble she was through the hole and sitting on the damp ground.

Unfairly fast, Bryce appeared next to her with no apparent effort. He seemed to be coughing, but she suspected he was covering up a significant amount of chuckling. She declined to react.

"Good! You wait here. If I not come get you in three quarters of hour, go to end of tunnel and make your way out to street. Mission will not wait." Matthias's face was just visible on the other side of the washing machine.

"Got it. Thanks." Bryce closed the hatch, shutting them into utter darkness.

What time is it, anyway? She'd left the detested replacement phone in her bag, still in her room.

Wait. Bryce gave me a light-up watch. And she wore it now.

One problem – the watch ticked on her left hand. With her right hand out of commission, she needed help.

"Hey, can you light my watch? I want to check the time." She extended her left hand until it touched his shoulder. His hands wrapped around the watch and he fumbled with it. Then a blinding light pierced her vision from the direction of her wrist and Bryce yelled. "*Ow!*"

"What happened?!"

"I set off your help signal. Because we're next to each other, the electric pulse was magnified."

"Sorry." *That must have hurt!*

"Don't apologize, it was my own fault." She could hear him shifting position. "Yeeouch. It really zapped me. I think my hair's standing on end."

She could see the watch face now. 6:14 PM. A shiver moved through her shoulders. It was chilly down there in the dark, sitting on moist basement earth.

"What was that?" Bryce sounded jumpy.

"What?"

"That noise you just made."

"I shivered. Sorry."

Silence. Then his arm slipped around her shoulders. "It's cold down here… you should be wearing a heavier jacket."

"Sorry, I didn't think to grab one."

"Cara, will you just stop apologizing already?"

A thicker silence, pitch-black air between their faces. All around them, for that matter. And then something brushed across her left hand.

"Eeek!" She screamed, jerking her hand away.

"It's me! I'm sorry. That was me." His arm tightened protectively around her. "I was wondering where your watch was. I think I should disable that shock function."

"You could have asked!"

"Sorry."

"Now *you're* apologizing too often. Stop it."

"Sorr- I mean, I will. Where is the watch?"

"Here." Their hands softly bumped into each other in the dark. Bryce's closed around hers, enveloping it in a warm, comforting grasp.

A gentle sigh escaped her before she knew it was going to, and a flush of embarrassment at having revealed her feelings flooded her cheeks. There, a reason to be glad about the darkness – he couldn't see her blushing.

They sat there, connected and silent, for what felt like about a year. Their hands fit together as if they had been perfectly molded for each other.

And then she had to ask. "Are we seriously sitting here in the dark, holding hands?"

~*~

Yes. In spite of all his good, godly intentions, he was holding her hand. *Lord, I'm sorry!*

Then let her go.

Let her go? As in, figuratively as well as literally? If Cara left his life now it would feel like something vital had been ripped out.

But the still, small voice wasn't messing around.

But letting go of Cara might be the hardest thing he had ever been asked to do in his whole life.

But it was what God was asking him to do.

Therefore… he had to do it.

He slowly lifted his hand away from hers.

"It… it wasn't that I *minded…*" Cara's voice sounded plaintive, wistful.

"I didn't mind either." *Hah! Understatement of the year!* "But you're right, we shouldn't be holding hands."

He felt her lean slightly away from him. "What? *Why*?"

"Well…"

If I tell her it's because God doesn't want me to, because I'm focused on saving myself emotionally as well as physically for my future wife, she won't understand, that's not the way the world thinks. And the last thing I want is to pressure her into accepting God because she wants… me.

"…I have cooties."

A bubble of Cara's gorgeous laughter burst inside the tunnel and trickled into soft giggles. He laughed along, accepting the emotional release of the pent-up tension.

"How can you make me laugh in the middle of situations like this?" Cara sniffed, and he heard her dabbing at her face as if she had laughed so hard it brought tears to her eyes.

"It's a gift."

~*~

Time seemed to crawl along slower than molasses in January, in Alaska, but at last the watch dial read 6:54. They were scheduled to move at 7:15 on the Ravenmeister compound, and he was supposed to be leading the charge. He had to leave now if he was going to make it there in time... but there was Cara.

The original plan had been to leave her at the safehouse. But it wasn't so safe at the moment. So...

He sighed. "Well, time for me to go. Want to come along?" *Not that you really have a choice, but...*

"Yes!" He was surprised by her immediate answer. "Take me with you."

Oh, come on, do you have to be so lovable...? "All right. But I need to warn you. This is not a picnic. This is a high-risk assignment. We'll be on the offense, trying our hardest to rescue Freddie. Understand?"

"Yep." He could almost imagine her biting her lip in concentration. Besides, she was faintly visible in the dim light from the watch face... which promptly turned off again.

"Good. Do what I do, walk where I walk, listen to me, be careful, and above all – Caviar."

A faint laugh. "Obey first, ask questions later, huh?"

"You got it. Come on." He grasped her hand and held it behind him as he navigated their way down the tunnel, stooping as they went.

Her hand felt cool and slender inside his.

I'm not 'holding hands', God. Just helping her out of the tunnel.

"*I know.*"

Thanks for understanding, Lord.

"Prepare her."

What? What is that supposed to mean?

"Prepare her."

Prepare her? Good grief! Prepare her for what? The worst? Did this mean his time had come? He didn't think so. It didn't seem like that. He felt deep in his heart that God had more adventures ahead for him. He had work to do. But that didn't mean Cara shouldn't be ready in case of …an accident.

"Hey, Cara? Listen-"

"Listening!" She replied promptly.

"Yeah… um… if something should happen…"

He heard a quick intake of breath.

"Not like *that*... well, anyway, if we should get separated from our team members whom you'll meet momentarily, or if anything happens to me, get in touch with Montrose at IFP, International Federal Publishing." He recited Monty's number for her. "Repeat that a few times, you'll need to remember it."

She murmured the number to herself as he led them toward a faint light at the end of the tunnel. "Okay. I think I've got it. What will I need to say to this Montrose?"

"Just say that Ashburn needs him. He'll understand."

~*~

Cara's mind was swimming with questions. The mystery of Bryce just kept getting deeper and darker and more mysterious. 'Team members'? Who would be helping them rescue Freddie?

Does Bryce think something's going to happen to him? The thought chilled her to the bone.

"O-kay." In the dim light near the end of the tunnel, she could see Bryce pull something out of an inner pocket in his jacket. "Let's find out who's playing peeping tom."

He held a miniature box-like device with joysticks and buttons on it. Near the outer edge was a circle with a tiny raised dot, about the size of a ladybug. Then he reached in his pockets again and pulled out his sunglasses, slipping them onto his face.

"What are you *doing*?" He wouldn't need sunglasses, there was hardly enough light to see where they were standing.

"Hang on, a second." He tapped the side of the sunglasses a few times, and then flipped a switch on the side of the box in his hand. The tiny white dot rose in the air like a flying insect, emitting a soft hum.

Bryce pushed the joysticks, and the dot responded to his movements. It lifted and soared out of the tunnel and into the sky.

"That is a micro surveillance drone, which I am now viewing with on a holographic screen in my glasses." Bryce's eyes remained hidden behind his shades as he explained.

Oh. My. Goodness. "Where did you get that?"

Bryce's mouth grinned. "Belongs to a friend of mine." Then he bit his lip as if in concentration. "Yep. There's one of them ... oh, wait... there's another guy. Anybody else?"

His fingers nimbly switched the joysticks as if familiar with the task. "That looks like it. Two men. I'll bring it back now."

Within seconds, the white dot returned to its miniscule circular landing pad.

Bryce removed the glasses and packed them away with the drone inside one of his pockets. "Ready?"

A nervous tickle ran down her spine, but she shrugged it off. "Ready."

Chapter Nine

To Die For

Escaping from the safehouse was simpler with Bryce's foreknowledge of the watchers. He sneaked Cara around a few corners and hopped into a plain brown sedan with the keys in the ignition.

She didn't ask any questions, just scrambled in after him, and they took off. Bryce drove them to another little farmhouse where a man and a woman waited for them.

The petite woman looked vaguely familiar, but Cara had never seen the man before. Taller than Bryce, which was saying something, he had long bangs that swept down over his forehead, brushing his eyebrows, though the rest of his head was cut shorter.

Bryce made her stay in the car while he talked for a few seconds with them. Then the two led Bryce and Cara into the new house, where they changed their clothing into heavy dark brown jumpsuits and lace-up hiking boots with thick tread.

Is this what military uniforms feel like? Is Bryce part of some elite force?

"All right. Move out!" Bryce gave the order.

Only miles from the center of Munich, they drove deep into the heart of the 'Perlacher' forest. Abandoning their cars, they tromped through the evergreen-scented woods on foot, searching for the Ravenmeister Compound.

Cara stayed close to Bryce's side, wary and watchful. Plentiful sunshine still streamed through the trees and birds trilled and chirped, filling the air with lighthearted music. *If only I were as carefree right now as those little birds.*

The tall man and the woman split off from them, fanning out to cover more ground.

She looked up at Bryce as they hiked along. Clad all in darkest brown, he looked like a rugged mountain towering beside her. He seemed impenetrable, immovable. What could possibly happen that he couldn't handle?

Pop-buzz. The walkie-talkie on Bryce's belt crackled to life. "Ashburn, we have something at 2:00."

Their heads snapped towards the direction indicated. Barely visible through the sparse undergrowth, a wire-and-metal fence glinted.

Bryce lifted the walkie-talkie to his lips. "Roger that, Markdown."

"Got it." Now the woman's voice buzzed from the walkie-talkie.

They converged at one point along the fence. Bryce whipped out a wicked-looking pair of wire cutters from the knapsack he wore. "All right. Let's go get our man." His voice growled with ferocity.

It didn't take him long to cut through the fence.

They crept through the compound and slunk from building to building, staying well out of sight. The whole place was deserted except for a couple of easily-avoided watchmen near the front entrance of a warehouse.

"There it is." The woman lifted binoculars to her heart-shaped face to verify. "In the west corner on the slope."

Cara gasped. She'd recognized the girl. She was the gorgeous brunette that Bryce had been 'chatting' with outside the pub. Minus the eyeliner, dangly earrings, and flashy sunglasses perched on her head. Now she wore a knitted grey ski cap pulled down on her chestnut-brown tresses.

The woman looked at her and quirked an eyebrow. "What?"

"I... just realized where I saw you before, that's all." Cara stepped a little closer to Bryce. *So all that flirting – was fake? Or was it?*

The woman smiled and sent her an approving look. "You're pretty sharp."

"Okay. Let's move in on that hut." Bryce caught the eye of the other man and nodded. "A 10-85 maneuver."

"Right." The other man agreed. His blue eyes, beneath his thick, wavy hair, gleamed in anticipation. "Game on!"

~*~

Bryce grunted his approval. The team moved like clockwork, a graceful dance through an area fraught with uncertainty.

Cara shadowed him, moving when he moved, freezing when he stopped, as quiet as a mouse. He'd never had to shelter somebody at the same time he was rescuing a captive, but it was working so far... thanks to Cara's obedient cooperation.

At last the hut lay before them, a mere five yards away. He looked at Cara and motioned for her to stay back. He caught the eyes of both Angelwing and Markdown, and they silently counted together.

One. Two. *Three.*

He ran up to the doorway of the hut, slipping his bolt-cutters out as he went, and chopped open the padlock on the door in one smooth "chink!" The cutters dived back into his suit as the M1911 handgun resumed its natural place in his right hand, and he pushed himself up tight against the wall, shoving the door open with his free hand.

A storm of gunfire erupted out the opening like lava spewing from a volcano. Way too much to belong to just one or two guards watching Freddie.

Ka-Blam-Bang-blam-rat-a-tat-tat-tat! Fur-r-r-r-BAM! BOOM…

They had run right into a cleverly baited trap.

~*~

"*Bryce!*" Cara screeched as he recoiled from the stone hut and fired into the hole. Bryce dodged to her and yanked her down on the ground as bullets whistled above their heads and pounded into the wall behind them. He fired a few more shots at the door and scooped her upright again with an arm around her waist almost before the shots left the chamber of his gun.

She hit the ground already running as Bryce pulled her around behind the hut with not a second to spare. Men poured out of the other buildings in the compound and started zeroing in on their location. Mysterious shots fired from a nearby copse of trees and a tin tool shed to the east halted the enemy's progress, and Cara caught a muffled "Backup, get backup in here *now-"* from the walkie-talkie at Bryce's belt. His friends had reached safe locations and were calling for help.

We're gonna die! This is insane!

Bryce pressed her against the stone wall, making himself a human shield between her and the gunfire.

"Hang on!" He yelled into her ear over the din. "We'll be okay!" There was a grim set to his mouth, but earnestness in his gaze that made her actually believe him.

She accomplished a nod as he half-twisted away and fired around the corner, a pained yell echoing after the sound of the shot. He took a second to reload his gun and then fired again.

Thrup-thrup-thrup-thrup. She looked up to see a huge helicopter hovering above them like a dragonfly aiming for a lily pad. The cockpit shone, looking like a giant eye, as the copter landed on the roof of the warehouse.

A look to Bryce sent warm reassurance through her. *We're not gonna die.*

He grinned and wiggled his eyebrows. "Backup's here." He fired yet another shot, sending her eardrums buzzing again. Through the acrid smell of gunpowder, she caught a breath of his fresh-smelling cologne.

People dropped out of the helicopter and assumed commanding positions at different points of the roof as more people jogged down the steps and began to infiltrate the dirt alleys between the small buildings.

"Gib jetzt auf! Surrender now!" A voice on a loudspeaker boomed from the helicopter.

"It's over." Bryce announced, and then caught her as she went limp as boiled linguini.

~*~

"They're not even Ravenmeister employees, just hired thugs!" Angelwing's face slumped in disgust. "And guess who sold this hot piece of real estate just 24 hours ago and now doesn't own an inch of this dirt? Ravenmeister, Inc."

"Mm!" He grunted in frustration and swept the hair off his forehead. "They've slipped away again, scot-free. That stings."

"Bryce, come look at this!" Cara popped her head out of the stone hut they'd been contesting only minutes ago.

He trotted over to her and Angelwing marched off, barking orders to the subordinate agents securing the area.

"Ahem. Use my code name." He whispered when he reached Cara's side.

Her eyes widened. "Ok. But look-" She tugged his arm and led him up to the far corner of the hut, where Markdown kneeled, shining a penlight on the dirt.

Bryce bent for a closer look and took in the scratched message with one glance. He stiffened upright, feeling steamed.

"Oh *man*! This explains a lot. Inside information?!" He looked back at the dirt. Poor Freddie. Apologizing ahead of time, worried about them. He wished could contact the guy and let him know they had survived the perilous trap.

"We'll get right on this, looking for anything that could fit this 'fortress' description." Markdown rose from his position on the floor and jogged out the door.

Cara looked up at Bryce in the darkened hut, her eyes reflecting the light from the entrance. "Inside information?"

He knew she was thinking the same thing as him. Who had betrayed them? Silver Strand... or was it the Agency?

~*~

The fading sunlight still looked bright compared to the darkness they'd left inside that stone hut. Cara shivered when she thought about Freddie held hostage in that damp, cave-like space.

Bryce walked up to the Pub Girl. "I'll secure the perimeter. Have Markdown look out for Cara."

"No!"

Bryce and the woman turned to look at her, surprise written on their faces.

She cleared her throat, trying not to let the nervousness show. "I'll go with you. Please." She looked at Bryce as she spoke.

Amusement lit his eyes and lifted one corner of his mouth. "All right. Come on." He turned back to the brunette. "And get a message to Monty to send someone to see Gungerson about the leak."

The woman gave a smart nod. "I'm on it."

"Good." Bryce turned and paced over to Cara. "Let's make sure the badguys are all gone." He sent her a wink as she fell into step with him.

She smiled, but as soon as they were out of earshot of the brunette and the other people the woman seemed to be commanding, she asked the question. "Who is she?!"

Bryce's gaze followed the wire fence they were walking alongside. "You won't believe me if I tell you."

"Try me!" She fired back, darting a quick look around, and then cementing her gaze to his face again.

"Okay, here goes. She's a co-worker, 'Angelwing', whom I've known for years and has saved my hide a time or two."

Cara let that sink in as Bryce led them outside the front gate and headed for the other side of the compound.

"She's also married."

Her mouth dropped open like a loose-hinged drawer. She couldn't help herself. "She's not wearing a wedding ring!"

Bryce coughed, his face contorting in an apparent effort to hold in uproarious laughter. "You looked?" He turned to stare at her. "You were jealous." It wasn't a question.

"Caviar." Finally. A chance to use that stupid word on *him* with the original intent – no teasing!

He smiled. "Oh, all right. Sorry." He didn't look a bit apologetic.

"Is she *really* married?"

He chuckled softly and nodded. "I swear it's true. To 'Markdown', that handsome fellow who was helping you examine the shed, as a matter of fact. Both of them are good friends of mine."

They reached a miniature meadow, a clearing in the woods, with tiny white wildflowers sprinkled among the lush emerald green grass.

She reached out to touch his arm and they stopped walking. "I understand-"

"-*Aaah!*" In that same instant, Bryce was almost knocked off his feet from behind. Cara caught a flash of black hair and pale skin as Bryce's arm was pulled from her hand. Whirling, he and his attacker fought like a pair of crazed wildcats.

"*No!*" She howled as she realized Ryan Black was raising a menacing gun, and before she quite knew she was doing it, she sent a kick with her heavy boot to the back of Black's knee.

It buckled for a half-second, giving Bryce enough of an advantage to rip the gun out of Black's grasp and send it hurtling in Cara's direction. She dived and caught it up in her left hand. She screamed again when she saw Black reaching for another weapon at his side – a fat, ugly pistol that looked like a murder weapon if she'd ever seen one!

Ryan Black shoved Bryce away from him and turned to point the gun at her.

In a heartbeat, Bryce twisted back around between her and the villain as Black fired. Bryce dropped to the ground. The sound of a shrill, powerful engine approached.

Cara reacted instinctively, lifted the heavy gun in her left hand, propped it against her right arm, and sprayed the woods, air, and ground at Ryan Black's feet with paintballs. Only they weren't paintballs, they were real bullets. Even in this chaos, Cara couldn't bring herself to aim for Black's heart.

Black lunged away towards the sound that was almost upon them. Cara looked up to see a low-to-the-ground Ferrari, driven by a woman with raven hair and pouty red lips. Black leaped in even as Cara speckled the car's flank with shots from the gun, and they roared off, a taillight exploding from a direct hit as they lurched down a dirt road heading deeper into the woods.

She turned from watching their retreat to see Bryce unconscious on the ground with a crimson stain blossoming from the area of his chest nearest his heart.

"No! Oh no! No, no...!" Cara tossed the gun away and sank to the grass beside him, screaming until her air was gone, feeling his throat for a pulse. The gentle motion in the carotid artery beneath her fingers brought the breath back into her lungs as she realized that he was still alive. Barely. His spattered chest rose and fell in a scarcely noticeable motion.

"Bryce! Oh, Bryce...no..." Her words were a tortured whisper, knowing he had taken the bullet meant for her. Every second counted, so she forced her suddenly clumsy fingers to pull the radio transmitter from his belt.

She pushed what she hoped was the right button. "Please, oh, please, Bryce has been shot. Ashburn is shot."

The half-second of silence before the reply almost killed her.

"Cara, this is Angelwing, where are you?" It was the voice of the beautiful brunette.

"What happened?" The voice of the husband, Markdown, nearly cutting into his wife's words.

"In the woods somewhere near the front gate! We were attacked by *Ryan Black!*" Her voice shook from the force of her sobs, which continued unabated. "He's been shot in the chest, please come quickly!"

"We're on our way."

Cara dropped the walkie-talkie into the emerald grass and looked down at the man lying before her, still sobbing out loud.

The blood seeped in an ever-widening circle across his chest. She reached for the zipper at his neck and pulled it open down to his waist. The white cotton T-shirt he wore was ripped and turning scarlet. She needed to put pressure on it or Bryce would bleed to death.

She unzipped her own jumpsuit and ripped off her T-shirt, zipped herself back into the suit. She folded the shirt into a pad, pressed it firmly to the wound, and leaned on it, slowing the flow of clotting blood.

His head was turned to one side, his eyes were closed, not even one of his thick eyelashes fluttered. He lay still as a statue, pale and frozen among the wildflowers. Every moment in which she had been angry at him flitted across her mind and sent an aching pang of remorse through her.

The woods were still and quiet around them. Help was on the way, but nothing marred the complete and utter silence of the moment. Even his slight, shallow breathing was only audible if she focused on listening for it. She leaned forward and kissed his forehead, and then stroked the hair from his brow with her fingers poking from her cast.

How she loved him! And now he was dying.

"Oh God." Her breath caught in a gasp of surprise at the whispered words, but then a dam burst and she released a torrent of pleading. "*God!* If you're there, save his life! *Please.* I give up. I can't do this without you anymore! It's out of my hands!"

A tear rolled down the bridge of her nose and dripped onto her hand that pushed the compress tight against Bryce's wound.

"I know you are all-powerful, and that you can give him his life back. So I'm asking you to restore him, to heal him." She looked up at the sky, which was turning rosy as the sun retreated. Venus twinkled back at her.

Life was uncertain. No way to protect her world. It was either surrender all or fake it, trying to hold impossible things in her grasp. Either trust in God's perfect plan, or buck against it like a rebellious bronco, which did absolutely nothing but cause anguish.

"God." She whispered, more tears rippling down her cheeks in steady waves. "I surrender me, too." She breathed in, then out again. "All of me. You can have everything. I'm yours. I believe Jesus died for my sins. Please forgive me, for... everything horrible I've done." She bit her lip, recalling just how much of her life was useless and full of sin. She'd made so many mistakes.

She looked down into Bryce's motionless face, which was growing less distinct as the light faded. "And Lord," She murmured, "Even if he doesn't make it, I'm going to live for you, in his memory." *It's what he would want.*

Distant shouts broke in, and Cara looked up to see people swarming through the woods in her direction. Someone drove a Gator all-terrain vehicle, wheeling and revving through the dense forest.

"Over here!" She shrilled a whistle as piercing and loud as she could.

People surrounded them in half an instant. "He's been shot in the chest!" Cara shouted even as the man called Markdown relieved her of the job of pressing the makeshift pad against Bryce's wound. Angelwing already held Bryce's head in her lap as a medic examined the rest of the still form.

"They drove off in that direction in a black sports car!" Cara pointed deep into the woods, "Ryan Black and a dark-haired woman. It was a long time ago. I doubt you'll find them now."

"No injuries except for the shot. It's safe to move him, and we'd better do it fast." The paramedic stood and motioned towards the Gator. With painstaking care, Bryce was lifted by many pairs of hands and laid on a stretcher that was transferred to the bed of the chunky all-terrain vehicle. Before anyone could stop her, Cara was up next to him, squeezing herself into a tiny corner by his head, holding his hand in hers. Markdown and Angelwing joined her in the vehicle, taking up positions near Bryce's feet, as the Gator rumbled into motion.

Cara took a quick glance behind them as they left, and saw the remaining people melting into the woods, searching, as fireflies twinkled over the soft green grass where the man she loved had offered his life for hers.

And then her eyes met the liquid brown ones of Angelwing. "There's a hospital only a few miles from here if you zigzag through the woods." Her gaze held calm assurance. "We'll have him there in no time."

It was then that Cara remembered what Bryce had told her in the tunnel. She forced herself to let go of Bryce's hand and dug around in one of her deep pockets. *If only I had two good hands!* There. A spare cell phone. She flipped it open and dialed the number Bryce had asked her to impress upon her brain.

When immediately a woman answered, Cara knew what to tell her. "I need to talk to someone named 'Montrose'. This is in regard to an emergency that has happened to Ashburn."

Markdown and Angelwing were giving her strange looks. She didn't care one iota.

"Montrose here."

"Hello, this is Cara."

"What's happened?" Montrose demanded, cutting directly to the heart of the matter.

"Bryce has been shot in the chest by Ryan Black and is unconscious. We are driving him to the nearest hospital." The wind whipped past her ear and she turned to shelter the phone. Ice-cold tears tracked down her face. "Ashburn needs you."

"Oh my God." The man's voice shook.

"He told me to call you if something happened and gave me your number. That's all I know."

Cara noted that Angelwing and Markdown were now staring wide-eyed at each other. "He told her to phone the boss?" Markdown whispered in his wife's direction.

"Cara, you hang in there with him, do you hear me? Trust nobody but Angelwing and Markdown. I'm flying in. I'll be there in five hours. Until then, get him treated by an Agency doctor and then stick close to him."

"An Agency doctor?" Cara repeated, clueless. More funny looks were sent her way by Angelwing and Markdown.

"Markdown will know who to get... he should have called them in already if he's worth his salt." Montrose's voice rang with a hard determination now. "I'll get there as fast as I can. Pray for him!"

A gasp of cold air hit Cara's lungs when the line went dead. "Hello? Hello?!" She looked at the others in the cart, trying not to panic. "The line is dead!"

Markdown shrugged and shook his head of wavy hair. "That's just the boss's way of ending a conversation."

"Oh." *How strange.* Cara closed the cell phone, dropped it back in her pocket, and grasped Bryce's hand again. His pulse remained steady, if weak.

"And I already called an Agency doctor." Markdown shifted, continuing to put pressure on Bryce's chest.

"Don't worry, Cara." Angelwing's voice broke through above the engine noise. "He's a tough cookie. Something tells me that he'll pull through."

Cara looked up at the woman. Angelwing's brow wrinkled in worry and her face was wet with tears.

Sure. You're as scared to death as I am.

~*~

Cara would have been gripping her hands together tight, just to have something to hold on to, but her tender right hand in the cast couldn't take the crushing press of her healthy left hand. So she gripped the chair arm in the waiting room instead. Beige walls surrounded them. The room was devoid of any decoration, plain and functional.

Angelwing sat with her, lips moving soundlessly, eyes closed. Was she praying? Cara had been sending up snippets of prayer, starting out slow, but it was getting easier. It felt like there might really be someone listening.

Markdown had gone in with Bryce to the operating room. There wasn't an exit wound, so the bullet had lodged inside of him somewhere. The x-ray would help them pinpoint the location, but it was the surgeon's job to find and remove it.

Cara felt a sudden longing to talk to her mother. She turned to Angelwing. "Would it be all right if I made a call to my mom?"

Angelwing looked up. "Of course, as long as you don't tell her the details. You can't say *how* he got shot, *where* he was when he was shot, or *who* shot him."

"Right." Cara nodded, and walked into the tiny, windowless bathroom branching off the main waiting room, finding a small degree of privacy.

Her mother answered on the first ring. "Hello?"

"Mom, it's me."

"Cara! Oh baby, I've been so worried about you... what's going on? I couldn't reach you at your hotel."

Her mother hadn't called her 'baby' in a long time. *Time!*

"Wait a sec, Mom, what time is it over there?"

"4:12 in the afternoon. What time is it near you?"

"Um..." Cara pulled the phone away from her head and glanced at her watch. "10:15 PM."

"Goodness! How strange!" Her mother sounded surprised.

"I know." Cara took a deep breath. "Mom... I'm calling to ask for prayer."

The phone was silent for a few seconds. "For *what*? You're asking me to *pray* for you?" Her mother's voice was sad and confused at the same time. "You know I always pray for you, whether you want me to or not."

Cara hugged her broken wrist close to herself and clung to the phone. Her mother, always troubled by Cara's rejection of God, had continued in her gentle way to believe in the Lord through all the difficulties they'd faced.

"I... I've changed. Mom, I gave myself back to God today."

"Cara!" Unmitigated joy infused her mother's tone. "Praise the Lord!"

Cara swallowed away the sob that rose in her throat. "It took something very hard to push me to Him."

Her mother waited, listening.

"Bryce has been shot."

Her mother gasped. "Oh, honey!"

"Please, please pray for him. The bullet entered his chest near the heart. He's in surgery now."

Her mother didn't waste a single second, launching into prayer right then and there, beseeching God to spare the life of 'this precious young man', asking for mercy and healing on his body.

Cara sat curled in a little ball on the thin industrial carpet, tears washing down her cheeks, listening to her mother pray.

When she was finished, Cara spoke again. "Thank you, Mom." Her voice was barely a whisper, but her mother heard her.

"You're more than welcome, sweetheart. I'll keep praying for him and for you as well."

"I can't tell you how everything happened. It'll have to wait for later. But I love you."

"I love you too! Please keep me informed on Bryce's condition."

"I will. Goodbye."

After her mother said goodbye, Cara closed the cell phone and tipped her head back against the wall.

"Lord... you know what's best. But I'm begging you to save him. I love him, God. Living without him would be so, so hard. I would still have you, which should be enough, but... oh, God." Cara pressed tissue against her wet eyes and face.

Someone tapped on the door. "Cara?" Angelwing.

Cara stood and tossed the tissue into the wastebasket. "Yes?"

"He made it through the surgery!"

Cara nearly knocked the smaller woman over as she burst out of the bathroom. "Can we see him?"

"Yes! Come on, let's go!" Together they raced for the doorway that led deeper into the hospital.

Chapter Ten

The Windows to a Soul

"He's in a shock-induced coma." The doctor explained matter-of-factly. "But he could awaken at any time. His system has been traumatized, a not unusual consequence of a gunshot wound." The agency-approved doctor had a captive audience in Cara, Markdown, and Angelwing, who stood by Bryce's bedside.

"But will he make it?" Cara demanded, grilling the doctor with what she was sure must be a granite-hard gaze. *Tell me!*

He cleared his throat. "I am reasonably certain that he will survive. His excellent physical condition contributes to this. The blood loss could have been much worse. The path of the bullet hit no major organs or arteries, but it was only millimeters from touching his heart, lodging in the lung. He's a very lucky young man. One-quarter of all trauma-related deaths are chest wounds."

Cara had heard enough. As Angelwing and Markdown continued to quiz the medical man, she slipped to Bryce's side and seated herself in a nearby chair. His left hand was connected to an IV, and he lay completely still in his hospital gown. She slid her left hand under his right one and grasped it gently. His hand still fit perfectly against hers, but now lay heavy and limp. She lifted his hand and held it against her cheek.

I'm here, Bryce. Please, don't leave me.

~*~

"Thank you, doctor." Her husband shook the hand of the surgeon.

Angel added her own thanks and walked with him and Mark to the door of the hospital room. A last glance over her shoulder gave her a glimpse of Cara watching Bryce's face intently. She kissed Bryce's hand and then hugged it against her cheek once more.

Angel smiled as she exited the room. Once she, Mark, and the doctor were outside, Mark leaned against the door and crossed his muscular arms over his chest. He would be Bryce's bodyguard, on duty until safe backup was determined and assigned by the boss. Markdown was fully capable of guarding Bryce, but even he would need to take it in shifts.

The sound of the doctor's footsteps faded down the hall. Angel slid her arms around her husband's torso and smiled up at him. "I love you."

He looked both ways down the hallway, then uncrossed his arms and wrapped them around her. "I love you more." He dropped a quick, firm kiss onto her lips.

"Yum. I'm sorry… I'm distracting you on the job." She cocked her head playfully.

He pushed her aside, gently. "Seriously, get away from me, you temptress." He winked to let her know he was teasing.

She backed away and leaned against the far side of the hallway. "You do know he's not alone in there, right?"

"I am aware of the fact." He smiled. "She won't hurt him, Angel. She's in love with the man… saved his life, in fact."

"Yes, that was pretty smart of her to press her shirt against his wound."

"Yeah, that, and single-handedly forcing Ryan Black to get the heck outta there." He laughed. "Did you think about how he just *left* after shooting Bryce? Team Yellow checked out the area and found it showered with bullets from the Uzi they found on the scene. Cara chased him off with a cloud of gunfire."

Angel's mouth dropped open. "Whoa… I didn't know she had it in her." She tapped her chin. "You know, I think Bryce might have found his other half."

"At long last. And thank God, he'll be alive to enjoy it." Mark grinned at her across the hall. "Come here." They shared another short, sweet kiss, and then he shooed her off again. "Go find me a sandwich or something, wifey. I'm hungry."

"Will do, hubbs."

~*~

Cara opened her eyes to see the blank walls of the hospital bedroom. It smelled of antiseptic. She sat up, and a twinge traveled from her shoulder up through her neck. She rolled her head in a circle, hoping to work out the crick, and then looked down at Bryce. He lay quiet and still.

She'd fallen asleep holding his hand. Her watch read 3:00 AM. She moved her fingers and laced them through his.

As she watched his face, a trace of a smile appeared on his lips. She held her breath as his fingers tightened around hers.

His eyes opened. *Oh God. He's awake. He's alive.*

He looked around and found her eyes. "Hi." He spoke, his voice a faint echo of the rich depth with which it usually vibrated. But he was talking! And the expression on his face… he recognized her.

ASHBURN

"Hey." She laughed softly, the pure joy uncontainable. *Thank you, Lord!*

His gaze traced her face. "You're crying."

He was right. Warm tears flowed down her skin. She hadn't even noticed.

"I'm happy you're alive."

Faint surprise touched his features. "What happened?"

"It's a long story." She squeezed his hand gently. "It's so good to see you awake."

He breathed in and out. "My chest hurts."

"Well, you were shot. They pulled a bullet out of your lung just a couple hours ago." She shuddered at the thought.

He stared at her. "Who shot me?"

"Ryan Black. You jumped in front of the bullet he was shooting at me."

He stared at the ceiling for a few seconds. "It's coming back now. But that's the last thing I remember." He looked at her face again. "You're ok?"

"More than okay." The joy was filling her with warm effervescence.

He quirked an eyebrow, a silent question mark.

"I'll tell you more later. But, Bryce… God finally got me."

His eyes widened and he opened his mouth to speak, but the door opened.

She turned her head to see a solidly built black man with salt-and-pepper gray hair enter the room. He was quickly flanked by Angelwing and Markdown.

"Monty!" Bryce's face lit up in welcome. "Cara tells me I've been shot."

The black man adjusted his bow tie. "That you have. I'm just glad to see you're still alive to joke about it." He stared down at him through his square-lensed glasses. "You should be thanking God for every breath you take from now on."

Then the man's eyes moved to her. "Miss Stephenson. It's nice to finally make your acquaintance." He smiled kindly under his close-cropped moustache, eyes twinkling. "I've heard a lot about you."

A quick glance at Bryce revealed that he was looking around at nothing in particular. He cleared his throat, seeming slightly embarrassed.

Holding back the giggle that wanted to pop out, she grinned. "Please, call me Cara. I wish I could have said the same thing to you, Sir, but Bryce is very good at keeping secrets."

Montrose chuckled. "That's one reason he's one of my best agents, if not *the* best." He nodded to Markdown and Angelwing. "No offense, guys." They smiled.

Bryce took a quick breath, staring at his boss.

Montrose's eyes swiveled back to look at Bryce. "Yes. I've gotten clearance from Blue Leader to let you talk to Cara... about you. Her background check is satisfactory, she's saved the life of one of our best agents, meaning you, and it is believed that letting you spill the beans will aid your recovery considerably."

"Monty... I don't know what to say!" Relief and delight tumbled against each other in Bryce's expression.

"I'm sure you'll think of something." Montrose gave a dry laugh. "All right, lady and gentleman. Let's clear out for a while." He looked over his shoulder. "I'll have more to discuss with you later, Ashburn, and you too, Cara."

~*~

Oh God, I never thought this could happen, not in a million years. I never dreamed I'd be able to tell her. Thank you!

Cara was wearing the happiest smile he'd ever seen her put on. "I can hardly believe how blessed I am." She shook her head as if in amazement. "First I think you're dead, now you're alive, and you have free rein to finally tell me all your secrets that have been standing between us."

Then her gaze lowered. He looked down to see that they were still holding hands, fingers interlaced. Their eyes met again, and Cara's cheeks turned a dusky pink.

"*Blessed*, you say? ...We have a lot to talk about." He picked up his hand up away from hers and gently laid it against her cheek, smoothing away a tear that lingered.

She sighed softly and placed her hand over his, cupping it against her face. "Where should we start?"

Hmm. Great question. "Do you know who Blue Leader is?"

"No." she shook her head slightly.

He dropped his hand, wishing it had the strength to stay raised. But it didn't. He felt so weak. But Cara slipped her hand around his, resting against the hospital sheets.

"Blue Leader is the code name for the Commander-in-chief, A.K.A... the President of the United States."

She looked utterly shocked, but then turned bright red. "The *president* knows about... *us*?"

He laughed softly. "If you mean 'us' as in our..." he hesitated. "...relationship...with each other, then, no. I think Monty meant that he personally felt it would help me out to talk to you."

She sighed as if relieved. "Oh. I see." She let go of him for a moment to reach for a glass of water sitting on the bedside table and handed it to him.

He *was* thirsty, come to think of it. Taking long, cool swallows never felt so good. She took the water when he was done and replaced it on the table. He sank back a little deeper into the pillows while their hands found each other again.

God, I really want to know how you 'got' her. But I'll answer her questions first. Patience was the key.

"So, Cara, what do you want to know?" *I'm all yours.*

She didn't even need to think about it. "Who are you, and *who* do you *work* for, already?!" A little sass slipped out, delighting him.

He squared his shoulders. "I am Bryce Gregory Reynolds, A.K.A. Agent Ashburn, so nicknamed for my ability to 'burn through the ashes' of any situation and see what's going on, reading between the lines. I work as a special agent for the U.S. branch of the I.C.E, International Counterintelligence & Espionage, agency that's so top-secret that 'nearly nobody' knows about it. Monty is the head of the branch and he reports directly to the Director of National Intelligence, the same person the C.I.A. reports to, along with the top brass in I.C.E."

As she listened, her eyes grew wider and wider. *I'd give a lot to know what she's thinking.*

"It's *extremely* hush-hush. Even the office in D.C. is undercover, underground, with a fake front and ground floor as a publishing house called International Federal Publishing. Anywhere in the USA outside that building and the White House, on paper, *we don't exist.*"

"*Wow.*" She whispered so softly that he hardly heard her.

"Now, as to where you come in…" He stroked his thumb across the back of her hand. "When I first met you, obviously, I was not a secret agent. They don't allow kids to become agents."

Cara giggled, eyes dancing with her green-hued sparkle of amusement. He was still in awe of how her eyes changed shades. "But when you came back, and I saw you again?"

"When you next saw me, in your office one day, I was who I am now… a secret agent."

"What happened in between?"

"A lot." He grinned. "Mostly getting my degree from the National Intelligence University and the mandatory one-year probationary period as a new agent. But I've had a lot of experience in the years of active service I've had under Monty." A sigh slipped out. "*Long* story."

"What were you doing at Silver Strand?" Cara looked eager for the whole story, her lips slightly parted as if in anticipation.

"I was sent to infiltrate the company and discover if Silver Strand Technologies was connected to an illegal arms dealership that we're trying to crack. Our sources narrowed it down to two options. Silver Strand, or Ravenmeister, Inc." He gazed straight into her eyes. "Possibly both. We had one hint that they were connected."

Cara repeated her all-but-silent 'wow'. "And then?"

"And then… you know most of the rest. Mr. Gungerson sent us on this mission. I'd heard about Freddie's kidnapping before Monty arranged me getting hired at Silver Strand, but I was just as surprised as you when Mr. Gungerson picked you and me for his search party, or one of his search parties. I don't think we were the only hounds he set on Freddie's scent."

He studied the striped pattern of the blanket, then looked into her beloved face again. "I have a feeling he might have been trying to get you away from his son, without firing you. I just happened to be the first fresh, acceptable guy that stumbled into his grasp, so he threw us together and hoped we'd stick."

He watched carefully for her reaction to that. Her nose wrinkled, but the look in her eyes grew soft. Interpreted, it could mean that she was annoyed at Mr. Gungerson for playing matchmaker, but happy with the end result.

Or it could mean she wants a peanut butter milkshake. He couldn't know for sure, for Adam had lost the 'women's instruction manual' thousands of years ago in the garden, if he'd ever been given one.

He pulled her hand a little closer. "Cara, if I could have told you any of this before, I would have. I was under orders not to tell you *anything*."

She leaned towards him. "Bryce, I believe you. About all of it. And I *trust* you." She shook her head. "I always did, even when I told you I was holding off on a decision. I know… have always known, that you were a good man right down to your core. Even when I didn't know what was going on, or you were driving me crazy."

Really? "How did you know?"

She grinned. "You have 'good guy' stamped all over you with invisible ink, only visible to the female eye."

They laughed together, but then she spoke again. "No. The real reason I knew I could trust you?" Her stare was probing this time. "Your eyes."

My eyes? "What about my eyes?"

"The eyes are the windows to the soul. Yours are too pure to belong to a man with anything less than sterling integrity."

God, that was you she was seeing in me. "Thank you. You have no idea how much that means to me."

And then, quite against his own will, he felt himself starting to drift off to sleep. His eyelids dipped, all at once as heavy as lead.

"Oh, you must be exhausted. Get some rest." Cara squeezed his hand.

The last thought that crossed his mind before he fell into the abyss of slumber was that he hoped he never had to let go of her again.

~*~

She watched as his eyelids fluttered closed and his head tipped back into the pillow... and just like that, he was asleep. But alive. Oh, so alive.

I love you. She dearly wanted to say it to him, but wouldn't. Not yet. Not until he said it to her first. She wished she could stay here with him all night long, but Mr. Montrose had mentioned that he wanted to talk to her.

Cara stood up, slowly disentangling her hand from Bryce's grasp. A faint frown crossed his face with the removal of her hand, sending a tremble of remorse into her heart. He needed her, but she would go and see Mr. Montrose, and then come back. Or... perhaps find a bed somewhere and catch some rest before the sunrise. She was feeling the effects of the long day. Her legs felt like logs as she limped towards the door.

Markdown greeted her outside the room and told her where to find his boss. "Just a few doors down, on that side." He pointed out the way for her.

"Thanks." She walked down to the door indicated and knocked.

"Come in."

She opened the door to find Mr. Montrose and Angelwing seated across from each other at a round table. "Cara! Join us." Montrose stood and pulled out a chair, immediately earning points from her for being a gentleman.

"Thank you." She sat. Fatigue washed over her and she struggled to stay alert. A discreet glance at her watch told her it was almost five o'clock in the morning. "I hate to be rude, but it's been a really long day. If we could keep this short...?"

"Of course. I will be brief." Monty tipped back in his chair and folded his arms loosely across his chest. His solid build was reassuring, somehow. He looked dependable.

"Here's the scoop. We've put some of our best 'miners' on this gem of Freddie's note, but we haven't come up with anything about the location of the alleged 'fortress' yet."

Angelwing slapped the table, a dark scowl splashed across her features. "Where *is* this place, for Pete's sake?"

"For Freddie's sake, you mean." Montrose admonished her.

She sobered and lowered her gaze to the tabletop.

"Angel, I want you to discover where these rats have made their nest."

"I'll do my best, sir, you know I will. But boy, do I wish Mr. Laser-vision wasn't out of action." Angelwing shook her head as if in regret.

Cara perked up, interested. "Are you talking about Bryce?"

"Yes *ma'am*. He's the best we have when it comes to seeing through walls like the one that's in front of us now. It's like he has some kind of internal compass pointing in the right direction." Angelwing talked with her hands, making emphatic gestures as she spoke.

Wow. He's highly respected among his fellow agents. Cara looked to Mr. Montrose. "So what's my job now, Sir?"

He let his chair tip forward until it sat level again. "Good question, young lady. For all formal purposes, you're useless to us now."

What?! She felt her eyebrows nearly hit her hairline.

"Wait, wait, don't panic." He chuckled. "What I'm saying is that we don't need you as a link to Silver Strand. Mr. Gungerson has been warned about the leak and you won't be reporting to him anymore."

"Warned?"

"I sent a trusted agent to speak to him face-to-face and he has been ordered not to say a word to any person about your investigation."

"Oh. Wow." Cara tried to comprehend that.

Mr. Montrose set his clasped hands on the table. "Informally, I *need you*." His gaze burned directly into her face. "I need you to work with Ashburn. He needs somebody to watch his back, be there for him, and help sort things out." Then he muttered almost to himself. "Always has, really..." His voice strengthened again. "That's where you fit in."

Oh good. She felt like smiling but forced her face to remain serious.

"From what he's told me about you, my dear, I'm impressed." Monty sat back a bit and rubbed his chin. "You discovered the second message from Freddie, and were the first person to find him inside the Ravenmeister building in Paris." He eyed her with a strange expression. "Although Bryce has yet to explain how you came to be in the building when my... *suggestion*... was that you stay in the tech van."

She could feel herself blush, but then Monty winked. "You're obviously a very bright woman. And I can use all the smarts I can get on this case." His eyebrows curved up in a questioning expression. "So… are you in?"

Oh yeah. "I'm *so* in."

Chapter Eleven

Storming the Castle

Inside craggy rock walls was a haven of luxury. The room had been designed for comfort, and pleasure. Ancient tapestries hung on the walls, sunlight poured through an arched window with diamond-shaped panes of glass, and the stone floor was strewn with animal-skin rugs. A bearskin complete with head reposed in front of a massive fireplace, where great fires would have roared and crackled in bygone days when the Baron roasted chestnuts and apples gathered from his own lands.

The voice yelling from the cell phone in his hand could not have clashed more strongly with the surroundings.

"You bungled the job! It was a foolproof trap! They walked right into it and you had to go and ruin the whole thing by jumping the guy instead of doing what you were supposed to – just shoot him, and grab the girl!"

Black pinched the bridge of his nose between his eyes to relieve the pressure pounding in his skull. *It's true. For once in my life, I let emotion reign.* He hated Bryce Reynolds with a passion. It was this hate that caused him to attack his enemy with his bare hands instead of following the plan.

But he couldn't admit that to the person who had commissioned the job without ruining his professional reputation.

"Sir, I had the element of surprise, and if we could capture them both alive-"

"That was not what I told you to do! I don't care a whit about Reynolds. It's the girl I'm after." Heavy breathing. "And now my fount of information has gone dry... I have no way of telling you ahead of time what they're planning."

Big deal. He could handle it without being given a cheat sheet. "I assure you, we have everything under control. They won't find us here at the secret headquarters. I even had Tatiana feed Freddie false information, just in case." He permitted a short laugh. "She told him he was going to Berlin. Miles away from where we really are."

"Well. That's the first smart action I've seen from you in this whole stupid mess."

Black clenched his teeth. Then he tamped down the anger and forced his voice into its customary coldness. "Now, if you could get us those access codes you learned about, we can operate on our skinny friend and confiscate that chip without it exploding into dust."

"Oh, I've got that covered. I'll sneak them out tonight. And nab an X2-scanner device to signal the codes into his arm. You just worry about your end of this deal, I'll manage mine." The oily confidence in the voice was galling.

Beep. The line was clear of the obnoxious presence. Black hurled the phone into the cushions of the couch just as Tatiana slipped into the room.

She looked at the tasseled pillows the phone had sunk into, and then turned her luscious black eyes on him in sympathy.

"What did that *horrible* man want now?" She purred, slinking up beside him.

"He told me what a fool I'd been, failing to do what I'd promised… catch Cara Stephenson."

Her eyes flashed sparks of anger. "That girl! She fills the air with bullets, with your own gun, so I fear for your life! I hate her."

"I don't know why she didn't just shoot me, unless her aim was terrible." He shook his head. "It would have been an end to a life of evil." A black mood had descended upon him… the depression that haunted him, dogging him at every turn.

She reached up and caressed his face with a slender hand. "You are not evil! I am not evil. We both know what we want."

He softened at her touch. A hint of a smile moved his mouth as he looked down at her. "What do you want?"

She kissed him possessively, pulling him close with a hand to the back of his head. "Your love." Her voice held intense force. "And enough money to never be hungry."

He ran his fingers through her hair. "My little Russian cat. You grew up starved for both love and comfort… poor and neglected."

Her eyes studied his face as if memorizing every detail. "You never got any attention from that stupid old woman who raised you. I think this… this is why you do, what you do. Your work brings much attention and wealth."

This was why he kept her around – she was a master at soothing his ego. "It's a power game, and I've got lots of it, don't I, darling?"

Her grin exposed slightly crooked teeth. "Oh yes. Very much power."

ASHBURN

Julia Erickson

~*~

Cara awakened and then struggled to recall where she was. She lay in a hospital bed. But she wasn't hurt... except for the pain in her wrist, which she was almost growing used to.

She sat up. *Bryce!* Everything flooded back to mind. She'd told Mr. Montrose that she was in, would work with them for as long as they needed her. Then Angelwing, or 'Angel' as she'd told Cara to call her, had showed her to an empty room and told her to get some sleep.

Her watch said 10:00 AM. *Oh my word! So late!* She crawled out of bed. A fresh change of clothes in her exact sizes lay folded on the table by the bed. Underclothes, a silky-soft pullover sweater and a pair of jeans with a hidden elastic waist, all easy to pull on with one hand. She had a feeling Angel had something to do with them. *Bless her!*

She greeted Markdown at the door of Bryce's room and met the doctor coming out. "How is he this morning?"

"Doing remarkably well for someone with his type of injury. If I didn't know better, I'd say there was some secret healing force at work." He studied her for a few seconds. Then he winked. "Perhaps it's you. Go on in."

She walked in with a spring in her step. Bryce sat propped up with pillows, while sunshine cascaded in from the window behind him, glinting on his hair. His smile outshone the sunlight when he looked up to see her.

"Good morning, Sunshine." His dimple showed with his grin.

She ran forward and oh-so-carefully slipped an arm around him, bending down to give him a gentle hug. "Good morning!" She returned his cheerful greeting.

"A little bird told me you're on the team." He beamed as she seated herself beside his bed.

"Unofficially." She corrected, and then laughed. "For now, yep. You've got me."

His eyes glowed with something like wonder. "Was I dreaming last night when you told me... that *God* 'got you'?"

"You weren't dreaming. He's got me. All of me. I gave in." She sighed, remembering the complete terror that had engulfed her when she thought Bryce had died.

"I realized there's no holding back. At last, I let go of everything I was trying to hold tight... I confessed my sin and asked His forgiveness. I told God that I believed his Son gave his life for mine."

She watched the dust motes swirl in the sunbeam. "I'd known that, really. I went to Sunday school like a good little girl. But I never accepted it for *myself*."

She looked back to him. "So... then, I did. I actually promised him that even if you didn't make it, I would go on living for Him in your memory." Her voice shook with emotion.

He swallowed, as if deeply moved.

"... and then... He gave you back to me." The inexplicable joy flowed through her again. Would it ever stop? She hoped not. "You're alive."

~*~

So are you, forevermore. Into eternity. "And you have a new life in Christ." He was so overwhelmed that his voice came out a little wobbly.

Oh, God. I wanted this to happen so badly that I don't think I believed it ever would. I should have known better. Your ways are higher than ours.

She nodded. "I feel like I have so much to learn."

He smiled. "There is a lot to learn about God. I don't think any of us will find it all out before we reach heaven."

A quick knock sounded and then the door flew open. Angelwing entered, holding a file, which she handed to Bryce. "Here you go, dude. These are the options we've come up with for that 'fortress' in Berlin." She sighed. "None of them have anything like a tie to Ravenmeister that we can see. But take a look and let me know what you think." She was gone again almost before they had time to blink.

"Hmm." He flipped open the file on his lap. It was separated into four sections for the four forts and castles they'd come up with. He scanned each one quickly. Nothing. *Really, this is pitiful.* The info-crunchers must have been scraping the bottom of the barrel so hard that they'd have splinters underneath their fingernails.

"Good grief." He shut the file at last and looked up at Cara. "None of these fit what Ravenmeister would need for a secret base. One of them is still an active nunnery, for crying out loud!"

Cara leaned forward with a look on her face that begged for his attention, as if she was about to reveal something of great importance.

"Bryce, listen." She cradled her broken wrist in her left hand. "I've let you carry on your agency investigation without insisting we try out my ...'hunch', if you will, and we've gotten close. Very close. But not close enough."

It pained him to admit it, but she was right. "This is true."

"Freddie's done a great job so far of telling us where he'd be, but they're going to catch on eventually. He might have heard wrong about 'Berlin'." Her eyes were huge and full of sincerity. "We need to check out Mitch."

His mind raced. Mitch. Spoiled rich kid, seated at Mr. Gungerson's knee, probably catching dribbles of all the information they'd been reporting.

Mitch. Just because he gave them the creeps didn't mean he was involved with kidnappers and would-be murderers, but then again...

Mitch. The person Cara felt 'stalked' by.

"You know what... let's do some digging. We just might have found our traitor."

~*~

She and Bryce ate lunch together in his room, laughed about the bland hospital food, and pretended they weren't nearly jumping out of their skin in impatience while they waited for other people to investigate Mitchell Gungerson, Jr.

Montrose burst through the door without even knocking. Angelwing and Markdown followed him as he marched right up to the foot of Bryce's bed and gripped the metal bedframe with both hands. "Ashburn, we've got it."

Bryce sat bolt upright, sending his cherry Jell-O sliding into the mashed squash on the lunch tray. "What did you find out?"

"We tapped into Mitch's phone records and found that he's been calling numbers in Venice, Paris, and Germany!" Angelwing shouted in triumph. "Right where you've been!"

Bryce looked at Cara and gave her a delighted grin, then yanked his gaze back to his boss. "And did you trace the numbers in Germany?"

Monty nodded, almost sending his urban-styled glasses flying off his face. "Yes!" He pushed the glasses back up the bridge of his nose. "The last call was made to a number in Rheinland-Palatinate. A landline. We've found it."

"Wait, Rhineland... whatever you said... is that the city where they are?" Cara piped up.

Mr. Montrose laughed good-naturedly. "No, Rheinland-Palatinate is one of the German States. Within that state, the exact location of the place that Mitch called is on the Mosel River near the town of Koblenz." He leaned forward. "Entführt Castle, to be precise."

Bryce burst into an excited whoop as Cara yelled "Woohoo!" and leaped to her feet.

Montrose looked around the little circle of people. "Come on, everybody, let's move. We've got a castle to attack."

~*~

Cara had a difficult job to do.

Mr. Montrose had ordered her to keep Bryce from overexerting himself. He was not to let himself get excited, nor could he move around overmuch. He was supposed to stay still and rest... which he seemed very disinclined to do.

Before they left Munich, the agency doctor had given strict orders about getting as much sleep as possible and being careful not to stretch or disturb the wound site that he had so neatly stitched up. Cara had listened, eager to absorb the information, while Bryce yawned.

Now they were at some kind of top-secret outpost approximately twenty miles away from Entführt Castle. Outside, it looked like an ordinary mid-size german house – small by American standards – and was surrounded by a diminutive fenced pasture with three dairy cows grazing contentedly.

On the inside, marble flooring. Sterile, no-nonsense light gray walls. Fluorescent lighting. And technology *everywhere.*

They'd moved a plump leather couch for Bryce into the hub of the enterprise, the innermost room where Mr. Montrose was laying out their plans while technicians studied satellite imagery of the fortress site.

She and Bryce sat on the couch while Angel and the others hovered like bees around a table spread with maps, lists, geological readouts, and miscellaneous important papers concerning the castle.

Cara marveled at the masterful way that Mr. Montrose was managing the operation. Three surveillance squads were scouting the area around the castle with long-range sensors and telescopes.

Mr. Montrose waved a computer printout of a zoomed-in satellite picture in front of Bryce's face. "Does this man look familiar to you?"

ASHBURN

Julia Erickson

It was an image of a man standing in front of an old wooden door in a stone wall, holding a pair of binoculars at his side.

Bryce grabbed the sheet and studied it. Then he looked straight up at his boss. "This is one of the guys that chased us through Paris. I'm 100% sure."

Mr. Montrose snapped his fingers and a smile sprang to his coffee-colored face. "A connection to Ravenmeister already!" He fairly skipped back to the table, humming to himself as he shuffled through papers.

Cara looked up at Bryce's handsome profile. "You know what? I thought your boss was a little old-school with his bowtie and moustache... not to mention the loafers..." She kept her voice to a low murmur, which blended in with the cacophony of noises in the room so that the others couldn't overhear.

He turned his head to look down at her. "Yeah, he does give you that impression at first. But as old-school as he might appear on the outside, he's got cutting-edge technology under his belt, and he knows how to use it."

"Experience blended with modern conveniences, eh?"

"Precisely." Bryce sent an admiring glance at his boss, who was talking in an excited manner to one of the technicians seated at the computers.

Mr. Montrose paced over to them. "Have a look at this, you two."

Bryce took a piece of paper from him. "Geological stats?"

"...Which nicely corroborate an ancient document that Angelwing unearthed. Don't ask me where she got it. I suspect she had to bribe some librarian."

Cara leaned over Bryce's shoulder and looked at the color-coded rendering of the land around Entführt Castle. "Interpretation, if you please?"

He looked up. "Oh, I'm sorry." He used two fingers to stroke areas of the map as he began to explain. "These bands of color represent the depth of the land, the rise and fall of the hills. What's interesting me are these purple areas here-"

"-Which mean underground chambers." Mr. Montrose smiled as if in great satisfaction. "There's an underground river that runs below the castle to join up with a tributary of the Mosel River, which curves around the whole point of land on which the castle rests."

Bryce rolled his eyes. "Way to steal the punch line, boss."

Monty grinned. He swiped the paper away from Bryce again. "You stay put like a good boy, and I'll see what we can cook up with this." He whacked the paper in his hand for emphasis as he strode away once more.

A low sigh drifted from Bryce as he sat back against the couch.

She leaned a little closer to his side. "If I didn't know better, I'd say you were sulking."

He glanced down at her without moving his head. Then he grinned and lifted his arm to settle it around her shoulders.

"Oh, oh, careful, we don't want you to stretch your wound-" She gently touched the spot where the bullet had hit him, as if that would help somehow.

"I'm fine. It hurts no matter what I do." He sounded irked, gazing with longing at the table heaped with papers.

"I just… care about you, that's all." She rested her cheek against his shoulder.

He gave her a meaningful look. Then he smiled, and proceeded to dub her with a new nickname. "Thanks, Carebear."

Carebear? Before she could comment on that, Angelwing let out a squeal worthy of a barnyard piglet. "Oooh! *Guys!* Come here!"

Cara hopped up, deserting Bryce on the couch, and dashed to her side, all but colliding with Mr. Montrose as they both reached her at once. "What is it, Angel?" the boss peered at the book that Angelwing held open.

"It's something that I doubt the Ravenmeister boys know." Angelwing traced a manicured maroon fingernail across one line of the text. "It says here that 'the Castle Entführt was supplied with water during a siege by a well dug in the center of the castle, allowing the inhabitants to procure water for washing and consumption without having to set foot outside the castle walls'."

She lowered the book. "Monty… if the well shaft is still there, it would connect to that underground river on the geo stats."

"All *right!*" Bryce shouted, pumping one fist in the air.

Mr. Montrose clapped his hands together once, an excited gleam in his eyes. "Great work, Angelwing." He turned to the whole assembly of people, who were watching him with attentive expressions. "Listen up, everybody. We've just found our way in."

~*~

Bryce could feel the tension building in the air. Angelwing and the other agents had spent most of the night verifying important details like whether or not the well shaft had been filled in – it hadn't, and the old well was clearly visible from the satellite imagery – and arranging for their watercraft.

Their boss gathered all the agents at the outpost into the dining room and briefed them on the mission.

The plan was intricate but simple at the same time. They would distract the guards on the walls and turrets with a diversion – a big, noisy tour boat would drive up to the side of the castle, looking like they'd gotten 'lost' and turned off the main river.

Meanwhile, the real attack force would move in from underneath. The underground river could be accessed through a cave about ten miles out, on the other side of the massive hills that formed the valley in which the castle lurked.

From there, 20 people – including four U.S. Navy SEALs that were flying in with special permission from the I.C.E. to help out with the job – would move in on two CRRC Zodiac boats, following the underground river until they reached the 85-foot well shaft. Once there, the SEALs would scale the rock walls of the well and send down lines with harnesses to haul the other agents up to the top. Once inside the castle walls they'd easily be able to subdue the Ravenmeister employees using the element of surprise and automatic machine guns, if necessary.

Hopes for the result of the assault on Castle Entführt were to secure Freddie – and his ID chip – capture Black, and incriminate Ravenmeister, Inc. should they uncover evidence of the illegal arms trade.

The German government was cooperating, but insisted upon imprisoning Ryan Black in German incarceration should the mission succeed.

"What are Zodiac boats?" Cara asked later, after the talk had concluded. She pushed him in a wheelchair as they were walking back to the 'planning room'.

"We call 'em 'Zodiacs', but the correct name for one is a F470 Combat Rubber Raiding Craft. They're specially fabricated rubber inflatable boats, often used by the Navy SEALs and Marines, among others."

"Man." Cara's eyes widened in amazement.

"Yeah." He could feel the grin spreading across his face. "Seriously. They're all black, low to the water, and practically invisible in the dark. Operations involving them almost always take place at night and depend on stealth."

They reached the door of the 'planning' room, and the door banged open and Montrose emerged, his face ashen.

"Ashburn." He looked surprised but glad to see Bryce. "Somebody just raised the stakes."

"What is it?" *Just when we thought things were going well...*

His boss rubbed a hand over his whole face, something Bryce had only seen him do when he was *really* upset. "We just got an encrypted message from our agent at Silver Strand. The open-access entry codes for the Personal ID Implant Chip have been stolen."

Cara turned white. "Freddie's chip?"

Montrose nodded once. "Gungerson is frantic."

Bryce pulled in a deep breath. "This is bad."

"Wait, wait-" Cara waved a hand as if trying to halt the conversation for a second. "This means that whoever has those codes can access the information on Freddie's chip?"

Monty's eyes were full of concern. "That... and whoever has those codes and the right device to send them into Freddie's arm can take out the chip and steal it without setting off the anti-removal explosion."

Bryce clenched a fist, feeling the blood pounding through his veins. "And that's the only protection that has kept Freddie alive so long."

"Oh, God." Cara breathed softly, pressing a hand to her mouth. It was a desperate prayer.

Monty set his mouth into a grim line. "We're moving up the invasion. The original time was tomorrow morning, a few minutes after sunrise."

He sent a bullet-like glance into each of their faces. "We're going in at midnight."

~*~

A freezing chill shot down Cara's back. The stars flashed by above as they zoomed towards their destination – the cave. She was second-guessing her request to come along... after all, only twenty people were going to fit on the two eight-foot by six-foot black boats, and that was at maximum capacity. But Mr. Montrose had immediately agreed, saying that Freddie might need a face he trusted. Anything could happen.

Both Bryce and Angelwing had backed her up, saying that Cara would be safe surrounded by Agency personnel and Navy SEALs.

And now here she was. Dashing through the cold night inside one of the two vehicles that raced through the dark in tandem. The van in which she rode seemed more like an extended 4-wheel drive SUV, and held most of the people who were on the mission tonight. The other one was a beefy truck with two deflated Zodiacs rolled up in the bed.

The four SEALS from SEAL team 5 had arrived at the outpost just after 9:00 PM, and seemed like nice guys, though definitely bigger and more hard-muscled than most. In their black suits, they looked dangerous.

I'm glad they're on our side!

The only familiar face in the van among the agents was Bryce. Cara felt comforted by his presence. He, like the other occupants of the van, looked serious and ready for anything. He still moved carefully, but was so determined to be a part of the rescue operation, that Montrose hadn't tried to stop him.

Angelwing and Markdown were stationed on the fake pleasure boat full of agents ready to swarm the castle. A veritable 'Trojan horse'. To fit the change in timing plans, the deck was strung with lights and strewn with empty beer bottles.

Everyone inside the van leaned against the pull of gravity as the van braked to a stop. Then the order came. "Everybody out."

Cara scrunched into the corner, staying out of the way as the SEALs and Agents deployed first. Then she followed them out. Waiting for her at the opening was Bryce. He smiled as he reached up a hand to help her down. She smiled back and grasped it with her unbroken hand. He grunted as she hopped down.

"Oh! Did I hurt you?"

He shook his head. "But we sure are a pair, aren't we? You with your cracked wrist and me with a hole in my chest." He winked. "Come on. Let's show 'em together."

The SEALs nearly had the boats inflated by the time Cara had walked to the entrance of the cave. Her curiosity about how twenty people were going to fit on the two small boats was answered. They stacked on top of each other, lying on their stomachs. She was just grateful she'd ended up on the end, leaning against Bryce.

Soon they were motoring through the underground tunnel, silent but for the lapping of the water against the triangular prows of the boats and the low hum of the engines. A specially-trained 'coxswain' controlled each boat from the rear.

All of the people on the boats wore inter-communication headsets, Markdown and Angelwing over on the Mosel River, and also Mr. Montrose, back at the outpost. Montrose would be coordinating the whole thing from on high with his satellite transmissions.

They traveled in the dark, and even through the night-vision goggles Cara wore, not much was visible. A few times they had to duck low as the earth above them drew within a few feet of their heads, and she felt like her heart was about to stop from the fear that they'd be crushed to their deaths.

But the river moved them on, and on. It felt like they were never going to get there when she heard Montrose's voice in her headset.

"Teams Yellow and Orange, you're about to come up to the well shaft. Prepare to stand by."

That was them, underground. Markdown and Angelwing were 'Team Red'.

And then, ahead, the walls opened up into a space about twenty feet across and seven feet high, tapering up in a cone to a circular shaft that stretched up, up, up.

They'd entered the well.

~*~

"Okay boss, we're in position at the end of the tributary." Markdown reported in as the helmsman brought the boat to a halt. "Ready to move when you say the word."

Angel and five of the other agents stood on deck, dressed in tourist clothing, already getting into their cover of partiers as they drew near the castle. The rest of the team hid down the hatch, along with all the guns.

"Okay. Get going. I'll alert the others."

He nodded to the agent at the helm, who shifted the throttle and steered for the tributary. Angelwing flipped on the twinkling lights and started up the pounding stereo, bobbing her head in time to the hip-hop music. "Whooo! Let's get this party started!"

~*~

In the near-silence, every tiny sound was magnified. The river sloshed past them and swirled on into the darkness. Bryce could smell the clammy dampness of the air and see the roof of the tunnel glistening.

"Team Red is moving in. Stand by." Signal clicks sounded as the agents and SEALs responded to Monty's directive.

The adrenaline rushed through his body faster than the water running under their boats. As a result, he felt 'good' for the first time since he'd been shot. His chest ached with a dull throb, but he'd endured worse in his years as an agent.

Besides, he'd made a promise to Freddie. He would see this one to the finish.

~*~

The music pumped an infectious beat as they motored up to the castle, which towered hundreds of feet tall in the moonlight. The agents on deck were laughing and singing along, one of them even drunkenly smashing a bottle against the deck for authenticity.

"We're approaching the Castle." Angelwing whispered into her microphone.

"Good. We've got action. The guards on the walls are starting to move to your side. They're all watching your boat now. I'm sending in Teams Yellow and Orange." Montrose's voice undulated in the smooth tones of the professional.

~*~

"Go."

It was as if the short word from Monty was the fuse that set off an explosion of activity. The four SEALs hoisted themselves up and scaled the rock sides of the shaft as easily as if they were cave spiders.

Cara shivered as she watched them crawl up towards the light. They had eighty-five feet to go in as short a time as possible, for it wasn't certain how long the party boat would hold the attention of the guards up top.

Then they were only specks moving towards the height of the shaft. Within minutes, four lines were sent down attached to harnesses that four people could buckle themselves into at a time, all in a row like legs belonging to a caterpillar. The two coxswains would remain below to manage the boats. Everybody else was going up.

Bryce secured her into a harness behind two other agents with lightning movements and then snapped himself in at the back. All four harnesses full with four people each, they clicked their headsets with the 'ready' signal and began to move. Assisted from above, they clambered up the rock walls. At last, they reached the top and climbed over the edge of the old well.

They emerged in a courtyard in the heart of the castle. Three wings of the building branched off, with innumerable stairways, doors and windows dotting the surroundings. The few guards on duty in the middle of the night had all moved to the outer wall, and even now could be heard shouting at the boat down by the river, telling them to go away.

The SEALs moved out to disarm the guards, who wouldn't see the silent shadows moving near until it was too late. The group of Agents separated into the three parts of the castle, watching for any movement as they went.

Bryce grabbed her left hand and tipped his head towards a darkened archway. They moved through it together and found a room with three doors. Trying each one in turn, Bryce chose the one with stairs leading steeply down. She followed him as they curved down through the spiraling stone steps, soon entering an even darker part of the castle where almost no moonlight penetrated.

One fat candle burned in a holder on the wall of a stone hallway that sloped down. It was quiet all around but for their soft footsteps.

"Something's telling me that Freddie's being held in the dungeon." His words came out as a low rumble. "It fits Ryan Black's usual modus operandi."

She shuddered, and he squeezed her hand. "Come on. Let's go rescue him."

~*~

Tatiana led the man along the cavernous corridor by the yellow light of the oil lamp, trying to conceal her disgust. He was a truly horrible puffed-up windbag oozing a foul odor of greed.

"I suppose your Mr. Black was too much of a wuss to meet me himself, so he sent you to take me to Donaldson."

"When you arrive in middle of night, you take what you get." She sent him a cold glance. "I not know where Ryan is – he has gone for walk around grounds to clear his mind. He could not sleep. And now you come with no warning."

The big man raised his free hand. "Hey, I'm not complaining. Far be it from me to gripe about spending time with a hot babe."

Insufferable boor! Tatiana sniffed, pulling the jangling keys out of her pocket. They were almost to the cell. One more flight of stairs and then she could leave the man with the prisoner.

"Here he is." They were at the innermost low point of the castle, deep underground. Tatiana unlocked the heavy wooden door braced with iron hinges and swung it open with a loud creak.

Freddie looked up at them from the floor scattered with moldy straw, fear leaping into his eyes.

She shoved the lamp at the man she'd escorted. "You take this. I will find my own way back. Tatiana is not afraid of the dark." She turned and sashayed away.

~*~

Shock and dread crashed against each other in Freddie's mind.

In front of him stood his boss's son, wearing a frightening smile and carrying an expensive briefcase, leather sides reflecting the flickering light from the oil lamp.

"Mr. Mitch?" A shred of hope filtered in. Maybe he was here to rescue him!

The hope fled with Mitch's laugh. It wasn't a happy sound, but full of ire and bitterness. "I see my reputation precedes me."

Oh no. Anger frothed in his chest. *He's one of the badguys. HE'S the one who's been feeding the information to them! Dirty traitor.*

~*~

Bryce knew they had to be getting close. The condition of the castle deteriorated as they descended.

Cara grabbed his arm and tugged, pulling him to a stop along the side of the hall. "Shh." She breathed, a finger to her lips.

Then he heard it too. A man's voice. A familiar one.

It belonged to Mitch Gungerson.

"I've brought something special along. You should recognize it... you helped develop it, after all." A clicking noise, like a latch opening.

"See? An X2 scanner. Programmed especially to mesh with that lovely little piece of technology in that skinny arm of yours. And I was able to snitch those all-important little codes from dear old dad, so we'll be able to remove the thing without setting off a blast. Isn't that nice?"

"You're... you're making a mistake." *Freddie's voice!*

Bryce's heart leapt into his throat and lodged there.

Electronic beeps. "I think not. With the money from the sale of this little chip, I'll be able to live in comfort for the rest of my days, surrounded by good food, bright sunshine, and plenty of beautiful women."

Then an angry grunt. "Too bad I couldn't get the one girl I really wanted. But Black may come through yet."

"Are you talking about Cara?" Freddie spoke up again, the tremor in his voice diminished.

A few seconds of silence. "Why you little... how did you know I meant her?"

"Oh, I kinda heard through the office grapevine that you had a crush on her. She's pretty, isn't she?"

He stole a look at Cara. She closed her eyes and put a hand to her forehead as if she couldn't believe this was happening. Her cheeks were red.

"Just the cutest thing on two long legs I've ever seen. And I've seen plenty, lemme tell ya."

Now Cara had her good hand clenched into a fist. Fury flashed in her eyes. *"Jerk!"* She mouthed the word.

"All right, it's been nice chatting, but time to get down to business. First let's send these codes into the chip."

Bryce knew it was time to move. He stole forward in time to look through the open doorway and see Mitch Gungerson brandishing a slim white device in the direction of Freddie's arm.

In a motion that felt as natural as breathing, he'd drawn his Colt M1911 and had it aimed for Mitch's head. "Okay Mitch, drop the scanner."

The back of Mitch's head stiffened. "Reynolds." He gritted the word out from between his teeth like he was cursing.

"Yup. In person."

Freddie gave him a big smile. "I knew you'd come-"

Mitch whirled, throwing the scanner in his direction. He dodged it and shot at Mitch's hand that was reaching for the gun in his pants pocket, stinging the back of it with a red scrape.

Mitch shrieked like a little kid and slapped his other hand over the bullet nick. "Owww!" He whined.

"That was the warning shot. Now pull the gun out slowly and *drop it on the ground.*" He infused his words with threatening fury.

Mitch narrowed his eyes, but slowly began to comply, removing the gun from his pocket with two fingers, but at the last moment he tossed it into the oil lamp that sat on the floor, crashing the glass globe and spilling kerosene and flames across the highly flammable straw-covered ground. Fire whooshed through the room as Mitch charged for the opening with an animal-like cry.

He had no choice but to pull the trigger.

Mitch collapsed forward onto the floor of the corridor, and Bryce looked up to see Cara already through the door, darting through the flames to Freddie's side.

He leaped to help them, screaming her name. "*Cara!* Get out of there!" She had her good arm around Freddie and was dragging him as he stumbled for the door. He grabbed them and tugged, pulling them through the door, then heaved it shut behind them, encasing the fire in the cell, for now.

Coughing and choking, Cara pointed to the limp mountain of flesh that was Mitch Gungerson. "Is he *dead*?" She gasped out, horror on what he could see of her face.

He bent next to the fallen man. "I don't know." And then he felt his pulse, beating steadily. "Nope. I'm getting a pulse. He's alive."

"Oh!" Freddie leaned against the wall, looking like he didn't know what to say. He stared nervously at the door with the fire behind it. "Um…"

"Everybody stay calm." Bryce turned on the radio in his headset. "Monty?"

"Ashburn! Where in blazes are you?"

Hmph. Interesting choice of words. And suddenly his code name was very apropos. "We have Freddie, and Mitch Gungerson, on the lowest floor down here. Mitch has been shot and will require some medical attention. There is also a small fire in the dungeon."

"We'll be right down." It was Markdown. "Great work, Ashburn. We have things under control up here."

"Roger that." He turned to Freddie and Cara. "They've got the upstairs wrapped up."

Cara looked stunned, eyes huge. "It's all over?"

He grinned at her, bracing himself for another swoon. "We did it."

She surprised him by jumping at him and throwing her arms around his neck. "Yes!" She yelled in victory, and then laughed, her features relaxing in relief.

He hugged her back, hiding his face in the hair piled on top of her head. She smelled like smoke, but a hint of sweet perfume still lingered. Then he peeked up to see Freddie standing awkwardly on one foot.

He shifted Cara to one side and held open his other arm. "Group hug!"

Grinning, Freddie hobbled closer and looped one arm around his shoulder and the other around Cara's back. "Thanks, guys." The grateful look in his eyes said more than words ever could.

~*~

The main floor of the castle was completely lit by electric battery-powered lanterns by the time Cara followed Bryce up into the open air again. Pairs and groups of Ravenmeister employees sat on the ground against the walls wearing handcuffs behind their backs while the SEALs and other agents stood guard. The roses planted along the edges of the courtyard released a sweet, heady fragrance in the moonlight.

Both Freddie and Mitch got carted off by the medical staff and were on their way to the nearest hospital. Mitch for his gunshot wound, Freddie for two broken ribs and a severely sprained ankle, not to mention malnutrition and dehydration.

She watched as Bryce smoothly meshed into the hubbub, checking with an agent here, talking to another there, and catching up on all the action that had gone down while they'd been having their own fiery adventure below. He barked orders and made quick, chopping gestures, and people jumped to obey. This side of him was a hard, sharp, competent *agent*.

Cara flinched when a wide medieval-arched door banged open and clanked against the wall. Out came Angelwing, pushing in front of her the same woman that Cara had seen at the clearing where Bryce had been shot. She held a pistol to the woman's back and was prodding her with it to get her to move.

The woman locked eyes with her as they stood in the middle of the courtyard. "*You!*" She hissed and screeched, flailing against Angelwing's grip on her elbow.

Three other male agents ran up to assist Angelwing, grabbing the woman, who fought like an enraged tigress until one of them fired a warning shot straight up into the night sky. Then she froze, panting for breath.

"Hey, Markdown, we found the weapons stash. The illegal arms dealership HQ is a tricked-out room down there." Angel tipped her head towards the door she'd just exited.

Markdown nodded quickly and clattered down the steps inside the doorway, four other agents filing after him.

"Okay, Tatiana. *Where is Ryan Black?*" Angel demanded, walking around to the front of the woman and sliding her gun back into the holster she wore on her hip.

Tatiana's gaze eerily centered on Cara as she spoke. "He is gone. He went to find *her.*"

Bryce's attention, like everyone else in the area, had been drawn to Tatiana's struggle, and now he stepped closer to Cara and moved an arm around her, sheltering her against his side.

"Where did he go?" Angel folded her lean arms across her midsection and grilled Tatiana with her brown eyes.

"I do not know, he would not tell me! He left. He has gone away." She burst into a storm of wild sobbing. "I will never see him again now!" She bowed her head, her black hair falling across her face like a veil as she wept.

Angelwing jerked a thumb towards the front of the castle. "Get her out of here."

The three men dragged Tatiana away. Her shrieks faded down the hall.

Angel pressed a hand to her headset and began talking to Command Center as she paced a track through the gravel flooring in the courtyard.

Bryce turned to Cara. "You're leaving. Now."

She wanted to stay with him. She felt safer at his side. "No, please–"

"Black is on the loose, Cara. He could be anywhere, ready to kill you. Please, listen to me. You need to get to a safe place." His eyes filled, and shock tingled down her spine as tears spilled down his cheeks, glinting in the white light from the lanterns. "Don't do this to me, Cara. *I don't want to lose you!*" He shouted the last words, gripping her arms.

A flash of lightning electrified the sky and a roll of thunder boomed overhead. A storm front obscured the moon and stars with slow fingers of dark cloud.

Stunned, Cara ignored the bustle and movements of the agents around them, and reached up a hand to wipe the tears from his face.

"*You* are my safe place." She laid her hand and broken wrist against his chest, melting against him as his arms encircled her. She gently pressed her cheek against his chest, in the same place the bullet had nearly killed him.

"He wants to kill *you* too." She whispered. He rested his chin against the top of her head. "If you don't come with me, I'm not going." *And I mean that.*

With another burst of thunder, rain began to patter down on their faces.

"I'm needed here-"

"No, you're not. The others are wrapping things up. Come with me."

"All right. I'll come." As Bryce lifted his head, a gunshot echoed across the courtyard and Cara felt Bryce's whole frame jerk forward from the force of the blow.

She had a view over Bryce's shoulder and the image burned into her brain in an instant. On the topmost wall, Ryan Black stood silhouetted against the moonlit sky with his hair whipping in the night wind, a gun lifted to his shoulder.

But the bullet ricocheted off Bryce's back and bit into the gravel at their feet.

"*Down!* Everybody *down!*" Bryce roared as he dove behind the raised stone circle of the well four feet away, pulling her with him. The agents and SEALs in the courtyard hit the ground as Ryan Black sent more bullets through the rain.

Cara heard a whimper off to her right, and jerked her head to see Angelwing clutching her right forearm, her face drawn with pain, curled up next to the stone wall.

~*~

His thoughts were scrambling worse than eggs on a skillet. Black had them pinned. While they sat there in the light from the lanterns, he perched up there in the dark with his gun, waiting to pick off anything that moved, angling for a shot at him and Cara.

The Dragon Armor he wore underneath his jumpsuit, a thin stretchy layer of bulletproof material that felt like rubber, had saved his life. He'd suffer from nothing worse than a bruise. Monty had insisted he wear it, and now Bryce was beyond glad that he'd listened.

The rain pelted down like it was shooting at them too, with hard drops that bounced off the ground.

He nestled his face close to Cara's. "Listen to me, Cara. You have to listen. *Stay. Here.*"

God, please let her obey me!

"I may be your safe place, but right now I have to save some lives, and to do it I have to leave you here. Will you trust me?"

"I trust you." Her words were soft and swift.

Thank you. "Good. I'm going to run up there and stop him. Stay here, you'll be ok, he can't get you from this angle." *Unless he moves, in which case a Navy SEAL will probably send a bullet through his head, so he won't.*

"Hurry. Angel's been shot in the arm." He followed Cara's gaze to a small form huddled in the fetal position next to the courtyard wall. At the sight, pain lanced through his chest.

She could bleed to death in a matter of minutes. Limb hits were some of the worst gunshot wounds because of the danger of blood loss. "Don't worry, I'll move fast."

He pressed his nose against her neck. "I love you." He whispered.

And then he made his move. He pushed to his feet and streaked for the courtyard wall. A bullet buried into the gravel next to him on his way there but he reached the wall's temporary shelter unscathed. He took two breaths before bounding up the first flight of stairs. So far, so good. Now to work his way up farther.

Routine. This is just part of your routine. He willed his racing heartbeat to slow down, trying to trick his mind into a state of cool calculation.

He crouched by the craggy, cliff-like side of the wall and then took off across the open space between him and the second stairway. Another shot bounced off his arm just before he reached the stairs, and he was up them before Black could shoot again.

Now Black had figured out that his torso and limbs were bulletproof. He would be aiming for the head next, which was unprotected.

Bryce crept inside a circular turret with stone window frames. Ivy curled through the crevices of the rock. The leaves were wet from the rain blowing through the breaches in the wall.

Out came the M1911.

He wouldn't be able to use the window to fire at Black. It was too exposed. But then he saw it.

An arrow slit.

He wedged the barrel of his gun into the narrow opening and stared straight at the crooked black silhouette where Ryan Black crouched, facing in his direction.

He fired.

Black crumpled. Bryce moved to the window openings and looked down on the still form of his enemy.

He walked through the turret and opened the creaking door on the other side, coming out on the narrow walk from which Ryan Black had been waging his one-man war.

He took three steps towards the man and halted.

It was then that Black sprang up like a panther and blew a shot straight for his head. Bryce jerked aside and from instinct, shot from the hip.

Black let out a strangled cry, twisted, and met space with his outstretched arms, falling down the castle wall hundreds of feet until his body bounced off the cliff and plummeted into the river.

He did not surface.

~*~

Chapter Twelve
The Diamond

He swept her into a hug as he stepped off the last stair and his boots crunched onto the gravel. Cara's arms locked around him so tight, it seemed like she'd never be able to let go. And he was fine with that.

"I saw the whole thing." Cara sobbed into his black jumpsuit.

"Shh. It's okay. *I'm* okay." He pressed his hands against her back.

"Did he die?" Her voice trembled.

"Yes. He's dead." They would find the body, verify it. At least twenty countries would be clamoring for proof of the man's demise.

"What about Angelwing – is she okay?" He didn't see her anywhere in the group of agents mulling around.

Cara lifted her head. "Yes, they said she'll be fine. Markdown is escorting her to the hospital." She smiled proudly. "You saved her life. They said if she'd had to wait there much longer – through a standoff, for instance – she would've lost too much blood."

The rain had abated and now fell as a soft mist. People were arriving in a continuing stream to collect crime scene evidence and document the area, lights glaring everywhere.

Their work here was done. "Time for me to escort you away too." He turned and she followed, still keeping her left arm wrapped around his back with a firm grip on his belt. He supported her with an arm around her waist.

They nearly walked into Montrose near the front bridge. "Ashburn! Cara! Glad to see you all in *one piece*." His brown eyes sparkled with humor.

A laugh welled up from his soul and tumbled out of his mouth. His boss would never let him forget this one. He and Cara were holding each other so tightly that it truly did look like they were one piece instead of two different people. He liked the idea. *And they shall become one flesh...*

"Monty, what are you doing here down on the scene instead of back at Command Center?"

"I wanted to keep a close eye on things and make sure everything went according to procedure. There's gonna be eyes on this one, Bryce." He leaned forward. "In fact, I hear someone's up for a medal for bravery."

"Diamond here sure deserves one." He looked down into Cara's oval-shaped face. "She literally ran through fire to help rescue Freddie."

Montrose nodded. "I heard about that. I'm glad none of you were burned."

Cara turned her face up to look at him. "Let's go now."

Monty waved them towards a waiting car. "Best idea I've heard all evening, Diamond. You two get outta here and go get some rest."

"Diamond?" Cara whispered with a curious expression as he opened the door for her.

"Your new code name. I'll explain later." He grinned before closing her door and walking around to the driver's side.

His exhausted little sparrow fell asleep in her seat before he could even start the car.

~*~

After a hot shower and a German breakfast of cold sliced sausage and cheese with a buttered roll and a cup of strong coffee, Cara felt like a new person. She'd given in and borrowed Angelwing's hairdryer. Her hair would just have to forgive her. She managed to fashion it into a simple ponytail with just her left hand.

Matthias and Myra had kindly sent on her suitcase from their house, so she'd been able to wear her own clothes this morning, something she never knew she'd appreciate so much. She slipped her fingers inside a pocket and found the *Paris Amour*.

I wonder if Bryce liked it. He didn't say. She stared at the bottle. *Oh, why not.* She spritzed a light mist onto her throat.

A knock came at the door, making her start and drop the perfume. "Come in." She snatched the bottle and chucked it into her suitcase.

Bryce entered, dressed in a blue polo shirt and khakis. Her resident butterflies decided to make their appearance known.

"There you are!" He looked pleased, as if he'd made a great discovery.

"There *you* are, you mean." She pointed a finger in his direction. "I wondered where you'd run off to."

"I had a lot of wrap-up paperwork to finish." He smiled at her as she rose and walked up to him. "Did you bring a pair of sneakers?"

Cara looked down at her sock feet. "I did, but I won't be able to tie them."

"I will." He winked. "Go ahead and get them out."

She obeyed, pulling the shoes from her case. "What is all this about?" *He's acting a little... mysterious.*

"I've got a pretty spot to show you." He tilted his head. "Feeling up for a walk along the river?"

She was still tired from yesterday, but peaceful scenery was just what she needed. "Yes, I'd like that." She sat on the bed and slipped the sneakers onto her feet.

Bryce kneeled in front of her and tied her shoes, pulling the laces to just the right degree of snugness.

How can you be so sweet? She thanked him with a warm smile.

He slapped the shoe he'd just secured to her foot as if finishing it off with a flourish. "Let's go."

~*~

A warm breeze caressed their faces and the sun shone down through a blue sky decorated with puffs of white clouds. Towering green hills hung over the river valley, which dived down to meet the waterfront. The surface of the water was so smooth and glassy that the sky and clouds were perfectly mirrored on it.

Boats cruised lazily down the Mosel, transporting passengers hither and yon wherever they cared to go, which just might be nowhere in particular, considering how lovely the surroundings were.

Bryce looked over at Cara's profile. That tantalizing fragrance she'd been wearing in Venice drifted from her this morning.

"I have to say, whatever you're wearing, it smells great." He risked telling her his thoughts.

She blushed most becomingly, with a demure smile. "Thank you. It's some perfume Penny gave me."

They walked hand-in-hand down the riverside until they came to the end of the path.

"Come on." He walked forward into the grass. "Let's climb a little."

The woods greeted them with the fresh scent of spruce. He led her by the hand as they walked single-file through the lush growth, following the river that dropped below. Then they came to an open shelf of land that had a beautiful view downstream. He waved to a huge flat-topped rock that lay half-sunken in the earth. "Have a seat, milady."

Cara sat and primly crossed her legs, cradling her broken wrist in her lap, then sent him a playful smile. *Wonder what she's thinking right now?* She intrigued him. He wanted to find out all her secrets, unlock the mysteries of her heart.

~*~

Cara watched, curious, as Bryce began to pace back and forth in front of her. Then he stopped with a sudden halt and stared intently at her.

"The life of a secret agent is rough. There aren't many perks besides the knowledge that you're serving your country in a manner few are brave enough to."

She nodded. "I can't say that I understand, not being one myself, but I can definitely imagine." *It must be so hard.*

He let out a short laugh. "Yeah. We have to make sacrifices for our job's sake. We put our lives on the line on a regular basis."

He walked a little closer. "Our families live in constant fear of us getting hurt… or worse."

She listened in silence. His meaning was starting to get across. "You're wondering if I would ever consider putting myself in that position."

He gave an emphatic nod, then froze. A bird started up a lilting tune in the woods nearby somewhere.

Cara looked down the river. "I have to be honest."

He gulped. "Go ahead."

"If I was a mother, I wouldn't want my children knowing that any day they could get a call telling them that their mom had been killed in the line of duty."

A light flickered in his eyes. He resumed his energetic pacing.

"Exactly. I have promised myself that I would be there for my kids, if I ever have any, and I would really, *really* like to. I wouldn't be able to continue my current work in that case. I'd have to move to a desk job within the Agency, instead of being a field agent."

He turned to face her squarely. "...Which I would be willing to do when the time came."

Her heart trembled inside her chest as she realized they were discussing *children*. She bit her lip and hid her gaze in the view down by the river. The desire to be a mommy one day surged within. She had dreamed of holding her own precious babies.

"What do you think about that?" His soft whisper broke through her consciousness.

She looked up at him again. The yearning on his face nearly brought tears to her eyes.

"I could live with that." Her answer was true. She would be willing to risk someday being the wife of a secret agent... if that agent was Bryce.

He clasped both of her hands in his, using great tenderness with her right hand in its cast, and helped her to her feet.

"I want to know everything about you." He smiled. "I'd like to spend lots of time together, meet your family, and find out how many colors your eyes can change."

She laughed. Her eyes had always had a weird trick of doing that. "Oh, you noticed. Isn't that funny?"

"It's fascinating." His grin changed into a more thoughtful look. "But I'm serious about wanting a relationship with you. Cara... will you be my girlfriend?"

Yes, yes, yes! Oh wow, I am so lucky. No – blessed. "Of course I will!"

"Yes!" He pumped a fist in the air, and they laughed together. "I was hoping you'd say that."

Bryce leaned forward and kissed her on the forehead. "Come on, let's head back and get some lunch." He drew her left arm through the crook of his elbow, and they followed the river back through the woods.

~*~

Cara thought it sweet how Bryce always drove her around, rather than vice versa. She didn't mind… but she missed her Jetta.

They stopped at a red light on their way back to the Agency outpost, and Bryce looked over to her and saw her smiling in his direction.

He slapped his knee. "Oh, I almost forgot! Cara, I'm so sorry-"

"Whoa, wait, look, the light's turning!" She pointed out the windshield, hating to interrupt him, but it had to be done.

"Oh, thanks." Horns beeped as he accelerated. "What I meant to say is, Cara, I'm so sorry about that time in the car when you smiled at me and I looked away. I had a good reason."

Now this is interesting. "Let's hear it."

His eyes followed the road ahead as he drove. "It might take some time to explain, but I'll try to keep it brief. The Bible tells Christians not to become unequally yoked."

The mental light bulb clicked on.

"Oh, I know what you're going to say. I heard a sermon preached on that when I was a teenager."

She shrugged. "I stopped going to church after I left home." A regretful sigh drifted from her.

"I see. So you understand the metaphor. Two oxen pulling at one yoke have to be traveling in the same direction, or their walk through life will be total chaos, and it's the same thing with us."

"Yes. Christians and unbelievers are walking different paths and won't be equally yoked in a relationship."

"Precisely." Bryce thumped the steering wheel. "That's why I knew I had to discourage you from becoming attracted to me. You weren't in a relationship with God at that point, so I couldn't be in a relationship with you."

The tiny rip that had been made in her heart at the previous rejection smoothed out, perfectly healed. "I understand now."

He took another moment to look at her before returning his gaze to the road.

"I didn't tell you that before because I didn't want you to... come to God because you wanted me." He dipped his head. "As prideful as that sounds, it's the truth."

"I don't think it sounds prideful. It was beautiful and selfless." She grinned. "Though, at the time, it made me mad enough to spit nails."

~*~

They took a quick stop at the hospital to visit Angelwing and Markdown before lunch. Angel told them that she was expected to be released that day, and looked mightily pleased at the prospect. She was already back to her spunky self.

Back at the agency outpost, Mr. Montrose called them into his office. He and Cara stood in front of his boss in the small, compact room, surrounded by the stacks of paperwork.

"Hey Monty, guess what lovely lady agreed to be my girlfriend?"

His boss looked up at him. "It doesn't take a special agent to figure that one out." Laughter echoed, Cara's a lovely melody, his in the middle, and Montrose's providing a mellow undertone.

"I'm happy for you both." Monty straightened his bowtie with one hand. "And I have some news for you as well." He shuffled through some of the topmost papers until he found the one he wanted.

"Cara, the agency is so impressed with you, that you have been given an official code name – "Diamond"." He beamed. "And should you choose to accept the offer, there is a part-time position for you as the assistant to one Agent Ashburn."

Cara looked blown away. "I'm honored! Let me consider it."

Benny nodded. "That's fine. We'll wait for your answer." He shifted in his chair. "Also, I have a paper here informing me of the promotion of one of our Alpha-3 Agents up to Alpha-1."

Bryce explained it for Cara. "Alpha-1 is the top rank in the Agency. Only a few agents have ever made it." He shook his head. "Even getting into the Alpha class is an achievement." He didn't mention that he was in the Alpha class himself.

Montrose grinned at him, waiting.

And then it hit him. "What? No, Monty, you can't be serious."

"Dead serious." He nodded once. "It's you."

Cara's mouth dropped open and she looked up at him. Her gray eyes sparkled.

Part of him was gratified by the recognition, but most of him was thrilled about one advantage that came with this promotion... a significant raise in pay. *I'd be able to support a family. Thanks, God.*

"That's not all." His boss wasn't done. "You're also being awarded the White Star Medal, for... and I quote... "Unflinching Bravery in The Face of Peril"."

A tickle of delight touched his heart. The private award wouldn't be announced anywhere outside the Agency –and the White House – but what did he care about that, when some of the dearest people in his life knew?

The smile softening his boss, friend, and mentor's strong features was full of pride. "Well done, Bryce."

~*~

"So..." He looped his arm around Cara as they walked through the airport. "How does it feel to set foot on American soil once again?"

Her beautiful smile was accompanied by a charming wink. "Almost as good as it feels being your girlfriend."

"Now there's an answer I like." He grinned. *She is such a rare jewel.*

Cara let out a little cry of joy. "There they are!" She took off through the people and ran to a threesome of ladies that wasted no time in engulfing her in an all-girl group hug.

It was easy to judge who was who. The plump, elderly woman with white-blond hair cut in a short style was Cara's Nana, her grandmother. The younger, slimmer version of her with honey-blonde hair down to her shoulders was Cara's mother, Naomi. And the vibrant young thing with the auburn hair, wearing a flowing fuchsia crocheted poncho, had to be Penny, Cara's best friend.

What was it about the fact that he was shortly going to introduce himself to these ladies making him, the hard-core secret agent, so ridiculously *nervous*?

~*~

Cara felt like crying, it was that wonderful to be back in the loving embrace of the three dearest women in her world.

"Now what happened to your wrist?" Her mother questioned her when they finally all released each other. The flow of travelers moved past through the airport unchecked, and they were forced to half-shout.

"You didn't tell them, Penny? I broke it." Cara waved away their looks of dismay and rolled her eyes. "Can you believe it? I fell on a tile floor in Paris. I finally get to go to Europe and what do I do but break my wrist!"

Then she looked over her shoulder to see Bryce, standing behind her with a smile on his face.

"Mom, Nana, Penny, may I present Bryce Reynolds." Cara took Bryce's hand and drew him nearer to the circle of women.

Naomi extended her hand. "Bryce, it's good to meet you again. I haven't seen you since you were thirteen years old."

Bryce grasped her hand and gave a little dip of his head. "Mrs. Stephenson. So nice to see you again." Bryce didn't have to shout. His clear, deep voice cut an undercurrent through the airport noise.

Nana was next, and as Bryce took her hand she warbled "It's nice to meet you, young man."

"It's a pleasure to meet y'all, ma'am."

Nana beamed. "A southern boy! How nice."

Cara laughed. *Dear Nana.* She liked Bryce already, for one of her highest compliments was labeling someone a southerner. Cara *knew* Bryce had let slip that 'y'all' on purpose.

"You probably don't remember me a bit, but I certainly remember you!" Penny stuck out her hand, bangles jingling merrily on her wrist.

Bryce took her hand and bowed over it, giving her a wink as he stood upright once more.

"But I do remember you, Penny – in art class, your paintings completely outshone all of ours."

Penny's cheeks turned bright red under her glittering green eyes. She tucked her hand through the strap of her trademark gigantic purse.

"Oh gosh, you're as amazing as I remember – did your brother turn out anything like you? I sure hope so."

"Penny!" Cara exclaimed, unable to control the giggles that tickled her ribs.

Bryce laughed heartily, flashing his white teeth. "He'd probably be insulted if I said yes. He's much more fun than I am, and better-looking, too… I'm the plain one in the family."

"Great heavenly days, if that's the case, I'll just faint dead away if I ever lay eyes on him!"

~*~

Cara regretted that Penny had to go home after seeing them at the airport, for she lived in Peachtree City, south of Atlanta, and wouldn't be going with them to Cara's apartment.

She and Penny went to grab iced coffee to go from *one* of the Starbucks' that the Atlanta Airport boasted while Bryce, Nana, and her mom went to get the luggage.

As soon as they were out of sight of Bryce and the ladies, Cara grabbed Penny's arm. "Penny, I have something to tell you."

Penny studied her, for once wearing a sober expression as they speed-walked towards the coffee. "For some reason, I'm getting the vibe that this is something bigger than, like, that you've found a new favorite brand of nail polish."

Cara smiled and shook her head. "It's a bit bigger than that."

The rich scent of fresh hot coffee drifted through the air as they entered the Starbucks.

Penny dragged her over to a quiet corner and then plunked her down on a leather couch, seating herself beside Cara among the trendy pillows. "Okay. What is it?"

"Bryce asked me to be his girlfriend, and I said yes."

"I *knew* it! He's a great guy, I can tell, but does he treat you well?" Concern wrinkled Penny's button nose after her initial excitement.

Images of Bryce's tender, protective actions flashed through Cara's mind. He was ready to lay down his life for her, a man after God's own heart. "Are you kidding? He saved my *life* on the trip."

Penny's eyes widened.

Um... Oops. Can't tell her all that. "You should have seen how he took care of me when I broke my wrist." *There. That I can talk about for hours.*

"Awww. Well, I'm thrilled and delighted. That's fabulous!"

"I wonder how Blake turned out – remember, his brother? He used to be a goofball, but if he's anything like Bryce..." Cara trailed off and nudged her friend with an elbow.

Penny giggled, but looked away. "I was just kidding out there." Suddenly she gasped. "Your mother and grandmother! The coffee!"

They leaped up from the couch in unison and hastily got in line.

~*~

Cara's mother and grandmother were staying with her for a few days to celebrate her Nana's birthday, and Bryce was invited to dinner, so they all drove over to Cara's apartment together.

They managed to keep the conversation flowing in light channels. Cara let him handle any tricky questions that came up about the trip.

One brief moment brought a strained look to Cara's face, when her mother asked one important question. "Bryce, I got a call from Cara asking for prayer because you had been shot in the chest. How did that happen?"

He inhaled a deep breath, still feeling twinges of pain in his chest. "Well, ma'am, it seems to have been a freak accident. The shot had been aimed at-" He slipped his hand over Cara's and squeezed it. "-someone else. The shooter is now in the hands of the authorities." *The ultimate authority. God.*

"My goodness. Well, I'm so sorry you were caught in the middle of that!"

"I'm just glad he's okay." Cara looked at him, and in her eyes that were shining with a soft blue-gray, he read her gratefulness for saving her life. That was all the thanks he ever needed.

~*~

Cara prepared a splendid feast of rosemary-thyme roasted chicken, cheesy baked potatoes, and salad with fresh greens, although her mother and grandma insisted on helping because of her broken wrist.

She was grateful, but a tiny part of her had wanted to show Bryce what she could do all by herself.

Bryce ate enough for two men, and showered compliments on all three cooks. They took the opportunity over the course of the meal to tell her mom and Nana about their relationship, and the women were elated.

Insisting that Cara not lift a finger to do cleanup, the ladies shooed them out of the kitchen, so Cara accompanied Bryce over to the Agency apartment where his Mustang was parked.

Atlanta sparkled as the sky darkened overhead, and the streets glowed in the golden light of the streetlamps.

"Well, not only do I have a lot of vacation days stacked up, I'm also on forced leave due to the chest wound." He shrugged. "So it looks like I'm going to be spending some time away from work."

She tucked her arm around his elbow and smiled up at him.

He looked over to her and winked. "How would you like to go on a date with me?"

"I'd love it!"

~*~

Back at Silver Strand technologies the next morning, Cara met with Mr. Gungerson – in his private, comfortable office, not the imposing conference room – and brought her mother along for moral support, as Bryce had a doctor's appointment that morning.

She thought her boss would be surprised at her proposal to shift all of her work online, freeing her to spend more time at home and with Bryce, but it turned out he had a bigger surprise for her.

"I'm naming you as my sole heir, Cara." Mr. Gungerson's voice was subdued, but confident. He almost seemed like a different man, with a new air of humility about him.

The shock in her mother's face, she was sure, reflected her own. "Sir, I don't know what to say... what about your son?"

Mr. Gungerson cleared his throat. "Unfortunately, Mitch has passed away due to the injuries he suffered in his... accident."

The cover story was that Mitch suffered internal injuries in a car accident somewhere in Europe, but Cara hadn't heard of his death.

"I'm sorry." Cara reached out a hand and squeezed Mr. Gungerson's arm lightly.

He patted her hand. "Thank you, my dear, but don't waste your pity on me." He straightened his posture. "Life must go on. But when mine is eventually over, I want my money left in good hands, and there are none better than yours, Cara. I wish I had been blessed with a daughter like you."

"She is the best daughter I could ask for." Her mother smiled sweetly.

"And her mother is also a very genteel and lovely woman. I am most pleased to have made your acquaintance, Naomi." A shy smile lifted Mr. Gungerson's handsome mouth.

Was her mother actually *blushing*?

"I would be honored if you ladies would join me for dinner sometime. And bring that young man of yours, Cara."

~*~

ONE MONTH, 25 DATES LATER

Bistro Niko entranced Cara with the delectable smells of French-inspired cookery, glimmering lights embedded in a ceiling embossed with curving white trim, and gleaming red leather booths. Soaked with bustling elegance, the modern restaurant was packed.

Bryce had told her that he'd made reservations for their lunch date, so she asked the hostess if he'd arrived yet. She was to meet him there.

Her face brightened. "Ah, the Reynolds reservation. Right this way, please." The short lady led her to one of the dark wood tables along the gold-textured wall underneath a Parisian painting.

The table was empty, but a square pink envelope marked "Cara" lay on one of the plates.

"Wait here." The woman fairly skipped away.

Hmm. She seems excited about something. Odd.

She seated herself and used one of the silver butter knives to open the letter, grateful that her wrist was healed and her dexterity restored.

"My dearest Cara,

I know you thought this would be an ordinary Saturday, but today is a special day. I've got some surprises for you, and I can't wait to hear what you think of them. The first one will be waiting outside in a yellow taxi. Wait for the waitress to bring you your lunch, and then go discover it!

Yours, Bryce"

A waitress appeared and handed her a posh to-go box and lidded cup with a straw. "Enjoy your lunch, mademoiselle!"

Befuddled, Cara returned to the entrance and peered down the street. Up drove a yellow taxi. Bursting from the backseat, a familiar red-headed whirlwind engulfed her in an exuberant embrace.

"Cara!" Penny squealed.

"Penny! What in the world-?"

"-isn't this just too much fun?! That boyfriend of yours-"

"-Where *is* he, anyway?!" Cara looked in the back of the cab, but it was empty.

"Oh, don't worry! He'll turn up!" Penny winked, sending the fairy-dust freckles dancing. "Now get in the cab!"

Cara obeyed, climbing in. "You know more about this than you're letting on! What's up?"

Penny laughed uproariously. "Your man told me to say "Caviar". I have no idea what that means but I think it's just adorable."

Cara rolled her eyes, but couldn't help giggling. "It means I'm not supposed to spoil the surprise by asking questions."

"Oh fun! Yes, you be a good girl!" Penny wagged an admonishing finger. "What did he get for lunch?"

Cara opened the box, where two warm, artfully crafted *Croque Monsieur* sandwiches reposed, layered with grilled ham, *gruyère* cheese, *pain de mie*, and *mornay* sauce.

"Bless that man." Penny lifted her perpetual thermos of sweet tea. "Vive la Bryce!"

Cara lifted her drink, which turned out to be *Fraise Limonade*, strawberry lemonade. *My favorite!*

"Now, here's your next clue." Penny handed her another square pink envelope.

Inside it, another note.

"Hope you liked the first surprise – it's going to be hard to top! But I'm up for the challenge. Instruct the cab driver to escort you to this address, and when you arrive, go on inside."

Below was an address on Piedmont avenue, which Cara related to the driver, and then sat back to enjoy the ride. Easy to do, with Penny next to her.

The girls devoured the delectable lunch, the last bite vanishing just as they arrived at the Piedmont Nail Salon and Spa.

Cara gasped. "He didn't!"

"He did!" Penny crowed, bouncing in her seat. "Come on, let's go in!"

Inside the door of the meticulously clean and chic salon, another surprise waited.

"*Bethany!*" Cara ran forward to hug Bryce's petite younger sister.

"Oh Cara, it's so nice to see you again!" Shy little Bethany's starry light blue eyes lit with excitement.

Cara had the opportunity to meet Bryce's mom, brother, and sister when they came for a visit a few weeks previously, all the way from Colorado. And they'd been delightful.

"What are you doing here, sweetie?" Cara was beginning to wonder what all this could be about.

"I'm supposed to say-"

"Caviar!" All three girls chorused at once, dissolving into giggles.

"All right, all right, no questions!" Cara gave in. "But I do wonder where Bryce is hiding himself. Maybe he's here for a pedicure?"

"Oh! That reminds me." Bethany handed her a pink envelope.

"Another one?!" Cara opened the note.

What's the perfect recipe for a happy girlfriend? I'm betting on friends + fabulous manicures & pedicures. Hint: Go with something light and beautiful for your fingernails, just like you!

Cara fanned herself with the envelope. *Okay, now I'm melting. He is so sweet.*

Out fell a gift card to the salon with her name on it.

...And generous. Aww!

They relaxed in massage chairs and drank chilled water and fruit juice while the manicurists and pedicurists created works of art on their nails after giving them sugar scrubs and soothing hand and foot rubs.

Cara chose a palest blush shimmer with French tips for her fingers, per Bryce's suggestion.

ASHBURN   Julia Erickson

When they went up to the front desk to pay, the cashier handed Cara another pink envelope just like the first three.

"No way." *This is crazy!* But she had to admit… she was loving every minute of this.

"Think I'm almost done? Think again. The fun has only just begun. Splish-splash – head to the Georgia Aquarium next to discover what awaits you there."

Penny and Bethany were just as surprised as she, saying they had no idea what would come next.

"But that's Bryce for you." Bethany smiled. "He works on a need-to-know basis, all the time!"

Cara and Bethany shared a look. Bryce's family knew that he worked for the government, but Cara knew they were unaware of the extent of Bryce's efforts.

It didn't take long to drive to the aquarium, and when they walked up to get in the entrance line, another surprise grabbed Cara – literally.

"Boo!" Angelwing exclaimed in her ear.

"Oh my word! Angel!" The two of them hugged each other tightly. "It's so good to see you looking so *well*."

"You too." Angelwing quirked an eyebrow, then smoothed her expression.

Yeah, last time we met you were shot and I had a broken wrist. Things have improved!

"Ladies." Angel nodded to Bethany and Penny.

"Girls, meet Angel. She helped Bryce and me on our trip."

"Oh yeah, Bryce and my hubby go way back. They're like this." Angelwing twisted two fingers together. "But we can't stand here jawing all day! I've got VIP passes for us." She waved a handful of tickets in the air. "No long lines for these ladies!"

"Is Bryce here?" Cara scanned the crowd in front of the enormous Aquarium building, but didn't see him anywhere.

"Nope, but he sent this."

Another pink envelope. Cara shook her head, laughing, and ripped it open.

Remember the awesome date we had here? You've got some time to kill, so go watch those whale sharks eat their krill. (Yeah, I should stay away from poetry.) Don't tell her I said this, but Angel's afraid of sharks – keep her away from the little hammerheads in the touch-tank! When you're done touring, stop in at the gift shop for the next hint."

Cara felt like galloping to the gift shop, but Angelwing insisted that they spend at least two hours touring the aquarium, though she wouldn't say why.

The gigantic place was separated into different themed sections, linked by darkened hallways to better offset the brilliantly lit exhibits and tanks, with one great room that accessed them all.

Cara remembered the date she'd had with Bryce here. He'd taken some amazing photos with his camera and they'd held hands and watched the tropical reef exhibit with realistic waves and a cloud of colorful fishes.

She and the girls spent hours watching the graceful white belugas and trailing jellyfish, riding the moving walkway of an underground tunnel of glass with a myriad of sea life above, and standing in awe before the colossal whale shark wall. The spotted giants cruised past through schools of smaller fish, a truly stunning sight.

At last, they reached the gift shop, and Cara retrieved yet another pink envelope – and the little stuffed plush beluga that came with it.

"Miss me yet? You're getting closer! Have dinner with me tonight? – wear a pretty dress. That's right! Time for some shopping. Hit the mall and buy yourself a whole new outfit – dress, shoes, the works! I'm sure the gals will assist you. Also, a special surprise will be waiting in the Ann Taylor store. If you're starting to think this is too much – trust me, it isn't. Not for you."

Tears welled in her eyes and Cara covered her face. She was starting to get an inkling about what this might all mean. *I don't deserve all this, Lord!*

"Come on, let's get going!" Angel patted her on the back and they all traipsed out the exit.

Catching a taxi over to the mall, the other girls seemed to sense her emotional state and told hilarious stories until her sides ached from laughter.

Sure enough, a very, very special surprise waited for her in the Ann Taylor dressing room. "Mother! Nana!"

"Cara, baby!" Her mother and grandmother squeezed her in gentle hugs, their faces aglow. "Surprise!"

"I *am* surprised! Is Bryce here?" She was almost ready for the "no" this time, but she was growing anxious to see her man and thank him!

There was quite a gaggle of women at this point, and with that many helping hands, it was no time at all before they'd created a gorgeous ensemble for Cara.

Her soft mint dress with a sweetheart neckline, cap sleeves, slimming fitted waist, and full skirt looked sweet with peep-toe heels and a single teardrop-shaped pearl on a delicate silver chain around her neck.

Another pink envelope handed to her by her mother contained a gift card to purchase the outfit, along with a note.

"Princess, I'm sure you look fantastic! Your chariot awaits you outside the mall. Pop back to your apartment to fix your hair and all that jazz you ladies do. One last journey, I promise. See you soon, my darling."

He'd drawn a heart at the bottom of this note, and Cara felt her own start to race.

She nearly swooned at the sight of the white limousine.

~*~

Angelwing smiled to herself as she listened to the cheerful banter ping-ponging around the limo. The girls were teasing Naomi, Cara's mother, about her 'new flame' – Cara's boss, Mr. Gungerson.

Cara looks beautiful. Penny had curled the glorious Rapunzel hair into soft ringlets and swept the hair away from Cara's face with a silver clip.

Angel herself had done Cara's makeup while Penny worked on the hair, and the result was mesmerizing. Lots of practice in the field, creating both disguises and alluring looks, had made Angel a skilled facial artist, but this was the happiest occasion she'd had to use her talent.

She checked her watch. They were right on schedule. *Bryce will be pleased – no, make that ecstatic.* She was happy for him. The man deserved a woman that loved him wholeheartedly. She'd often wished he had the kind of companionship that she and Markdown shared.

Cara laughed, her eyes sparkling.

Angel nodded. *She's perfect for him.*

~*~

A little over an hour later, the limousine turned down an old dirt road named Burberry Street. Verdant pastures dotted with pecan trees surrounded the quaint lane. Homes were few and far between. One special house rose before them, dignified as a grand old dame, with a wraparound porch perfect for sittin' a spell in the wooden rocking chairs.

"Nana's house." Cara breathed in and exhaled, gazing out the window at her girlhood home.

The limo driver rolled down the partition. "This is where you get out, miss."

The other women nodded encouragement.

Cara's feet left the limo and her heels crunched lightly against the sandy gravel driveway. She tiptoed up to the house as the limousine backed up and smoothly drove away, taking her mom, Nana, Penny, Bethany, and Angel with it.

Taped to the screen door was a little square of pink paper with an arrow drawn on it pointing to the right.

Cara followed the porch around the curve of the corner, her shoes thumping softly on floorboards.

Crickets and cicadas strummed their evening song and the sunlight slanted through the trees in the shady backyard. Then she saw him.

Bryce stood on the freshly-mown grass in a sharp gray suit, clasping his hands together. Behind him, a white arbor strung with twinkle-lights and garlands of white roses, a lacy wrought-iron chair beneath it.

He flashed white teeth with his huge grin and extended a hand. "Cara!"

She ran to him across the grass and he caught her around the waist, lifting her in the air, and spun in a circle, laughing.

"Bryce!" She gasped when he set her down, "Today has been amazing!"

One of her shoes had slipped off mid-whirl, so Bryce bent to retrieve it.

"Oh, this is perfect." He waved to the chair. "Have a seat, Cinderella."

She laughed and seated herself in the chair. "Thank you, my prince."

He knelt and tenderly cupped her foot in his hand, brushed some stray grass blades from it, then slipped on her shoe.

"I see you've been to the nail salon. Your toes are pretty."

ASHBURN   Julia Erickson

She held out her hands. "I certainly have."

He took both of her hands in his and made a show of examining the nails. "*Very* nice. Great choice." Then he looked into her eyes. "I have something to ask you."

Oh my word. He's on one knee.

~*~

He reached into his jacket pocket, and realization dawned on Cara's face when he pulled out a small velvet box. Her hands flew to her cheeks.

"Cara, I love you. You are the bravest, cleverest, most talented, and most stunningly beautiful woman I have ever known."

Her face flushed a dusky rose.

"The Lord is at work in our lives, and I believe I have clearly seen his hand in our relationship. And I've watched you grow in your faith with inspiring speed in the past month."

It was true. Cara studied the Word with a passion that took his breath away. She deeply desired to know God. Her Bible was thickly underlined and highlighted already.

"We've been through the worst of situations and the best of times together, and leaned on each other through it all. We make an awesome team."

She laughed, nodding in agreement.

"So..." He tilted the lid open, and the princess-cut diamond flashed and sparkled in the evening light with the barest hint of an aqua hue – her favorite color.

"...Cara Anastasia Stephenson, will you marry me?"

Bright tears welled in her eyes and spilled down her cheeks, but her smile shone brighter. "*Yes!* A million times yes!"

She stood and they embraced underneath the curve of the arbor, arms tightly wrapped around each other. On their first date, they'd discovered that they shared a mutual desire to save their first kiss for marriage – so Bryce only gently kissed the cheek of his fiancée.

At last he released her, holding her at arm's length. "Smile for the camera!" He grinned in the direction of the bush that the photographer hid behind.

Cara gasped, shock splashed across her features. "You didn't!"

The photographer, who happened to be Blake, his younger brother, bounded out of the bush. "He did!"

Cara's laughter rippled through the air, again reminding him of a bubbling brook. "Blake! What are you doing here?"

Blake jauntily swaggered a few steps closer, tossing his molasses-brown hair out of his eyes. "Capturing your perfect moment, of course, you silly girl." He pointed up to a tiny upstairs window. "The videographer is up there."

Cara swiveled her head to stare at the window of her old bedroom. He knew it was hers – he'd thrown pebbles at it in bygone days.

Markdown waved from his perch on high and gave them a thumbs-up.

Cara laughed, then looked at him in awe. "You planned *everything*." She leaned close to whisper in his ear. "Now I know why your missions go off without a hitch."

"Most of them!" he whispered back, with a wink.

"Gag. If you're going to whisper sweet nothings, I'd better get the engagement photo-shoot set up." Blake clicked a button on a remote in his hand.

Instantly, high above their heads, crystal chandeliers dazzled in the fading twilight, hanging on wires threaded between the pecan trees.

"Oh my *goodness!*" Cara looked absolutely wonderstruck. She peered up into the treetops with pure, childlike happiness.

He tucked an arm around her waist and gazed up at the sight.

"Click." Blake took a photo. "Nice. Work it, work it!"

They laughed, and Blake took more pictures, leaning and shifting to get a better angle. "Let's get some great shots, then we can join everybody at the banquet hall for dinner. I'm starved."

Cara smiled into Bryce's face. "The Alvaton Banquet Hall?"

The biggest building in the tiny town, it was also where they had first danced together, as teens in English Country Dance class.

She slipped her arms around him. "I love you."

"I love you too!"

Mission accomplished.

~The End~

Ready For *More?*

DIAMOND, sequel to ASHBURN, #2 in the I.C.E. Agency series

Penny's last love story ended tragically, so she hides among her paints and brushes while keeping a bubbly façade firmly in place. Could a dashing realtor with a sidesplitting sense of humor be the first step of her fresh start?

Blake has always lived in the shadow of his older brother, using jokes to mask his insecurities and uncertainty. Searching for purpose and direction, he runs into a red-headed stop sign, and wonders if she might be the key to open his locked doors.

When calamity hits Cara, Penny's best friend, and Bryce, Blake's brother, they'll have to lean on each other and race to the rescue, and a bitter billionaire planning a major terrorist attack on America might turn out to be the smallest of their problems.

...Coming Soon!

Acknowledgements

Mama, I can't start by thanking anyone else but you. You have not only laid down your life for me and your other two children, homeschooling us brilliantly and allowing our creativity to burst forth, but you've done it pressing through the many hardships of an auto-immune disease. You are so strong and courageous, a *true* Proverbs 31 woman, and my biggest inspiration. I love you!

Daddy, you are the kindest man I've ever known. You are always there for me, ready to help me out with a twinkle in your eyes. I don't think you'll ever know how precious it feels to listen to you teach us from God's Word and explain the beautiful verses therein. I am incredibly blessed to have you as my father. I love you!

Mark and Steven, you amaze me. Not only are you tall, handsome, and hilarious, but you're also the best brothers in the world. I owe many hours of laughter and practice in the skill of bantering to you guys. I love you!

To the many online friends and blog readers who have provided sweet encouragement and support of my writing (You know who you are!) … a resounding THANK YOU! Love and hugs!

Google, I salute thee. You make me sound like I know what I'm talking about.

And finally, thank you, Lord, for the breath I breathe, the overwhelming blessings, and your everlasting love for me. I am nothing without you. May my writing praise your name and draw others into your presence!

About the Author

~

Julia Erickson has always adored reading. As a little girl, she even read while rollerblading, floating in the pool, and climbing trees. Her love of words and expressive personality naturally flowed into writing her own stories. Off the pages, Julia is also a budding graphic designer, photographer, and blogger. She loves to sing and dance and has her own handcrafted-jewelry business. Sparkle and style and colors are some of her favorite things! Growing up homeschooled all the way (Thanks, Mom!) allowed her to nurture her many hobbies. She loves her Lord and Savior, and believes the Bible is the best and truest story ever told.

Connect with her here:

On Facebook:

http://Facebook.com/JuliaErickson

On her Lifestyle Blog:

http://sparkle-song.blogspot.com

On the blog she and her mom share:

http://resourcefulgals.blogspot.com

Her jewelry-making eBooks:

http://jewelsbyjuliashop.com

Made in the USA
Columbia, SC
13 October 2017